Hate Mail

An Arranged Marriage Romance

Paper Cuts
Book 1

Winter Renshaw

Copyright

Important!

Also By Winter Renshaw

<u>THE NEVER SERIES</u>

Never Kiss a Stranger

Never is a Promise

Never Say Never

Bitter Rivals

<u>THE ARROGANT SERIES</u>

Arrogant Bastard

Arrogant Master

Arrogant Playboy

<u>THE RIXTON FALLS SERIES</u>

Royal

Bachelor

Filthy

Priceless (Amato Brothers crossover)

<u>THE AMATO BROTHERS SERIES</u>

Heartless

Reckless

Priceless

<u>THE P.S. SERIES</u>

P.S. I Hate You

P.S. I Miss You

P.S. I Dare You

THE MONTGOMERY BROTHERS DUET

Dark Paradise

Dark Promises

PAPER CUTS

Hate Mail

Yours Cruelly (September 2023)

Dear Stranger (October 2023)

BOX SETS

The Best of Winter Renshaw

His & Hers

STANDALONES

Single Dad Next Door

Cold Hearted

The Perfect Illusion

Country Nights

Absinthe

The Rebound

Love and Other Lies

The Executive

Pricked

For Lila, Forever

The Marriage Pact

Hate the Game

The Cruelest Stranger

The Best Man

Trillion

Enemy Dearest

The Match

Whiskey Moon

Stone Cold

The Dirty Truth

Love and Kerosene

You or Someone Like You

All Books Available here!

Free Content Available here!

Description

In the Wakemont family, it's tradition to arrange a marriage before the ink is dry on your birth certificate. I was five hours old when my father promised me to the son of a man with "more money than God."

As we grew older, my future groom and I were encouraged to exchange "love letters" to get better acquainted—except the correspondence he sent read more like hate mail.

Slade Delacorte hated the arrangement.

But more than that, he hated me.

He was moody, intense, arrogant, and darkly gorgeous. A villain—not a prince. The last man on Earth I'd ever marry (if I had the choice).

On my 24th birthday, we exchanged vows in front of six hundred guests who had no idea we weren't every bit the blissful couple we pretended to be.

But as we began our new life together, I soon learned there was only one thing worse than marrying the man I'd hated my entire life: falling in love with him.

To staunch optimists—and the broody assholes who love them.

1

Campbell

"Please tell me this is some kind of joke." My mother's face falls the instant I emerge from the fitting room in a black lace wedding dress.

The soft filtered sunlight streaming through the lace curtains, racks of designer gowns, Chopin faintly playing from hidden speakers, endless flutes of Veuve Clicquot, and perfumed, lily-of-the-valley air should be enough to make this one of the most beautiful moments of anyone's life, only this has to be one of the worst moments of mine.

Six months from today, I'm to be married to Slade Delacorte—an arrangement my parents made with his before either of us were old enough to protest.

"Nico said black is the trending wedding dress color this year." I wink at my fitting room attendant, silently willing him to help me out here, only he looks like a deer in headlights. "Right, Nico? Weren't you just telling me that?"

"It ... it's true, Mrs. Wakemont," he stammers in his

posh English accent as his hooded gaze settles on my mother's horrified expression. "There was an article a while back in Bride magazine. I could find it if you'd like to have a read."

Turning, I step onto the raised platform and examine my reflection in the three-sided mirror, ignoring the commotion going on behind me as my mother attempts to get my bridesmaids on her side.

"White is classic though," Tenley, my best friend since preschool, chimes in. Love her to death but she's always been weak-spined, especially when it comes to powerful, intimidating women like my mother. "You can't go wrong with white."

"Black is bold and sexy," my former college roommate, Elise, offers. She's always been quick to take my side in all matters—even when I've been wrong—because that's the kind of person Elise is. "You could wear traditional white for the ceremony and do an avant-garde black for your reception."

"I like it," Stassi, my best friend from high school, chimes in. "I wouldn't wear it personally, but I like it. It makes me think of a black swan. Chic and elegant."

Stassi offers a pained smile, though her pain has nothing to do with my dress or this awkward situation we're in. Last year, she found out her fiancé was cheating on her a few months before the wedding. They were about to buy a condo in Manhattan together and everything. Their entire lives were ahead of them and I'd never seen her happier—until it all came crashing down.

Inevitably the wedding was called off and Stassi moved back home to Sapphire Shores for a "break," but her sabbatical has turned into something akin to a semi-permanent situation.

She used to take the subway to work and broker high-dollar deals.

Now she makes crappy pizza at a local parlor and lives in the run-down apartment above it—by choice.

But I digress.

"You girls are doing Campbell a disservice by being generous with your praise," my mother tells my friends. The girls exchange looks, though not a single one of them dares to rebut her. Mom clasps her French manicured hands in her lap, over her elegantly slanted crossed legs. "Let's get on with this, darling. Please."

I run my hands along the silky onyx lace that hugs my hourglass hips and makes me feel rebellious and brave.

There's not a single piece in this entire boutique that could hold a flame to this one.

Not only that, but it's a statement.

Marrying Slade is essentially a funeral for my future.

I'm in mourning, even if I have to plaster a smile on my face and pretend I'm not.

Also, a woman has to have a sense of humor about these kinds of things if she wants to stay sane—a decision I landed on years ago, when I learned my parents were never going to change their stance on this ridiculous marriage arrangement.

"Is there a matching veil for this?" I ask Nico.

He glances at my mother, who rolls her eyes.

Hesitating, he mutters that he'll be right back.

Poor guy—stuck between a rock and a hard place.

Welcome to my world ...

"Campbell Elizabeth Wakemont, I'm *not* buying you a *black* wedding dress." My mother tosses back a mouthful of champagne before checking the glimmering diamond Rolex on her left wrist. "We have brunch reservations after this and then we're meeting with the florist to finalize flowers. Please don't waste any more of everyone's precious time. Take that horrid thing off and try on some of the gorgeous gowns Nico pulled for you."

I twist around, peering over each shoulder as I examine myself from every angle in the mirrors. The dress is sexy yet understated, the way it hugs and drapes and exposes the perfect amount of decolletage and bare shoulders. It moves when I move, fluid yet fitted, holding me like it never wants to let me go.

I feel like I could conquer the world in this thing—or run away in it.

It's not constricting. The lace makes it breathable. I could do a lot of exciting things in this.

"Can one of you take a picture for me?" I ask my friends.

Tenley reaches for her phone, but my mother places her hand out to block the move.

"All right, while I don't have an exact match for that dress, I do have these lovelies." Nico returns with two black veils—one so long it drips to the floor and the other, a shorter, chicer option.

"My apologies for wasting your time, Nico, but she won't be trying on any black veils," Mom says. "This is a wedding for crying out loud, not a funeral—a celebration that six hundred guests will be talking about for years to come. We're going for classic, timeless, elegance—not Victorian graveside chic."

Tenley shoots a sympathetic wince my way.

Or maybe it's apologetic.

Either way, she's been around my family long enough to know that disagreeing with Blythe Wakemont is the quickest way to land on her personal shit list, which is akin to existing on the dark side of the moon.

My mother can move mountains for the people she adores. Even if you don't love her, you need her to love you.

"I'm obsessed with this dress though," I say with a dreamy sigh, placing my hand over my heart. My flawless seven-carat engagement ring glints under the soft ambient light. Its Edwardian setting representative of the woman who wore it first—Slade's great-great grandmother. "It captures me perfectly."

"Sure, if you were a tragically young widow in the 1800s," Mom says, topping off her champagne. At this rate, she's going to be blitzed before we make it to our brunch reservations. We'll be hauling her *and* all of her Chanel accessories into the Joie de Vivre Café and Patisserie on Claremont Avenue. "Fortunately, you're a beautiful, modern day bride-to-be, so let's dress like one, shall we?"

Stealing one final glance at the moody obsidian number hugging my body, I retreat behind the changing room curtain where Nico has carefully hung the first white dress for me to try on. With its fitted satin bodice and skirted plume of never-ending organza and tulle, it's something Cinderella herself would approve of. But the difference between Cinderella and me is that she got to marry the man she loved.

Not only that, but she married a prince.

I might as well be marrying a bona fide villain.

"Love is not a fairytale, Campbell. Not even close," my mother told me once, when she was reading me a book of bedtime stories. It was late, we'd just finished Sleeping Beauty, and with bleary eyes I told her I hoped to find a prince like Phillip someday.

It wasn't much longer after that when she and my father

sat me down and told me my "prince" had already been chosen for me. I couldn't have been more than seven or eight, still very much in my princess era.

I beamed with excitement and elation as they told me his name, that he was the son of an old family friend, that I'd be meeting him soon, and that his family was "practically royalty" which made him as good as a real-life prince.

After that, they explained that he and I would be exchanging letters to get to know one another.

Months later, as they handed me the first piece of correspondence—a letter sealed in a scarlet red envelope—I carefully tore the flap, my stomach in knots with anticipation and the first flutters of what I could only imagine was true love.

Boys had written me love notes at school, but I'd never received one from someoneone who was almost royalty ... one who promised to be *my* prince someday.

"*Campbell, what's wrong?*" my father asked when tears sprang from my eyes after I read it. Rushing to my side, he swiped the red envelope and its matching letter from my little hands. "*Oh, for crying out loud.*"

"*What does it say?*" Mom asked.

Dad released a heavy breath, handing it over to my mother so he didn't have to read the words out loud.

A few seconds later, she cupped her hand over her mouth. "*Why would he write that?*"

But what did it matter?

My future husband wrote it, signed it, stamped it, and sent it, and there was no taking it back.

They say you never forget your first love or your first kiss.

But no one ever tells you that you never forget the first time a boy tells you he hates you.

Campbell—
I hate you.
Slade (*age 8*)

Slade—
I hate you times infinity and you will never, ever,
<u>ever</u> be my prince.
Campbell (*age 7*)

2

Campbell

"What about this one?" I point to a heart-shaped wreath composed of pink and white carnations as my mother follows the florist around a heavenly-scented shop that's been a Sapphire Shores mainstay for almost seventy years.

Mom stops cold in her color-blocked Chanel heels and shoots me a death look. "*Campbell.*"

"Those are actually meant to go beside caskets," the florist says before clearing her throat and adding, "at funerals and memorials."

I know this, but I play dumb.

If I can't have a funeral dress, what about funeral flowers?

This entire celebration is about uniting two families who would have united us regardless of anything. I could have had eight extra appendages and Slade could be exclusively attracted to men and our parents would still be forcing this unholy union on us.

If this day isn't about either one of us, can't I at least have something?

I don't think funeral flowers are asking too much—I saw the invoice for the elaborate ice sculpture my mother chose for the reception.

This heart wreath costs a fraction of that, plus it's a *heart*.

It's practically wedding-themed.

"What about those?" I point to the planters of peace lilies lined up against the wall. Pretty sure I've seen those at funerals before.

Years ago, when we lost Granddad, our entire great room was filled with baskets upon baskets of them until my mother started passing them out to various staff members just to get them out of her sight.

"Darling, you're in the wrong section. Come over here." Mom waves me her way, though if the florist weren't watching, she'd be snapping and pointing to the floor, treating me like a disobedient puppy. It's not that she means to be like this, it's just who she is. She's a matriarch. A first-born female. She calls the shots everywhere she goes and she doesn't have time to wait around—or play these little games. Over the years, I've learned to adapt to her whims, mostly via my sense of humor. Anything else runs the risk of landing me in hot water, and who has the energy for that?

Certainly not me.

If only my bridesmaids were here ...

I could sure use Elise in my corner right about now, but I sent them all on their way after brunch. They'd already spent a perfectly good Wednesday morning with my mother and her antics—I wasn't going to punish them by commandeering their perfectly good afternoons as well. They'd have stayed, of course, but I couldn't do that to them.

"I'm absolutely in love with these ivory roses mixed with the lilacs and lavender," my mother gushes to the florist. "Pale violet has always been Campbell's color."

Years ago, my mother took me to have my 'colors' analyzed. We walked away with a booklet full of mostly pastels and the second we got home, my mother proceeded to yank everything out of my closet that wasn't a pastel.

For the months that followed, as I slowly rebuilt my wardrobe piece by piece, I walked around looking like a teenage Easter egg—not a flattering look by any stretch of the imagination.

"Wouldn't these roses complement the ivory beading in your veil, Cam?" Mom carefully lifts a long-stemmed white rose to her nose and inhales before passing it to me. She closes her eyes, smiling gently, as if it's the first time she's ever sniffed a flower in her five decades on this planet.

"I mean, it does match the dress you chose for me," I say. I won't lie, the gown we settled on is gorgeous—a stunning ivory number with lace overlay, a curve-skimming trumpet skirt that pools out into a tasteful train, and a tiara veil with just enough teardrop pearl beading on the tulle to make my mother stop nitpicking every other detail.

The dress wasn't as frou-frou as she'd have liked, but it was the last one I tried on and there was no denying it fit that whole American blue-blooded princess illusion Blythe Wakemont salivates over.

All Nico had to tell her was that Meghan Markle had once considered that very same gown before ultimately going with the Clare Waight Keller number, and Mom was sold. Her eyes lit like Christmastime in July.

If it was good enough for a princess—er, duchess—it's good enough for the daughter of an American steel magnate marrying the son of an American media magnate.

"Shall we make this easy on Addison?" Mom bats her mascara-coated lashes, and while she's speaking to me, she's looking at the florist. I've only known Addison a handful of moments—long enough to ascertain she's a people pleaser, a tiny bit shy, and very passionate about all things floral. But I can already see the dollar signs adding up in her eyes—not because of the flower selections, but because my mother has already mentioned at least half a dozen times that this will be one of the grandest weddings the state of Maine has ever seen. "Can we both agree on the ivory roses, lilacs, and lavender? I thought about maybe throwing in some of those gorgeous purple hydrangeas, but depending on the light, those can sometimes read more blue or blue-violet, and that's too intense for what we're wanting. Plus, hydrangeas scream spring to me and this is a late summer wedding. Anyway, are we settled? Can we move onto designing bouquets and centerpieces next?"

"I didn't realize flowers could scream," I tease. "But sure. Let's go with the ivory and purple. Sorry—lilac."

I force a smile, quickly running out of energy to amuse myself by resisting her at every turn.

Maybe it's childish.

Okay, let's be honest—it *is* childish.

I'm a twenty-four-year-old college educated young woman about to be married. I've been to both finishing school and a debutante ball. I spent an entire year living abroad in Europe when I was seventeen. I can speak three languages fluently and am currently working on a fourth. But since no one else dares to give my mother an ounce of any kind of guff and I'm her only child, that duty lands solely on me.

"You two mind if I step out and grab an iced coffee?" I fight a yawn. The closer we get to the "big day," the more sleep evades me. I'm lucky if I got four mediocre hours last night. "Addison, can I grab you anything? Mom?"

Annoyance flickers in my mother's intense deep blue glare, but she says nothing. She doesn't drink coffee anyway (it stains her snow-white smile), but I had to offer or else I'd never hear the end of it on the car ride home.

"I'm fine, but thank you, Campbell," Addison says.

"Don't be long, please." Mom turns back to the florist, motioning with her hands as she describes her vision for my bouquet.

The jangle of the bells on the door as I exit sounds like freedom, and I drag in a lungful of damp late February air as I hit the snow-melted sidewalk. Maine winters are particularly never-ending, but today feels like the tiniest preview of spring.

The line at the coffee shop next door is at least seven people deep, maybe eight. I let an older woman go ahead of me before holding the door for a tired-looking mom pushing identical twin girls in a double stroller. She offers to let me go ahead of her once we're inside, but I insist on taking my place at the very end of the line. Even if I weren't stalling, I'd still let her go first.

Motherhood (unless you have a staff of ten on your payroll) looks hard as hell—twins or not. I imagine she needs all the caffeine in existence and then some.

Ten minutes later, I'm walking out, iced caramel latte in hand, when my phone chimes. I don't need to look down to know it's probably my mother wondering what's taking so long.

But I check anyway.

Only it isn't a series of question marks like I expected.

SLADE: Flight got cancelled. Coming in tomorrow at six.

I refuse to believe His Royal American Highness is flying commercial when he has a private jet at his disposal 24/7. Private flights get delayed all the time, but cancelled? Doubtful.

ME: [thumbs up emoji]

I've learned over the years, the fewer words we exchange, the better—especially when it comes to anything in written or texted format.

Thank goodness for emojis ... doing the Lord's work.

When I return to the flower shop, I find Addison and my mother in the back, paging through some photo album with ornate gold edges. The two of them are so deep in conversation about centerpieces they don't notice me for a solid three minutes—long enough for me to mentally sing the newest Taylor Swift song in my head.

"Oh, Campbell, when did you get back?" Mom chuckles, her manicured hand splayed over her chest like she wasn't just shooting me daggers fifteen minutes earlier. "We were just discussing centerpieces, and I think we should do a whole spray of lilacs at the bridal table and then smaller versions at the tables in the front, you know, where family and our guests of honor will be sitting."

Addison nods, feverishly jotting notes in a pale yellow notepad. She flips to a clean page and continues scribbling as my mother waxes on about her ideas for the bridesmaid bouquets. Her handwriting is tiny but elegant, much like my mother.

"Sounds good," I say before taking a sip of my iced latte. "Oh. Slade changed his flight to tomorrow."

Her red lips flatten and she peers my way, squinting as if she's attempting to read between lines that aren't there. But she will find neither excitement nor relief on my face.

For years we went round and round on this whole

arranged marriage thing. I even showed her how awful Slade's letters were, illustrated how miserable we'd be together, painted pictures of how wonderful my life would be if it were filled with real love and babies born to two loving parents ... but nothing I said or did convinced her or my father to budge.

If anything, the more I resisted, the more they doubled down on their convictions, keeping me under their thumb even more and micromanaging my whereabouts and controlling my extracurriculars in any way possible. They even went so far as to send me to all girls' schools to ensure I wouldn't be tempted to meet a boy and run off with him. When it came time for college, my choices were narrowed down to a handful of the only all-female universities in the country.

Fighting my parents will always be a losing battle.

"I'm sure there's a perfectly good reason for that," Mom says, her voice as pleasant as watermelon mint punch on a hot summer's day. "I heard we might be getting some snow tonight? Always better safe than sorry."

Judging by the sun blinding the clear Maine sky and melting all the snow, I'm doubtful on that forecast. Regardless, I couldn't care less what his reasons are for postponing his trip. If anything, I'm secretly celebrating the fact that I don't have to entertain his insufferable presence tonight.

"Excuse me, Addison. I'm terribly sorry. I just need to make a quick phone call to the house." Mom trots off with her cell in hand, her coiffed blonde bob bouncing with each hurried stride. I imagine she's calling the chef to tell him the family dinner we were supposed to have with my *beloved* will now be tomorrow night. If she's lucky, he hasn't already started on the beef Wellington and baked Alaska—Slade's two favorite dishes.

Slade's visits before were always few and far between, but now that we're full speed ahead on the wedding, his presence is required for various meetings and parties thrown by our families. I've seen him more in the last six months than I had in the last six years, and from now until August, he'll be making monthly trips here.

At some point soon, I'll start flying back with him as we set up our new life together in his hometown of Palm Beach, Florida where I'll, no doubt, stick out like the sorest of sore thumbs.

"Are you excited?" Addison asks while we wait for my mom's return. She scrunches her shoulders in and flashes me an awkward smile that tells me she hates small talk just as much as me. I wish I could tell her she doesn't have to do any of this ... make small talk *or* treat me like a regular bride.

But alas, I can't.

In fact, the whole arranged marriage thing is protected with an ironclad NDA baked into a brassbound pre-nup. All it's missing is a notarization from the devil himself— though our longtime family attorney is close enough.

Regardless, it *kills* me knowing that everyone around us —from my closest friends to my darling sweet elderly ladies I volunteer with—thinks I'm head over heels in love with Slade, that I would choose him *on purpose*.

All they know is "we're old family friends" and "our parents are thrilled that we're marrying."

"They say opposites attract," Stassi told me when I first shared the news with my girlfriends. We were having dinner and I showed them a handful of photos I screen-shotted from some Miami magazine that did a lifestyle photo shoot with Slade. I didn't have a single candid shot of him in my phone, nor did I have anything of us together.

As she passed my phone to Elise, Elise squinted before saying, "He looks expensive."

Internally I rolled my eyes because Slade would take that as a massive compliment, but then Elise clarified by saying she meant "expensive" as in "being with someone like him might require a lot of therapy if it ever blows up in your face because holy-effing-shit he's gorgeous."

"Okay, ladies, I'm back." My mother takes the chair between us. "Where did we leave off?"

As she and the florist talk amongst themselves, I zone out, thinking about all the things I'd rather do than marry Slade Delacorte—if only fate would allow.

But the thing about fate is that it has never been on my side.

I don't expect it to start now.

Campbell—
My mom said I had to write you a nicer letter
this time.
But I don't have anything nice to say to you.
Slade (*age 8*)

Slade—
Do you have friends? Because you sound like a
jerk. I would never be friends with someone
like you.
Campbell (*age 7*)

Campbell—
Good. I don't want to be friends with you either.
Slade
(*age 8*)

3

Slade

We're wheels down at the Sapphire Shores municipal airport at exactly 6:02 PM. While I'd love to fly into, say, Portland, or anything with more than a few thousand inhabitants, my trusted flight crew insists this is the most efficient path. And they're not wrong—it'd just be nice to see some semblance of city lights now and then as opposed to a place that could be wiped off the map in a heartbeat and no one would even know it's gone.

Why anyone would choose to live in this godforsaken one-stoplight town is beyond me.

It looks like a 1980s postcard and it smells like the ocean—in a rotting seaweed and trash island kind of way.

Palm Beach at least smells good.

Like money.

Ambition.

Confidence.

Freshly waxed sports cars.

Italian cologne.

Exotic flowers.

Top shelf liquor.

The electric energy in the air is palpable the moment you step outside.

Sapphire Shores is the kind of place people go when they want to pretend we're not living in a world two seconds from some nuclear war every second of every day. The kind of place where people have vegetable gardens in their back yards and potato sack races at Fourth of July picnics. The kind of place where people eat at the same mediocre restaurants for decades because even though the food sucks, it's all about tradition and history. The kind of place where it doesn't matter who the president is because they're all in their own little world anyway.

Maybe it's for some people—but it isn't for me.

I'm not entirely unconvinced that this place doesn't exist in real life.

Maybe I'm stuck in some lucid dream and one day I'll wake up and I won't be flying here once a month in preparation to marry Campbell Wakemont?

A man can dream.

Then again, if I'm dreaming now, I'd love to wake the hell up sometime between now and August twelfth —specifically.

By the time I step off the plane, a shiny black Lincoln Town Car is waiting on the tarmac. If this were Palm Beach, there'd be swaying palm trees waiting to greet me and not this cold, salty excuse for a breeze.

"Mr. Delacorte," my driver, a different man than last time, greets me while another man loads my suitcase in the trunk of the car. "Welcome to Sapphire Shores. I'll be your driver for the next four days."

Four days with the Wakemonts ...

It would've been five, but one of my colleagues scheduled a last-minute emergency teleconference with our Berlin office yesterday, which allowed me to postpone my trip one more day.

Thank God for small favors.

"First time here?" The driver glances at me in the rearview as I check my email on my phone for the millionth time today, a task that feels like playing whack-a-mole lately since Blythe Wakemont copies me on each and every wedding-related piece of correspondence.

"Unfortunately not." I return my attention to my phone, quietly wishing I could snap my fingers and make a privacy partition appear out of thin air.

"Business or pleasure?" he asks.

He must be new here. Most of the time these drivers are quiet as mice—exactly the way I like it.

Small talk is a nuisance even on the best of days.

"Neither," I answer without looking up.

"Huh." The man sniffs a laugh and flicks on the turn signal. "That's a first for me. Any plans while you're in town?"

"Yes," I answer, though I'm not talking to him. Lifting my phone to my ear, I pretend to take a call. Talking on the phone to absolutely no one isn't my finest moment, but a man's got to do what a man's got to do.

The drive to the Wakemont estate takes a leisurely eight minutes thanks to the severe lack of stoplights in this town.

By the time we pull up outside the hundred-year-old brick colonial mansion with its six marble columns, Mrs. Wakemont is already trotting towards the circle drive in her heels, her arms outstretched as if she's greeting her favorite person in the entire world.

"Slade, so wonderful to see you." She wraps me in a Dior perfume-scented hug, and when she pulls away, I notice the soft fur of her jacket has left a few remnants on my cashmere Armani coat. I resist the urge to pluck them off out of respect for my future mother-in-law.

While Blythe has been nothing but gracious to me for as long as I can remember, there have been times I'm not unconvinced she wouldn't swap lives with Campbell if given the chance. As excited as she is for this wedding, it's almost as if she's the bride-to-be in this equation. Then again, she's been planning this affair for decades now and Campbell is her only child. I suppose she reserves the right to be excited about it.

"How was your flight?" Blythe asks, her eyes glimmering as she wears a grin so wide it might get stuck like that. "No delays or turbulence?"

Even if there were, I'm not here to complain.

I'm only here to fulfill an obligation.

"Flight was good," I say. "Where's my best girl?"

Mrs. Wakemont rolls her eyes and laughs. She loves it when I refer to Campbell with any kind of term of endearment. Lately I've been making a game out of seeing how many cheesy monikers I can say with a straight face. So far I've used "my Juliet," "my beloved dove," "my gorgeous doll," and my personal favorite, "my heart's dearest."

"She's inside," she says, swatting her hand. "Said it was too cold to wait out here."

Judging by the flush in Blythe's pale cheeks, I don't want to know how long she's been standing outside waiting for my car to pull up.

"If she hates the cold, she's going to love it in Palm Beach," I say as the driver wheels my luggage over. I hand him a twenty and thank him before following Blythe inside the house that always gives me an intense sensation of claustrophobia.

There isn't a single wall in this twelve-thousand square foot monstrosity that isn't paneled in mahogany or wallpapered to the ends of the earth. Antiques adorn every square inch of shelf or tablespace and there's enough seating in every room to host a diplomatic meeting. And the pictures—there are so many oil paintings and family portraits, a person could easily mistake this place for an art museum.

My home in Palm Beach is ... simpler.

Modern.

Cleaner.

Brighter.

Designed for both work *and* play.

"Campbell? Cedric?" Blythe calls out for her daughter and husband before taking my coat. "Slade's here."

The buttery, savory scent of beef Wellington fills the air and the sound of shuffling feet trails from one of the many recesses of the home.

"Hope you brought your appetite," she says while we wait in the foyer. "I'll have someone take your bag to your room while we eat. Dinner's almost ready."

"Perfect timing." Cedric makes his way through the tiled foyer, his right hand outstretched as if we're about to make a business deal—which is essentially what this arranged marriage is: two powerful American dynasties becoming one.

"Mr. Wakemont, good to see you." I meet his handshake.

Cedric squeezes my hand hard before covering it with his left—the same power move my father does ... a little trick they learned back in their Yale days.

While it tends to make them come off like assholes, a

person could argue that no one ever closed a multi-million-dollar business deal by being a nice guy.

"Oh, my. Campbell's taking her sweet time, isn't she?" Blythe toys at the strand of pearls affixed around her elegant neck, making zero effort to hide her annoyance. "Let me run and find her ... why don't you two go on ahead and meet us in the dining room?"

I follow Cedric to the old school country-club-esque dining room, where an elaborate setup is waiting for us. Crystal goblets, polished silver, ornate china plates with coordinating saucers, and more mahogany than should be allowed in one area at the same time.

"How's old Tupper doing these days?" Cedric asks about my father, a gleam in his eye as he uses an old nickname from their college years and some insufferable story involving a Tupperware container and God only knows what else. As such, my father loathes being called Tupper, but if anything, that only motivates Cedric to call him that even more. The two of them are like brothers who bicker like an old married couple but have each other's backs at the end of the day. "I'm sorry—it's only funny when he's here. How's Victor? Recovering from that shoulder surgery still?"

"He's anxious to get back on the golf course." I take the seat to his left. "Doctor hasn't cleared him yet."

Cedric offers a sympathetic wince. "That's what he gets for trying to best me at Pelican Bay last year. Serves him right. And your mother? The incomparable Delia Delacorte? Still tearing up the tennis courts at the Polo Palms Club?"

"When she can."

Cedric acts like we didn't just have this exact same conversation four weeks ago ... and four weeks before that ... and four weeks before that. For a while, I was worried there might be something going on with him neurologically, but I've recently deduced that he simply doesn't know how to talk to me because we have nothing in common other than my father and his daughter, and what can be said about either of them that hasn't already been said? That isn't already known?

Still, I humor him by engaging in this brain-numbing small talk while we wait for my future wife to make her fashionably late appearance. But it isn't long before our conversation reaches its inevitable lull.

I've never been a fan of silence.

It gives a person too much time to think, and too much of anything (with the exception of money) is never a good thing.

My phone buzzes in my pocket. The urge to check it is overwhelming, but I push through it.

I'd rather be working.

I'd rather be in Florida.

I'd rather be anywhere but here, pretending I don't hate every waking moment of this dog and pony show.

I'll never forget the day my parents told me about this absurd arrangement. I'd finished second grade with top marks, so as a reward, my parents took me out for ice cream at this place on the pier. A few doors down, there was a bridal party taking photos. I watched them, my nose scrunched in disgust as the woman in white kissed the man in black. My mother laughed and nudged my father, who also seemed amused by my reaction.

"That's going to be you someday, son," he said.

"Never," I told him between licks of Rocky Road. *"Girls are disgusting."*

"You won't always feel that way," my mom chimed in.

The two of them exchanged looks before my father cleared his throat.

"What would you say if we told you we knew who you were going to marry?" he asked.

At the time, I didn't understand what he was asking. It didn't make sense. I thought everyone got to choose their partner—which meant they could also choose not to have one at all.

"There's a girl," my mother said, *"and her name is Campbell."*

"Like the soup?" I laughed.

Mom smiled a soft smile. *"Yes, I suppose. But it's a family name."*

"Campbell Wakemont," my father said. *"She's the daughter of an old friend of mine. Her father has promised her hand to you."*

"I don't want to hold her hand," I said, studying my cone to optimize my next bite. The more the conversation continued, the closer I was getting to the sugar cone—the best part.

"Hand in marriage, my love," my mother clarified. *"It means the two of you are promised to each other. She'll be your future wife and you'll be her future husband."*

My parents had done some weird stuff before—like the time my father hired someone to dress like Santa and sneak into our house Christmas Eve because he thought I still believed.

But this didn't feel like that.

"You're going to meet her this summer," my mother said, studying me. *"We're going to Maine to visit the Wakemonts. I'm sure the two of you will hit it off. You might actually become good friends. The best marriages are built on a foundation of friendship."*

I'd never had a girl *friend* before.

I sure as hell didn't want one either.

"*We thought maybe the two of you could start exchanging letters?*" my mom continued. "*To get to know each other better?*"

"*Like pen pals?*" I asked before crunching into my cone.

"*Exactly,*" my father said. "*And we know how much you love to write.*"

It wasn't that I loved to write—it was simply that I was insanely good at it. The English language had come early and easily to me as a child. By the time I was one, I was speaking in complete sentences. Short but complete. By two, I was writing my name. By three, I was reading at a kindergarten level. By first and second grade, I was devouring middle grade chapter books.

At school, I insisted on writing everything in pen, not because I liked the way it looked—I did—but mostly because I never made a mistake. Pencils were a waste of space in my already crammed desk.

"*When we get home, maybe you could write the first letter?*" my mother suggested.

"*I think we've thrown too much at him too soon,*" my father said, leaning into her. "*Let's just let the boy enjoy his ice cream.*"

They didn't bring it up again—for a week.

For days, I dragged my feet writing that stupid letter. And by the time I did, I was so annoyed with the whole thing that I simply told my "future wife" that I hated her. In my eight-year-old mind, I was certain that if I was a jerk, she'd call off our wedding. That's the kind of stuff that happened in the movies, anyway. It seemed logical enough.

A month later, our jet touched down at some hole-in-the-wall airport in Maine.

Standing next to an idling Escalade were a man and

woman my parents' age, and a little girl with ice-blonde pigtails and a scowl on her face.

For the entire first day, she wouldn't talk, look, or so much as breathe in my direction.

I was certain my hate mail strategy had worked, that it wouldn't be long before she told her parents she didn't want to marry me and I'd be off the hook.

God, I was a naïve little shit back then.

"Ah, here's the young woman of the hour," Cedric announces, pulling me out of my bittersweet reverie. "Fashionably late, of course."

Like a proper gentleman, I rise until she takes the seat across from me, and I pretend not to notice that her lips are slicked in the palest pink balm, her lashes are painted dark, her blonde waves are pressed to silken perfection, and her entire look is rounded out by a curve-hugging little black dress.

Black must be her signature color because lately it's all she wears.

She'll stand out in Palm Beach if she continues to dress like she's in mourning, but I'll let her learn that on her own.

My gaze pierces hers for a single endless moment before we sit down.

"You look beautiful, Campbell," I tell her while her parents watch with bated breath and stars for eyes. "As always."

It's as if they've forgotten this entire thing is unnatural and orchestrated.

But *we* haven't.

Campbell's steel-blue eyes flash, as if she thinks I'm lying—as I've done before with various compliments.

But the thing is, this time I'm telling the truth.

She's, unquestionably, one of the most sinfully gorgeous

women I've ever laid eyes on. Feminine in all senses of the word. Every detail of this obnoxious creature—from her delicate collarbone to her Coke-bottle silhouette to her long runner's legs to the delicate arch of her size 7 feet—is sheer perfection.

She could wear a paper bag and still turn heads.

This woman—without question—is the very definition of a bombshell.

I'd have to be blind, stupid, or crazy to state otherwise.

"You look tired," she says with a coy smirk, instantly reminding me that the game we're playing here has never been checkers.

It has *always* been chess.

And it will always *be* chess.

For better, for worse.

'Til death do us part.

Campbell—
My parents are making me send you this
Valentine's Card. It was not my idea. It came
with a Spiderman tattoo, but I kept it.
Slade (*age 9*)

Slade—
I already got cards from other boys. Plus six
tattoos, five erasers, three pencils, a Dora
sticker, and a pink flower ring.
Campbell (*age 8*)

Campbell—
Maybe you should marry one of them instead
of me?
Slade (*age 9*)

Dear Slade—

Maybe I will.
Campbell (*age 8*)

4

Campbell

"I have something for you," Slade reaches into the pocket of his dress slacks, pulling out a small, dark object.

After dinner, my parents suggested we "cozy around the fireplace" on the back deck with some dessert wine, except as soon as we all got situated, they suddenly decided to call it a night and left the two of us alone to catch up.

I'm sure they think they're doing us a favor, fostering romance or something, but my alone time with Slade is only ever filled with barbs and one-liners and each of us checking the time every two seconds.

"Why?" I ask.

He snickers. "Usually when someone gives you a gift, the first thing out of your mouth shouldn't be the word *why* ..."

I clear my throat and straighten my posture. "I just mean, we don't do gifts. You've never given me anything. Why now?"

"Wasn't aware I had to have a reason ..." The crackling fire paints shadows on his handsome face as his dark eyes glint the way they do when he's up to something.

My stomach turns upside down, against my will.

I've always loved and hated it when he looks at me. It's as if he's mocking me yet undressing me with his gaze simultaneously, and I'm not quite sure how I feel about that. I've yet to wrap my head around the fact that we're going to have to consummate our marriage at some point in the near future—we haven't even held hands. Not because our families are ultra conservative or anything like that ... we simply haven't wanted to.

But in less than six months, his lips will be on mine in front of a sea of friends and family.

Perhaps it wouldn't be the worst thing in the world if we started being semi-nice to each other as we march toward our inevitable doom.

I mean, at the end of the day, we're on the same team.

He drops a small leather object in my hand. Attached to it is a shiny gold fob.

"What's this?" I examine my gift in the dark.

"My house key," he says.

I run my fingertips along the leather key ring, realizing there's some kind of inscription on one side. Upon closer inspection, I realize it's a capital D flanked by a C and an E ...my soon-to-be monogram.

Campbell Elizabeth Delacorte.

As much as I hate the idea of taking his last name, I have to admit Campbell *Delacorte* has a nicer ring to it than Campbell *Wakemont*. It's softer, rolling off the tongue easier than it should.

"It was my mother's idea," he says before I can comment.

"Thank you." I close my palm around the key ring.

The plan has always been for us to reside in Florida after the wedding—not only is it a notorious tax haven for the uber-rich like the Delacortes, it's the headquarters of Delacorte Media Group, one of the most powerful media conglomerates in the world with thousands of employees. I wouldn't dream of making a single one of those innocent people relocate for my sake, so I agreed to the move. Besides, Slade would be miserable in Sapphire Shores, and he's already going to be miserable enough in this marriage. No need to double down.

"It's not too late to call this whole thing off, you know." I study his face as I reach for my wine.

"And walk away from my inheritance?" Slade counters without hesitation, reminding me that this has always been about money and nothing else. "I would never."

I've read the contract a million times, backwards and forward, over the years, hoping I could find some kind of loophole or way out of this, but the thing is airtight. Not only that, but Slade has more to lose than I do. Should he choose not to marry me, he'd walk away from his entire inheritance, a fortune estimated to be worth just north of ninety-eight billion dollars (if Google is to be believed).

If this arrangement falls through, his father plans to dismantle Delacorte Media Group piece by piece—a fate worse than death for Slade as he's made his family name and legacy his entire life's purpose.

Nothing—and I mean nothing—matters more to Slade than this company, which is why Slade's father placed a series of stipulations into the contract, stipulations that span beyond the simple marriage itself.

By our first anniversary, I'm expected to be with child—assuming there are no verifiable medical issues to prevent such a thing. Once a baby is born, Slade is slated to receive a ten percent interest in Delacorte Media Group.

By our fifth anniversary, as long as we have two children, Slade will receive another twenty-five percent.

By our tenth anniversary, as long as we're still married, Slade will receive another fourteen percent of the company, with the other fifty-one percent controlled by a board of trustees.

By our twentieth anniversary or Victor's death (whichever comes first)—Slade will receive the remaining shares of Delacorte Media Group.

For Slade, I'm a means to an end.

He needs me more than I need him.

My parents have, naturally, threatened disinheritance should I back out of this arrangement. While our family fortune is comfortably in the millions, it's considerably small compared to the Delacortes'.

Our prenuptial agreement guarantees me five million dollars for each year we're married, plus "bonuses" of twenty million per Delacorte child that I bring into the world.

While I've no doubt I could be happy living the simple life and I'm fully capable of figuring things out on my own and making my own way in this world, I know I could bring about more change and make differences in people's lives— and the world—with a bank account that size. In that regard, I'm choosing to look at the one and only bright side that comes with spending the next twenty years as Mrs. Slade Delacorte.

That, and I've always wanted to be a mom.

Slade might be a bona fide prick ninety-nine point nine percent of the time, but having him as a father would be like setting my future children up to win the genetic lottery.

He's intellectually brilliant. Driven. Athletic. And beautiful. Not to mention, he'd ensure the entire world was at their fingertips. What mother wouldn't want that for her babies?

I'll have to work double time to keep them humble, of course, but I have no doubt it's doable—especially if I involve them in my philanthropic efforts. I'm thinking we could start out with an animal sanctuary and expand into affordable housing for the masses before launching a nation-wide campaign to ban harmful chemicals from American foods.

I've got a long list ...

All I have to do is marry the man sitting next to me.

"Have you ever been in love?" I ask him the question that's been on my mind the most lately. The closer we get to the big day, the more I've been grappling with the notion that I've yet to know what it's like to love or be loved, and marrying him means I may not get the privilege of knowing what that feels like for at least twenty more years.

"Never." He takes a drink of wine, his lips pressing flat as his eyes squint. "You?"

I shake my head. The crackle of the fire and the darkness that engulfs us makes this moment seem more intimate than it probably is, and I'm tempted to confess to him I'm still a virgin, that I've only ever kissed a small handful of guys before. But instead, I swallow my words and decide to play my cards close to my chest as I've done all along with him.

There's an intelligence about this man that's as unsettling as it is sexy.

The last thing I should be doing is exposing my vulnerabilities unless I want him to play me like a fiddle.

"There's more to life than things like love." There's a

hint of confidence in his tone. Or maybe it's arrogance. "Besides, they say romantic love lasts a minimum of three years. It's just a phase fueled by hormones and novelty."

"How could you possibly know that if you've never experienced it before?" I ask.

"Your argument is weak. I don't have to murder someone to know that killing is a bad thing or that I have no desire to commit such an act."

"Apples and oranges."

"We're all entitled to our opinions. You asked mine and I gave it to you." He downs the rest of his wine in one swallow before abandoning the empty chalice on the side table. "It's getting late."

"It's barely 9 PM. I'd hardly call that late."

"Spoken like a true night owl," says the man who wakes up at 5 AM on the dot *without an alarm.*

I imagine the next twenty years will be filled with plenty of lonely late nights ... might as well get used to them now.

Pulling my throw blanket tighter around me, I remain planted in my seat by the fireplace. It's not like he needs me to show him to the guest room. There's no one else around. No need for us to waste our precious energy with phony displays of kindness.

"How bad do you think it's going to be?" I ask before he leaves.

He stops in his tracks. "Excuse me?"

"Our loveless marriage," I clarify. "How bad do you think it's going to be?"

Slade mulls my question with a moment of silence.

"Bad is the wrong word," he says. "It's not going to be *bad* so much as it's going to be the hardest thing either one of us has ever done."

I'm not sure what I was expecting him to say, but it wasn't that.

I nurse the remaining ounce of wine in my glass and ponder his words—and our future.

"What if it doesn't have to be hard?" I ask. "What if we can find a way to make it easier?"

Slade's full lips curl up at the side as he rakes his hand through his thick dark hair, and I can't help but notice the veins popping from his forearms. In the corner of my mind, I picture those hands in my hair and those muscled arms holding me tight.

"What?" I ask. "What's so funny?"

"Your optimism," he says. "Goodnight, Campbell."

Slade—
**Sorry to hear about your cat. Next time maybe
don't let it wander outside and then no one will
steal it?**
Campbell (*age 9*)

Campbell—
**You're dumb and you have no idea what you're
talking about.**
Slade (*age 10*)

**Slade—Maybe it was trying to run away on
purpose? That's what I would do if I was
your cat.**
Campbell (*age 9*)

Campbell—
If you were my cat, I'd let you go on purpose.
Slade (*age 10*)

PS—My cat came back … not that you care.

Slade—
It must have been hungry.
Or stupid.
Campbell (*age 9*)

5

Slade

"Oh, Slade, there you are." Blythe stops me in the hall, placing her hand on my sweaty shoulder as I return from my 5:30 AM jog. Running in this weather is brutal and my lungs feel like blocks of ice, but I'm invigorated, got my morning dose of sunlight, and now I'm ready to take on the day, and that's all that matters. "We're having breakfast in an hour in the dining room. I know you do the whole intermittent fasting thing, but will you at least join us for coffee? I was hoping we could discuss the itinerary for the rest of your stay?"

"Of course." It's not like I have anything else to do.

"Wonderful." Blythe's smiling gaze lingers on me a moment longer before she lets me go. "See you soon."

Continuing down the hall, I pass Campbell's bedroom. The door is half-open for once, so I steal a glimpse inside for the first time ever. The busy floral wallpaper and walnut-stained Americana furnishings makes the space look like it was ripped out of a Ralph Lauren ad campaign circa 1996. A desk in the corner is littered with framed photos, notebooks, and various ribbons—all serving as reminders that while I've known this woman almost my entire life, I still hardly know anything about her.

A glass curio cabinet in the far corner houses an expensive-looking doll collection—a strange thing for a twenty-four-year-old woman to fall asleep next to every night, but I have a feeling Blythe designed every square inch of this space, so I don't hold it against Campbell.

If anything, I feel sorry for her.

Every day of her existence has been micromanaged and orchestrated and dictated.

It's the one thing we have in common.

The only thing, truly.

"See something you like?" Campbell's voice sends a start to my heart. Between all the busy-ness going on in her room, I hadn't noticed her standing amongst it all.

"Yeah," I quip back. "Was just admiring your porcelain doll collection."

She fights a smirk, though her cheeks flush a pale shade of rose, as if she's both humored and embarrassed. I take a moment to drink her in. Even with her glossy blonde hair piled into a mess on top of her head and crumbs of sleep in her eyes, she's still a work of art—prettier than any doll on any shelf could ever be.

"Will your *collection* be joining us in Palm Beach?" I ask.

"That's up to your future mother-in-law. I have a feeling she'll say the humidity will be bad for their curls, though she really likes you, so maybe if you ask nicely, she'll concede?"

I'm leaning against her doorway, which I hadn't realized

I was doing until now. Crossing the threshold feels like an unnatural move, so I don't take another step. Six months from now we'll be sharing a bed—and our bodies. The irony of this moment isn't lost on me, but I don't have time to stand around and give it another thought.

Without a word, I head to my suite to take a shower and prepare for breakfast—and a day chock full of dreaded wedding planning activities.

I've never understood the antiquated concept of marriage or why people continually keep this ridiculous tradition alive when more than half of all marriages fail catastrophically anyway.

If I were a betting man, I'd bet against marriage every time.

Unfortunately, I don't have that luxury with our union. I meant what I said last night when I told her this was going to be the hardest thing either of us would ever do. Fortunately for me, I can do hard things. I can't speak for Campbell, though her optimism is admirable.

Foolish.

But admirable.

Campbell—
I'm only sending you this birthday card because my mom said I had to. I hope you have an awful birthday. I hope your cake is salty and the ice cream melts into a big puddle of sludge. If I got you a gift, it would be a bag of smelly trash wrapped with a puke green bow.
Slade (*age 11*)

Slade—
You're just mad you weren't invited to my party.
Campbell (*age 10*)

6

Campbell

"Are you sure you want to register for that?" Slade points at the gaudy fiesta-style chip-n-dip platter in my hand as we peruse yet another shop for our bridal registry.

"Are you implying that I have bad taste?" I keep a straight face knowing damn well it's the ugliest chip-n-dip platter in existence. Then I snap a picture and send it my group chat with Stassi, Tenley, and Elise who immediately reply with gifs and LOLs. At least someone appreciates my sense of humor.

He cocks his head, lifting a brow. "Well, I'm *not* implying that you have *good* taste."

"How great would this look at our annual Cinco de Mayo pool party though?"

"Pretty sure I didn't agree to an annual Cinco de Mayo pool party."

"Oh, but you did. I slipped it into the pre-nup," I say. "Article twelve, section three—festivities and celebrations."

"Must have missed that part." Gently he takes the dish from my hand and places it back on the shelf. "I get the impression you're just trying to waste time while your mom picks out our wedding china, but let me remind you we still have five more stores to hit after this."

I hate how well he can 'read' me.

It's cruel, really.

He picks up on more nuances than some of my closest friends ever have.

"You have a point," I say.

At breakfast this morning, my mother informed us we'd be spending the day in Portland completing our wedding registry. Never mind that Slade's house already has everything a person could want or need and then some. Most of the things we're registering for will likely be donated anyway, so I'm keeping an eye out for practical items.

I've only been to Slade's personal estate in Palm Beach once, and I wasn't exactly making myself at home. Beside the place being ice cold thanks to a plethora of air conditioning units running around the clock, it was wide open, expansive, and reminded me more of a modern art gallery than a place a person would find comfort at the end of the day.

"My darlings, what do you think of these?" My mother appears out of nowhere, holding up two plates: one with a baby blue floral pattern around the edge and the other with scalloped gold edges. "You can't go wrong with either, in my opinion. True classics. Though, Slade, I know you favor a more modern aesthetic, so I'm happy to look for more options."

Slade and I exchange looks, both of us silently daring the other to speak first.

Anything I say to her will go in one ear and out the other, so I lift my brows and wait for him to pick.

"To be completely honest, Blythe, I can't imagine we'll use the china at all. Even then, it feels a bit superfluous to ask for twenty place settings. I'd hate to have our guests waste their hard-earned money on something that'll be collecting dust in a drawer somewhere." He softens his expression as if it could possibly soften the blow he's just landed in my mother's speechless direction.

Still, I'm impressed.

Hard truths rarely go over with her, but so far she's maintaining her composure.

"Hmm." She examines the plates in her hands. "Well, I mean, it's tradition and all to register for wedding china, and most people display them in cabinets so they're rarely out of sight—but if you're absolutely positive you won't use them …"

Slade defers to me with a wordless glance.

Are we actually on the same page for once?

"I agree." I take a step closer to Slade, offering my support. "I appreciate the sentiment, but no sense in registering for something we'll never use."

"Fair enough." She stacks the plates in her hands. "At least select some stemware while we're here—they have some lovely champagne flutes over there. You can use them on your wedding day and toast with them on every anniversary, just like your father and I do."

The ease of which my mother pretends all of this is normal never ceases to amaze me, so I don't waste my breath reminding her there won't be any anniversary celebrations. At least not on my part. I have no doubt Slade will be joyfully commemorating the specific milestones in which he collects another percentage of his inheritance.

"Sure," I say. "We'll head that way in a second."

Mom trots off to return the plates to their displays, and I turn to my future husband.

"You can pick the flutes," I tell him. "I've never been big on champagne and I highly doubt we'll be celebrating anything, ever. I mean, with how hard everything will be and all."

His coffee-hued irises flash, but he doesn't offer a comeback.

"I need some air." I point to the doors and head that way before he has a chance to protest. Not that he would. I'm sure he wants a break from all of this together-ness.

Once outside, I drag in a lungful of crisp winter air and let the cold sunlight wash over me. Hard to believe in less than a year I'll be trading in the four seasons for alligators, well-fed mosquitos, and tropical storms.

I dig the toe of my leather boot into a blanket of nearby snow and listen for the satisfying crunch, a sound I imagine I'll be missing more than anything this time next year.

Years ago, when I was arguing with my parents about this arrangement, my grandmother pulled me aside and told me to focus on what I was getting out of this, not what I was giving up. She reminded me that her marriage was arranged, and that my parents' marriage was also arranged, and all of them were wonderfully happy with lives blessed beyond belief. She prattled on about financial security, a bright future for my children, and a family history that spans back to the gilded age since one of Slade's great-great-grandmothers was a Golden Age "dollar princess."

She painted a beautiful portrait with her words, one filled with hope and joyful future memories and all good things.

If Gram were still around, she'd have gotten a kick out

of my black wedding dress, though she'd have vetoed it as well.

Her penchant for tradition made my mother look like an amateur.

"There you are." A masculine voice interrupts my me-time after a few minutes.

I look over to find Slade standing outside the shop door, his hands in his pockets and his breath turning to clouds with each exhalation. I wouldn't be surprised if he hates the cold almost as much as he hates this arrangement.

"Did my mother send you to find me?" I ask, head cocked. If he says no, it'll be the shock of a lifetime because Slade's not the type to care about anyone's wellbeing other than this own.

"Of course."

"Tell her I went to grab an iced coffee down the street. She'll freak out. It'll be fun." I wink and he stands there, like he doesn't get it. And he wouldn't, I suppose. He only knows her on a superficial level and even then, that's barely scratching the surface of Blythe Wakemont. "I'm kidding. Don't do that."

There's a vague tightness in my chest when I realize he and I will likely never have inside jokes the way a *real* couple would. I don't need a crystal ball to know we're going to be two passing ships in the night for the next twenty years.

Maybe Slade's right—this is going to be harder than I imagined.

"I think she's ready to wrap everything up and head to the next place ..." he says.

"Right." I follow him back inside, and we find my mother at the registry desk, making pleasantries with the attendant as they go over a printed list.

We're patiently waiting a moment later when Slade leans in, his lips nearly brushing my cheek, and he says, "I chose the champagne glasses, by the way."

"Oh, yeah? What'd you go with?" I ask.

Pulling out his phone, he shows me an image he must have taken when I was outside.

"They're not flutes, they're technically champagne saucers," he says. "Drinking it this way allows for more surface area of the champagne to come into contact with air, which lets you taste more of the aroma flavors. Some people drink champagne for the bubbles. Some drink it for the full experience."

Typical Slade—intellectualizing every little thing down to the last detail.

"That's nice and all," I say, "but like I said before, I'm not a big champagne person."

"Have you ever tried it from a saucer?"

"Can't say that I have."

"Then perhaps you do like it, you just don't know it yet."

Slade—

My mom said we should tell each other ten things we want the other person to know so we can get to know each other better. She also said we have to be nicer going forward. I told her I'd try. Anyway, here's my list:

1. I'm a Sagittarius (which means we're incompatible since you're a Capricorn).
2. My favorite kind of food is any type of green vegetable—no one believes me, but it's true. Brussels sprouts and asparagus are my favorite, then arugula.
3. I speak both French and Spanish.
4. I'm distantly related to Ariana Grande on my mom's side.

5. My best friend's name is Stassi. She has two older brothers who play hockey and they're super annoying.
6. I love scary movies and they never give me nightmares.
7. The longest handstand I've ever done was three minutes and thirty-nine seconds long.
8. I make really, really good banana chocolate chip pancakes.
9. I've never broken a bone or gotten stitches before.
10. I almost drowned once, but my nanny saved me. Then she got fired.

Campbell (*age 11*)

Campbell—

Here are ten things about me that I think you should know:

I hate you.

I hate you.

I hate you.

I hate you.

I hate you.

I hate you.

I hate you.

I hate you.

I hate you.

I hate you.

Slade (*age 12*)

Slade—
Tell me something I don't already know.
Campbell (*age 11*)

Campbell—
My mom is sick. Bet you didn't know that.
Slade (*age 12*)

Slade—
You're right. I didn't know that. I hope she gets better soon.
Campbell (*age 11*)

7

Campbell

"This looks good. Want to watch it?" I point the remote control to a movie I have cued on Netflix in the family room —a brightly hued romcom called *Mr. Perfect* starring Rose Byrne. After ten hours of registry shopping in Portland finished by a five-course meal at my mother's favorite Italian haunt on the way home, I'm in coordinating baby blue sweats and in full couch-potato mode and I'm not even sorry. "I think it just came out today. The preview looks funny."

Normally I'd pick something in the horror genre, but not everyone has the same *refined* taste as me. That and Stassi claimed this was worth the watch.

"What?" Slade glances up from his phone, half-listening. "Yeah, whatever. That's fine."

I press play and the room flashes dark save for the giant red N on the screen and the dim light of Slade's cell in his hand. Whatever he's texting or emailing about, it must be serious because he's done nothing but sigh and huff since he sat down a few minutes ago.

I fully expected him to retire to his suite for the night when we got home earlier, but he muttered something about not wanting to be cooped up and asked what I was going to do. Before I had a chance to answer, my mother suggested we "relax with a movie in the den" and offered to have the house manager pop us some of her "famous" white cheddar popcorn.

The entire thing was as wholesome as it was awkward—and now here we are.

The sound of moaning and panting co-mingles with some chipper pop song as the film starts, and the camera pans to a bed covered in messy sheets and tangled, bare legs.

Oh god ... I had no idea it was going to start like this.

From the corner of my eye, I catch Slade's attention gradually lifting away from his email and towards the TV.

Rose Byrne's character grabs a fistful of her partner's wavy blond hair as she gyrates her hips beneath him. Her face is contorted and she's breathless and sweaty. Pretty sure sex is nothing like this in real life, but I wouldn't know for sure.

Maybe it is?

Wouldn't that be wild?

"Harder ... yes ... oh god ... don't stop," Rose pants as her nails dig into her co-star's muscled back. "Just like that ... yeah ... keep going ... harder, deeper ..."

I pull my merino wool throw blanket tighter around me and slink down into the sofa. I'm a grown woman, but if my father were to walk in right now, I'd feel very much like a humiliated teenager wanting to crawl inside a hole and die. Anyone walking past right now would no doubt think we were casually enjoying a porno together.

"You like that, Jasmine?" the muscled blond Casanova growls into her ear as he plows into her. "God, you're so wet. I just—"

Rose stops gyrating and panting, her brown eyes wide and her mouth agape.

"What'd you just say?" she asks, shoving him off of her.

The man, clearly confused, says, "I said you were wet ..."

"No, before that. You called me Jasmine. My name is Jessamyn," she says.

In one frustrated fell swoop, Rose's character pushes him off the bed, wraps her naked, sweaty body in the tangled sheets, and scampers off to the bathroom, slamming the door behind her. The man, cupping his junk, chases after her, knocking and apologizing for the gaffe while we get a perfectly framed view of his tanned, taut glutes.

"God, I hate when that happens ..." I tease in an attempt to make this less awkward.

Slade frowns. "What?"

"Never mind." I wave my hand. If you have to explain a joke, that means it wasn't funny enough to begin with.

I return my focus to the movie.

"I said Jessamyn!" the male star insists as he talks through the locked door.

"You said *Jasmine!*" Rose yells from the other side. "And that's my *sister's* name! I knew you liked her. *I knew it.* You tried to deny it when I asked you before, but I had a feeling ..."

The on-screen couple continues to bicker, and I fully expect Slade to mentally check out at any time, but he doesn't.

The montage that follows shows Rose's character kicking her beau out and tossing his clothes over the balcony railing of their Manhattan apartment. Not exactly groundbreaking stuff here, but I'm curious to see how it pans out because the next scene has Rose calling her sister —the real Jasmine—to tell her what happened. Only Jasmine's reaction isn't what Rose's character was expecting ... at all.

"Do you ever wish you had a brother or sister?" I ask, tossing a salty, cheesy popcorn kernel into my mouth. "Like, we'll never know what it's like to fight with a sibling."

"You say that like it's a bad thing."

"It's just some food for thought." I chomp another kernel before offering him the bucket we're supposed to be sharing.

He shakes his head, passing. I don't push it. More for me.

While Jasmine and Jessamyn quarrel over the blond muscled now-homeless guy, I steal another peek at Slade. The dark of the room and the flash of the TV screen illuminates his perfect profile, highlighting his strong, straight nose, his prominent jaw, full lips, and thick head of hair.

To think ... he's going to be the father of my future children.

Tuning out the on-screen drama, I whip up a visualization of what our babies might look like, swapping out various features like that Super Mario Brothers game where you have to match up the three parts of a star or mushroom or plant.

Our brood is either going to be beautiful ... or interesting-looking.

"Why are you staring at me?" Slade breaks his silence, his dark gaze darting my way.

"I wasn't staring at you." I scoff, fumbling a few pieces of popcorn into my mouth.

"You were. And you have been. Maybe you should watch this movie—the movie you picked out?"

"Okay fine," I say. "I was just trying to picture what our future kids would look like."

His brows meet. "Really? That's what you were thinking about just now?"

I nod, chewing. "Aren't you curious?"

"Not really."

"Do you even want kids?" I ask a question I'm pretty sure I already know the answer to. "Or is it just another obligation you have to fulfill?"

"You want to have this conversation right here, right now?" he asks while the sister drama continues to play out. He has a point—it'd make for an obnoxious soundtrack to this sort of discussion.

"No," I say.

The scene ends with the sisters hanging up on each other.

"Do you think we'll have them the old-fashioned way?" I ask another question that's been on my mind lately. The contract doesn't say we can't use IUI or IVF or even a surrogate. Technically we don't even have to consummate the marriage to have babies ...

But twenty-four years is a long time to be a virgin, and I don't want to go another twenty. I'm patient, but not that patient. I suppose I could have an affair given that the foundation of our arrangement was never built on love, but I've never thought of myself as that kind of person. The thought of it alone makes me feel ... sticky.

As insufferable as Slade is, I bet he can do some serious damage in the bedroom—in a good way, I mean.

Hate sex is a thing for a reason.

"That was my assumption, yes," he answers. His words send my stomach to the floor.

He actually *wants* to sleep with me ...

Does he think I'm sexy?

Does he find me attractive?

Or am I just a convenient hole to fill?

"How many people have you been with?" I ask as he reaches for his can of lime seltzer water.

He almost chokes on his drink. "Seriously?"

"No judgement. Just curious."

Clearing his throat, he presses his lips into a firm line. "I don't know that number off the top of my head."

"That many, eh?" I lift my brows.

"No, it's just not something I think about." He leans back against the sofa, running his palm along the top of his muscled thigh as he draws in a long breath. His lips move softly as he whispers to himself. "Twelve, thirteen maybe?"

"Which is it? Twelve or thirteen?"

"Does it make that big of a difference to you?"

I roll my eyes. "I just don't want to be number thirteen. It's unlucky."

"Says who?"

I place a hand over my chest. "Says moi."

"Never took you as the superstitious type," he says. "You know, superstitious people tend to be the easiest ones to manipulate."

"Says who?"

"Says the Journal of Political Science," he cites his source, like the hot nerd that he is. "People who believe things without proof, tend to believe more things than the average person."

"I'm not an idiot."

"I'm not saying you're an idiot."

"Anyway." I reach for the remote and rewind the movie a bit. "You're not as experienced as I assumed you'd be."

"Were you expecting my number to be higher?"

I laugh. "Much."

"How much?"

"Thirty, maybe forty," I say. "I mean, you're an attractive guy. You live in a city filled with beautiful women. You travel all around the world. I figured you'd want to sow as many wild oats as you could before you had to marry me."

"Thanks for stereotyping me. Appreciate it."

I chuff. "Any time."

"What about you?" he turns the tables before we can dig into his number any deeper. "How many have you been with?"

Holding up my fist, I form my fingers into the shape of a zero.

"Liar," he says.

"Give me a Bible right now and I'll swear on it."

"Seriously?"

"Seriously. I'm a virgin," I say.

"You ... saved yourself for *me?*" He squints as he studies me.

On the TV, Rose Byrne is tossing back her lemon drop martini and scanning a bar for someone to take home so she can have revenge sex. Whoever wrote this terrible script did Rose dirty. It's nothing but cliché after cliché.

"Not on purpose," I say. "Just ... the opportunity never came up. I always went to all girls' schools, then I went to an all girls' college. I never bothered dating anyone because I was afraid I'd get attached or he'd get attached and the whole thing would inevitably end in heartbreak since I was already promised to someone, so it was just easier to avoid it altogether."

"Have you ever been kissed?"

"Of course," I say. "Many times. And I've messed around with guys too."

He rests his elbow along the back of the sofa as he angles his body towards me. It's as if he's seeing me in a new light, though I can't tell whether or not that light is flattering or appalling. Half of me would pay a penny for his thoughts, but the other half of me is vehemently against it in case he's thinking about how my inexperience might lead to a disappointing wedding night.

"I almost lost it to this one guy my senior year at Wellesley. I met him at this house party and we were having a good time, hitting it off. And he was nice. And hilarious. And cute. But the more I thought about it, the more I knew I didn't want my first time to be with some random dude with beer breath. Plus, he kept calling me Cami, and I hate that. Took it as a sign. Also, he had a weird obsession with Modest Mouse. Was wearing a Modest Mouse t-shirt. Carried some Modest Mouse concert ticket stubs in his wallet. Even had a Modest Mouse ring tone *and* phone cover."

"Sounds like you dodged a bullet that night." His mouth lifts at the side as he drags his fingertip over it. He's giving me that look again, the one where I can't tell if he's undressing me with his eyes or analyzing vulnerabilities I didn't know I had.

Heat creeps up my neck, and I swallow hard.

In the background, Rose and some suit-wearing lothario are going at it in the bathroom of some nightclub. He props her up on the sink, tearing at her clothes as she throws her head back and groans like a sex-starved siren.

"It's not really like that, is it?" I point to the screen. "It's not that cringy and desperate, right?"

Slade sniffs a laugh. "Nah."

"Good."

Sex, to me, has always been this far-off concept. Other than paging to the smutty parts of drug store romance novels and feasting my eyes on sultry movie scenes over the years and listening to tales of my friends' late-night exploits, it's always been the kind of thing that everyone else did—except for me.

Strange to think that in less than six months, I'll be kissing my virginity goodbye once and for all.

"Are you good?" I ask, propping my head against my hand. "In bed, I mean."

Slade sniffs, insulted. "What kind of question is that?"

"What are you like? Are you attentive? Do you take your time? Or do you just do your thing, wait for her to fake an orgasm, and go on your way?"

"Sounds like you've seen way too many shitty Netflix movies."

"That doesn't answer my questions."

"I don't know." His face scrunches as he ponders his response. "I take my time. I don't rush. But I'm efficient." He lifts a hand. "But not too efficient." His tongue glides along his lips. "For me, it's not over until we're both satisfied. However long that takes."

My heart trips over itself in my chest.

Is it possible that Slade, in all his self-serving glory, actually gives a damn about other people's pleasure?

"So you always get your partner off?" I ask.

"Every time."

"How do you know for sure?"

"For starters," he begins, "when a woman comes, her entire body tightens. It's an involuntary response. I can actually feel her tightening about my cock. Her muscles tense up, her breathing changes. Afterwards, her body will shake a little, especially when I pull out or if I run my fingers along her sensitive parts. She'll tremble. That's my test. That's how I know."

The thought of his fingers between my thighs fills my head before I have a chance to stop it, and I squirm in my seat. I expected him to rattle off some egotistical statement like, "A man just knows" or some bullshit like that, but damn.

I clear my throat, which is as tight and clenched as, well, the rest of me.

"Is this conversation making you uncomfortable?" he asks.

Was my squirming that obvious? I suppose it is to a man who notices everything ...

"No," I lie. It's not making me uncomfortable so much as it's making me think about him in ways I never thought I could before.

To be completely honest, the times when I've imagined the two of us consummating our marriage, it was always along the lines of us in missionary position, in the quiet dark, our gazes pointed in opposite directions while we got it over with in five minutes flat.

Never once did I imagine Slade had an attentive bone in his body.

"You surprised me, that's all," I say.

"In a good way, I hope."

I ward off a smirk. All things considered, the man does have an ego the size of Jupiter and its eighty moons combined. Any more praise and his head might literally explode.

The movie scene playing across the room consists of Rose getting ready for a date with the guy she met at the bar. She wasn't expecting to like him. He was supposed to be a revenge hookup and nothing more. Now she's frantically shaving her legs and changing her dress every two seconds and cursing under her breath, trying to muster up the strength to cancel on him because she's not in a place to dive into another relationship—but the sex is good. She reminds herself about the sex. And her roommate chimes in, reminding her that love and sex can be mutually exclusive if you allow them to be.

A sliver of hope dashes through my middle in the mist of Rose's fictional chaos.

Maybe Slade and I will never be in love—but maybe, just maybe we could have a smoking hot sex life.

I could settle for that.

Especially if he's as attentive as he claims to be.

Focusing on the movie, I do my best to pay attention to what's going on, but my thoughts are all over the place, conjuring up all sorts of naughty scenarios involving the two of us.

But at some point between the start of this movie and now, the space between us on the sofa has narrowed. In fact, we're so close, I can feel the heat radiating off his body, invading my space along with a hint of his spicy cologne.

It isn't long before we're in the throes of another over-the-top sex scene.

I'm not sure if it's my own sexual repression or a combination of everything, but every atom of my body is electric and I'm pretty sure I'm going to explode if I don't do something about this soon …

I check the time on my phone—we're only thirty minutes into this movie with at least another hour to go. A tortuous hour of sitting here daydreaming of Slade's touch like the curious virgin that I am …

Sitting up, I reach for my Diet Coke and popcorn and try to keep my head on straight. In all the years we've known each other, our conversations have never so much as skimmed the surface of this sort of thing.

Rose Byrne takes her date home for a nightcap, which ends up with him ripping her clothes off and taking her on the kitchen island.

She comes not once, but twice—once by his mouth and again by his cock.

He doesn't say her sister's name.

He makes her pancakes when it's over because it's late, she's hungry, and all the good restaurants are closed. After that, he stays over and they lie awake talking all night about all the things they have in common—authors they love, places they've traveled to.

I blink and it's the two of us on that screen, lying in bed, laughing, eyes only for each other.

But my silent fantasies of Slade come to a screeching halt when I realize I'm getting ahead of myself.

This is what I get for having too much wine at dinner.

Just because a guy knows his way around a clitoris doesn't mean he's going to check all the other boxes too—that sort of thing only happens in the movies.

Slade and I will never be *that* kind of couple.

As the movie plays on, I find myself stealing more peeks his way, still wondering what our first time will be like. Curiosity has always been my middle name, much to my mother's dismay. She used to tell me my head was too full of questions and I needed to make room for other things, but I can't help it.

"Still wondering what our children will look like?" Slade asks when he eventually catches me. His dark gaze holds mine captive.

"No," I say. "I was looking at your lips this time, wondering what kind of kisser you are."

He laughs. "Why?"

"Kind of sucks that we have to have our first kiss in front of six hundred people," I say. "What if it's bad? What if I turn my head left and you do too? Or what if we bump our teeth together? Or—"

"I can assure you I'm an excellent kisser and you'll have nothing to worry about," he says. "Besides, who says you have to wait until our wedding day to find out?"

"What, like we're going to just kiss before then for the hell of it?" I laugh at his ridiculous notion. "Because we *want* to? Because we *feel* like it? Yeah, right."

He lifts a muscled shoulder and juts his chin forward. "You're laughing, but I don't find this funny at all. I'd kiss you right now."

My stomach drops—again.

The way he says that, so calm and confident, and the determination in his eyes—it's like he's hunting me, already knowing he has me caught in his net.

My face flushes and I'm grateful for the dark so he can't see.

Perhaps I'm imagining it, but the distance between us has narrowed once more.

His fingertips graze the top of my arm, leaving a trail of goosebumps in its wake. The realization that this is exactly what my mother probably wanted to happen intrudes on my thoughts and threatens to ruin this moment, but I force it away.

"You've always had the prettiest mouth," he says as he slowly brings his hand to the side of my face. Cupping my chin, he runs the pad of his thumb along my lower lip. This is—quite literally—the most intimate moment we've ever shared. "Heart-shaped. Soft. Fuckable."

His words deepen my blushing cheeks a full three shades, I'm sure of it.

No one has *ever* spoken to me that way before—like I'm a sexual being and not just someone's friend or daughter.

He holds my stare with his, and as much as I try to look away, I can't.

My curiousness has me powerless, frozen.

"Am I supposed to be flattered?" I strengthen my resolve and break my silence, refusing to melt in his hands. Even if I'm promised to him, he still has to work for me. Not to mention, this doesn't change anything. He's still rude. And arrogant. And self-centered. And obsessed with money. Nothing I'd ever want in a husband.

"I don't know," he says. "Are you?"

Flattered? No.

Turned on? Strangely ... yes.

But that's between me, myself, and I.

My mouth runs dry as my focus turns to his lips. His hand slinks down to my neck, his fingertips slipping into my hair while he looks like he's seconds from making a meal out of me.

"Oh, there you two are." A voice that belongs to neither Slade or myself slices through the viscous tension in the room.

It's my father.

Without hesitating, I lunge for the remote and pause the show on the off chance Rose Byrne gets down and dirty again.

"Your mother said you two were in here watching a movie," he says, completely oblivious to what was about to take place a moment ago. "Hadn't seen either of you since this morning. Just wanted to say goodnight before I headed to bed."

We exchange goodnights, and my father leaves, taking the tension we'd been building up for the last forty-five minutes along with him.

The moment is gone.

Though maybe it's for the best.

"I'm getting a little tired myself. Should probably call it a day." I fake a yawn. My body's still reeling and I don't trust myself to sit next to Slade for the next forty-five minutes without doing something stupid like offering myself to him on a silver platter because he's mastered the art of verbal foreplay.

"You never go to bed this early." He frowns. Of course he would know what time I hit the hay. The man notices everything I do.

"First time for everything." I rise, folding my throw blanket and resting it on the arm of the sofa. Collecting my Diet Coke and sticking the bucket of popcorn under my arm, I give him a wink. "Better luck next time."

Slade—
I haven't heard from you in a while. I hope your mom is okay. My mom said she sent your mom her favorite flowers—daffodils. They had to be imported from south of the equator because they only grow in the springtime here. Hope she likes them.
Campbell (*age 11*)

Campbell—
My mom is still sick. She said thanks for the flowers.
Slade (*age 12*)

8

Slade

I'm adjusting the starched white collar of my tuxedo Saturday morning when my phone vibrates with a text from my uncle.

OLIVER: How goes it? You alive up there? Making sure you didn't freeze to death.

ME: That joke is as lame today as it was last month. Need to come up with some new material.

OLIVER: Whatever. Just checking on you. Haven't heard from you in days. Forgive me for giving a damn about your uptight ass.

ME: Blythe has me on a tight schedule with all of this wedding planning shit.

OLIVER: Don't act like you're not enjoying every second of it. Every little boy dreams about his wedding day. This is your time to shine, buddy!! This is your moment!! It's gonna be the best day of your life!! [bride and groom emoji] [church emoji] [flowers emoji]

ME: Says the guy who left his bride at the altar four years ago. Also, what thirty-five-year-old man uses those emojis? I'm embarrassed for you.

OLIVER: In my defense, I'd just found out my bride slept with my best man. Traded one cliché for another. And I'm secure enough in my manhood to use those emojis. Feel free to take a page from my book.

I roll my eyes and place my phone aside so I can finish getting dressed. The sooner I emerge from this fitting room, the sooner the tailor can make his markings and we can be on our way.

"How's it going in there, Slade?" Blythe calls from the other side of the curtain. "Need anything?"

"I'll be out in a minute," I say.

"You sure about that?" Campbell adds from out there. "Because it sounds like you're on your phone in there."

"Slade, darling, please tell me you're not working on a Saturday," Blythe groans like it's the worst thing in the world. I vaguely recall years ago my parents talking about how Blythe gave Cedric an ultimatum about his work schedule and Saturdays were sacred. My mom would have never done that to my father.

Delacortes are work horses.

We never take a day off.

It's not in our blood.

Even my uncle Oliver, who lives off a small yet comfortable trust fund, runs a small yacht business as a side hustle despite not needing to work at all.

A few minutes later, I'm straightening my black satin bow tie and shrugging into a black suit coat.

God, I look like a grade-A prick in this penguin suit.

An expensive grade-A prick, but a prick nonetheless.

Shoving the curtain aside, I step out of the dressing room and into the area where Blythe and Campbell are waiting.

Blythe gasps, placing a delicate hand on her collarbone. "How handsome are you? My goodness. Look at that. Campbell, isn't he just striking?"

Campbell's pretty blue gaze flutters up from her phone screen, and while I attempt to gauge her reaction, she gives me nothing. I've yet to determine if she finds me good-looking. Last night she stated that she thought I'd slept with almost forty women because I was attractive, but that doesn't mean *she* finds me attractive. I don't suppose it matters. She's stuck with me regardless.

Meanwhile, Blythe continues to fawn.

"What do you think?" I ask my future wife as I turn around.

"It looks ... like a tux ..." She shrugs. "I don't know what else I'm supposed to say?"

Blythe jabs an elbow into her daughter's rib cage, leans in, and whispers something. Campbell's heart-shaped mouth forms a knowing smile that vanishes in an instant.

"Sorry. You look very nice," Campbell says without a trace of genuine emotion or excitement. "You'll be the belle of the ball—whatever the guy version of that is."

My gaze falls to that smart mouth of hers.

Twelve hours ago, that heart-shaped estuary was almost mine ... until her father ruined the moment.

I've thought about her cherry lips more times lately than I'd ever admit to anyone.

All I wanted was a taste ... a sample.

She's a virgin.

I wouldn't have taken it too far, too fast.

I'm a lot of things, but I'm not *that*.

I was hoping we'd pick up where we left off as soon as her father left, but no dice.

Campbell saw through me.

If we were chess pieces, she'd be a knight, never moving in any kind of straight line so you never know where she's going to go next.

Unpredictable in a sense.

"Black and white is such a timeless combination," Blythe muses as she rises and examines me from every angle. Tugging and pulling on various parts, she tells the tailor what to change and alter. "And you can never go wrong with Dior."

Campbell rolls her eyes when Blythe isn't looking. The more I'm around these two, the more I'm realizing how much name-dropping and brand-dropping Mrs. Wakemont does, especially in the presence of others.

It's a bit over the top.

An unquestionable sign of insecurity too—which is shocking considering how much money the Wakemonts have. Granted, they're no Delacortes, not even close, but they're up there.

Campbell, on the other hand, has yet to wear a single item of clothing or accessory emblazoned with any kind of designer logos. At least not around me.

Last night at dinner, when her mother was going off about the Oscar de la Renta bridesmaid dresses that are running late, Campbell stated that they wouldn't have had that problem had they gone with the local designer she wanted to support.

I stayed out of that battle, but remained quietly impressed with Campbell's stance.

"Did I tell you what your fiancée tried to do the other day?" Blythe places her hand on my arm, her face pulled into a wide smile like she's about to laugh at a joke she's yet to tell.

"What's that?" I ask.

"She tried to choose a *black* wedding gown." Blythe slaps my arm. "Can you believe that?"

I steer my attention to Campbell, my little chess piece.

"Yes," I say. "I can very much believe that, actually."

"And then she tried to pick out *funeral* flowers," Blythe continues, chuckling as she toys with the glimmering diamond pendant hanging from her neck. "She keeps me on my toes, this one. She'll keep you on yours too."

I don't tell her that Campbell already does.

Slade—
I'm starting to think there's got to be a way out
of this stupid marriage thing. I tried talking to
my school counselor about it, but she laughed
and thought I was joking. She told me nobody
can make anyone marry anyone else because
it's a free country. Maybe if we keep telling our
parents we don't want to do this, they won't
make us?
What are they going to do? Drag us down the
aisle on our wedding day kicking and screaming
in front of all those people?
Let me know what you think.
Campbell (*age* 12)

Campbell—
You don't think I've already tried? I'm ten steps
ahead of you. Let me know when you come up

with an idea that's smart and doesn't actually
suck.
Slade (*age 13*)

Slade—
If you're ten steps ahead of me and nothing has
worked, that means your ideas sucked too. In
case you've forgotten, we're fighting for the
same cause.
You don't always have to be a jerk.
Campbell (*age 12*)

Campbell—
My father always says being nice doesn't pay
yet I'm expected to be nice to you to get paid.
If you're so smart, make that make sense.
Slade (*age 13*)

9

Campbell

"You're seriously watching this without me?" Slade stands in the doorway of the den Saturday night.

"Oh, sorry." I pause *Mr. Perfect*. "I didn't realize you were into it."

"I wasn't," he says. "But I'm invested. I want to know if Jessamyn ends up with Mr. Perfect and whether or not her sister and ex get their comeuppance."

"Hmm." I tilt my head. "Kinda sounds like you were into it."

He takes the spot beside me, his body weight dipping the couch cushion just enough that there's some sort of gravitational pull that brings me a few inches closer to him than before.

Whether it's a strategic, intentional move or sheer happenstance is hard to tell, but I have my suspicions.

I press play and attempt to get comfortable despite the fact that my thigh and his thigh are basically fusing into one thigh and we're sitting so close I can taste the mint on his breath when he exhales.

He must have brushed his teeth before he came in here …

"Is it true you wanted a black wedding dress?" he asks when we're halfway into the next scene. Rose Byrne is showering with Mr. Perfect and in a span of thirty seconds, he goes from massaging the shampoo into her hair to massaging an orgasm between her legs.

"Yep." I drag in a slow breath, waiting for some smart remark, but it never comes.

"And funeral flowers?"

"Yep."

"Let me guess, you're mourning the life you'll never get to live."

I clench my jaw, hating how spot-on he is while also being wildly impressed with his consistent penchant for keen observation.

"Is it that obvious?" I ask.

"Little bit." He sniffs. A bout of silence simmers between us. "Some people have real problems, you know."

"Thank you for that enlightening tidbit of information. I had no idea."

"I'm just saying, there are worse things in life than marrying into a family richer than God and having the kind of privilege ninety-nine point nine-nine-nine-nine-nine percent of the world will never experience a fraction of."

"Not surprised you've done the math on that." I keep my gaze trained on the TV screen so I'm not tempted to look at his lips or his mouth this time.

"I'm just saying, sometimes perspective is priceless."

"That's rich coming from a man with quote-unquote

more money than God," I tell him. "By the way, who even says that? Do you hear yourself right now?"

"Not every truth can be wrapped in a pretty bow for the masses."

"For the record, I'm not the masses, I'm your fiancée. And please don't ever use that expression in my presence again." I reach for the remote and dial the volume up a couple of notches. I don't want to talk, bicker, or flirt. I've been with this man for two straight days. All I want is to escape reality for the next forty-five minutes by living vicariously through Rose Byrne and her sexual escapades.

"Noted." Swiping the remote, he dials the volume back down.

"What are you doing?"

"Rose gets a little loud when she, uh ..." His eyes dart to the doorway where my father essentially manifested out of thin air the night before. "I mean, unless you want everyone to think we're watching porn in here or something ..."

Fair point.

We continue the show, but in the minutes that follow, I can't stop thinking about Slade's comments, so much so that I can't focus on Mr. Perfect's eight-pack while he tugs his shirt off before baking Jessamyn pumpkin muffins for her neighborhood's charity bake sale.

"I hope I don't come off like some spoiled princess in a tower, crying over her good fortune," I break the silence. "I promise I'm not like that. I'm not a poor little rich girl. I'm very grateful. Beyond, actually. I just ..."

Slade pauses the show and turns his focus to me.

"The funeral stuff, that's my sense of humor," I continue. "I'm trying to make light of something that's arguably pretty heavy. No one knows about this arrangement. Not even my closest friends. I can't talk to anyone about it. There's no one I know who can relate to the strange assortment of feelings swimming through my head at any given moment. I'm alone. I don't even have *you* to talk to because you're this impenetrable fortress of a man."

I spare him the diatribe on how I've never had the choice as to where I was going to live, whom I was going to marry and have kids with, or even whether or not I'd keep my last name. All of those things were decided and all but written in stone before I took my first steps or said my first words. These ideas and expectations have been indoctrinated into me for as long as I can remember, presented to me as both a privilege and a threat at the same time.

My options have always been that I can "have it all" or I can have nothing at all.

There was never an in between.

My eyes search Slade's, though for what, I'm not entirely sure.

His gaze drops to my lips for a fraction of a second, causing my heart to come to a dead stop when I'm almost certain he's going to try and kiss me again.

"You can walk away," he says, sparing me the kiss I did (and didn't) want. "From me ... from all of this."

I exhale, releasing a lungful of tension. "Don't think I haven't thought about that a thousand times."

"What's stopping you?"

Years ago, I asked my father what would happen to Slade's inheritance if I chose not to marry him but he still wanted to go through with it. He told me more than likely his father would choose someone else for him to marry, that I'd be replaced in two seconds flat by someone who'd probably kill for the opportunity to be the next Mrs. Delacorte.

Despite not wanting to marry Slade in the first place, it

was with those words that I experienced my first pang of jealousy—which disappeared as quickly as it showed up.

"I don't know. I guess I made peace with this a long time ago, and I'm choosing to focus on the good that can come out of it," I say. "What's stopping you?"

"I think you already know."

"You want your father's company so badly you're willing to trade your future for it? Your free will?"

"Yes." He doesn't hesitate, not for a millisecond.

"What's it like not caring about anything except money?"

"Liberating."

I wrinkle my nose. "From what?"

"From *everything*," he says. "You should try it sometime."

Slade—
My mom gave me a Pen Pal book with a list of things we can write about to get to know each other better because apparently we've been doing a bad job of it the last several years. I don't really have anything else to say to you, so … whatever I guess I'll do it.
Three words that describe me are: curious, amused, and easygoing.
My role model is: Harriet Tubman because no one is braver than she was.
One thing I like about where I live is that we can ski in the winter and boat in the summer. I guess that's two things. Oh, well.
My favorite color is red.
Your turn.
Campbell (*age 13*)

Campbell—
That was probably the lamest letter you've ever
sent me, and that's saying a lot.
Slade (*age 14*)

10

Slade

"Where's the old man?" I ask Oliver Sunday evening. An hour ago, I arrived at Palm Beach International, picked up my car from the valet, and drove straight to my parents' house. The place is quieter than usual. No TV tuned into a steady stream of cable news. No classical music playing on hidden speakers throughout the entrance. No bustling sounds coming from the kitchen where the chef would normally be preparing an elaborate Sunday dinner.

"On the greens." Oliver swirls his brandy in a Delacorte monogrammed crystal tumbler as he leans behind my parents' bar. "Where else would he be?"

Four weeks ago, we got the unfortunate news that the rare neurological disorder my mother has been battling since I was a kid is back with a vengeance. This time it's progressing faster than the best doctors can stop it. It won't be long before it'll steal her vision and language and eventually, her life.

I slam my fist on the counter. "What the hell is he doing golfing when—"

"—relax, sweetheart. I told him to go. I insisted, actually." My mother shuffles in, her gaunt frame wrapped in a vibrant Pucci robe with a matching headscarf to disguise her thinning hair. Her sea glass eyes are especially shiny—a sign that she's having one of her good days. "I thought some sunshine and fresh air would do him good. We could all use a little more of that, couldn't we? Almost feels like spring-time already."

She slides onto a bar stool and gives me a sleepy smile.

"I thought the doctor hadn't cleared him yet?" I ask. It's one thing to take care of my ailing mother—it's another to have to take care of a stubborn, sixty-five-year-old man who refuses to wait a second longer to get back on the golf course.

"Cleared him this morning, actually. How was your time with the Wakemonts?" she asks, cupping her pointed chin on her delicate hand. The woman is wasting away by the second. Every time I see her—which is daily when I'm not traveling—she's smaller than the time before. The medications zap her appetite, she says, always followed by a comment about how she won't need food where she's going anyway.

At times, her dark humor reminds me of Campbell's.

"Maine was good," I tell her. Though I always tell her that. "We finished our registry and went over the guest list one last time. Did a tux fitting."

I pretend to be excited about these things, but only for her.

"I can't wait to see you in a tuxedo," she says with a dreamy sigh. "It'll be the best day of your life and the second best day of mine."

The first best day of her life was the day I was born —naturally.

Oliver and I exchange looks. Last month the doctors gave her three to six months to live. Odds are, she won't make it to the big day. I offered to move the wedding up, but she wouldn't have it. Save the dates had already been sent, and she didn't want six hundred people to have to rearrange their travel plans for her. That and she didn't want six hundred people knowing she was dying, nor did she want to steal an ounce of attention at our wedding.

"The Wakemonts send their love, by the way," I tell her.

Mom places a hand over her heart and smiles. "I can't wait to see them this August. It'll be the celebration of a lifetime."

Oliver tops off his bourbon and takes a generous sip. While he's technically her brother-in-law, he and I are a mere ten years apart and have more of a sibling dynamic. Growing up, Oliver spent most of his teenage years living under our roof and considers my mom more of a mother figure than his own.

He doesn't always show it, but he's struggling to come to terms with our inevitable loss as much as I am.

The realization that one day soon I'll wake up and not be able to call my mother or see her smiling face is something that has haunted my every waking second lately.

Over the years, my father has spent tens of millions flying her all around the world to consult with the best doctors and receive experimental care not yet available stateside. What good is having all the money in the world when it can't buy the one thing you want the most? The most precious and finite resource known to man?

Time ...

While I've never looked forward to getting married,

knowing how happy it would make my mother has played a huge part in looking past the absurdity of it all. She was excited to be a grandmother, too—a privilege she'll never have the joy of experiencing now.

"Oliver had a date last night," Mom lifts her brows and offers an impish grin. "Tell him about it, Oliver. What was her name again?"

Oliver chokes on his drink. "Her name isn't important because there won't be a second date."

"Tell him why though," Mom prompts. For a moment it feels like we're all back to our normal selves, chatting about Oliver's usual shenanigans like each of our lives aren't three to six months away from drastically changing forever.

"Remember that woman who was stalking me last year?" Oliver asks, rolling his eyes.

"The one who worked at your dry cleaner's? Then got a job cleaning your boats?" I ask.

"Yeah," he says. "So this was her best friend. Only I didn't know that until we went back to her place."

Mom covers her mouth as she listens, as engaged as if she's enjoying the story for the first time all over again.

"We were, um," Oliver clears his throat. "Having a nightcap. In her room. When I kept hearing this noise in the closet, like a rustling sound or something moving. I thought maybe it was in my head, and I ignored it for a while, but then I heard it again."

"Your stalker was in the closet watching?" I ask.

"Yep." He tosses back the rest of his bourbon before slamming the tumbler down.

"What about the restraining order?" I ask.

"She technically didn't violate it since *I* went to *their* apartment," he says.

"Wait, I'm confused—how did you meet the roommate in the first place?" I take a seat for this.

"She approached me at a bar the other week," Oliver says. "Pretty sure the stalker put her up to it."

"That's what you get for being such a man-whore." I pour myself a drink. "I don't feel sorry for you."

"Good, because I don't want your sympathy anyway." He grabs the decanter from me and refills his glass.

"I'm sure there's a perfectly lovely girl out there for you, Oliver," Mom interjects. "We'll find her one of these days."

Oliver has always skirted the line between being a trust-fund playboy to being utterly pussy-whipped. There's rarely an in between and because of that, he's earned a reputation in Palm Beach for being one of the most eligible bachelors. His only issue is he tends to self-sabotage when things are going too well.

"Slade, I was thinking, maybe Campbell could come out here sometime?" Mom changes the subject. "I haven't seen her since the engagement party last year, and I missed her when she visited last month since I was in the hospital. Do you think she'd be open to coming down soon?"

Her sallow expression is lit with joy that I'd never dream of stealing away from her.

"Of course." I can't imagine Campbell would come here for my sake, but she adores my mother.

I've yet to tell the Wakemonts about Mom's prognosis. Perhaps I should've said something this time, but every time I thought about it, I couldn't bring myself to utter the words "my mother is dying."

I couldn't give that statement oxygen.

When Campbell was here last month, I told her my mother was on a girls' trip in St Barths, and I implied that I was going to the office when I was really spending my workday at my mother's bedside at the hospital.

"How is our blushing bride these days? Is she getting excited? I bet her dress is gorgeous. I can't wait to see it." My mother clasps her hands. "She's going to be stunning, I just know it."

I don't tell her about the black mourning dress Campbell wanted.

Or the funeral flowers.

As far as my mother is concerned, Campbell and I made peace with the arrangement years ago and are in the throes of a budding and blossoming romance. I've become a professional at honing and perfecting this illusion where my mother is concerned, but only because I know how much it means to her.

To this day, she's still clueless about the mean letters I used to send to Campbell. I'd always write a nice one for her to read first, then I'd swap it out before mailing it. If Mom ever knew the things I said to my future wife, she'd be heartbroken. And while I only meant to send a few mean letters at first—convinced I could somehow dissuade Campbell from marrying me—the whole thing took on a life of its own. Once I started, I couldn't stop—especially as my mom battled a mystery illness.

I was angry.

And I expressed that anger the only way I knew how— with words.

But as we move closer to Mom's final days, continuing this illusion is paramount.

The only thing that matters to me is that she dies with a smile on her face and the peace that comes with believing her son will be loved and have a happy life filled with meaning, purpose, and babies.

"I can't tell you how happy I am that this day is finally going to be here." She places her cold palm over my hand, her crinkled gaze watering. "The Wakemonts are wonderful people, and your father and I couldn't have chosen a more perfect partner for you. Campbell's going to be a phenomenal wife and the best mother to your children."

"I have no doubt." The lies come easier now, the more I feed into them.

I tell her about how Campbell is dealing with the preparations, how we discuss everything together, make plans, choose patterns and colors, argue over little details... it's a reality I'm creating just for my mom, a separate universe where Campbell and I are just another ordinary couple in love, excited for our big day.

Years ago, I once asked my parents why they arranged us in the first place. It boiled down to the fact that over half of all marriages don't last, people in our circles are often targeted because of money, and pre-nups aren't always iron-clad. They were worried I'd choose wrong and our family would lose a significant amount of the things they'd worked so hard to achieve. My father viewed marriages as business deals—insisting the best partnerships happened when both parties go into it with eyes wide open and their signatures on the dotted lines.

"You hungry?" I change the subject this time. "You look hungry. I can order that soup you like—the lobster bisque from Chown's?"

Mom swats at me. "I ate about an hour ago, but even if I were still hungry, I'm perfectly capable of ordering my own soup, my love."

She may be wasting away physically, but her faculties are all still there.

She'll be stubborn as hell until she takes her last breath.

I should know that by now.

"Did you check out the fountain in front?" Mom changes the subject. "The landscapers just redid the flowers and I think it looks stupendous. Nice and bright and cheerful. First thing people see when they pull up."

I must have missed that when I arrived. Guess my mind was on other things ...

"I noticed," I say. "Did you choose the plants or did they?"

She bats her hand. "They know what I like. I told them to surprise me."

Standing here pretending like everything is normal sends a tightness to my chest, but I do it anyway. Never mind that I'm chomping at the bit to ask how doctor's visit went while I was away. While I'd prefer to be there with her, she refuses. She wants me to focus on the wedding and not her illness, which has already robbed so much of my life anyway—her words, not mine.

I was twelve when Mom's condition first reared its merciless head. It started with headaches, which were misdiagnosed as migraines. Then it progressed to changes in her speech and her ability to keep her balance, which earned her a neurology consult. After that, there were bouts of joint paint and debilitating fatigue juxtaposed with periods of insomnia and endless energy, causing one doctor to erroneously speculate that her condition might be psychosomatic.

My father must have flown her to at least three dozen doctors and specialists all over the world before they finally diagnosed her with an extremely rare autoimmune syndrome.

And that's what it was at first—a syndrome—a collection of symptoms.

It took years before they finally identified the root cause, and only after one of her specialists referred her to a genetic study taking place at Vanderbilt. After a series of tests, researchers there discovered she carried the two sets of genes for Palmer-Schoen Disorder, a condition affecting only one in every twenty million people around the world.

A condition for which there is no cure and the average life expectancy is forty years.

At fifty-one, she's on borrowed time and has been for the last decade thanks to my father's vast resources and connections. But all the money in the world still isn't enough to save her.

This past Christmas, her symptoms returned with a vengeance seemingly overnight, and her body stopped responding to the stem cell therapy and experimental transfusions that had been keeping everything at bay all these years.

"Oof." Mom places her fingers at her temples. "I've got a headache coming on. Room's starting to tilt a bit. Probably too much excitement today. I'm going to go lie down."

I rise to help her, but she shakes her head.

"I've got it, my love. Thank you." With her hand gripping the bar counter and then bracing against the wall, she makes her way into the next room.

Oliver and I linger in silence until we're sure she's out of earshot, and then we exchange looks.

"She's not doing so hot," he says.

"Really? Hadn't noticed," I shoot back, my tone rich with sarcasm.

He begins to say something else but stops. There's no need to point out the obvious. She's getting worse by the day and the way things are looking, it'll be a miracle if she gets to see us walk down the aisle come August.

"I should head out," Oliver says. "You going to hang out here for a bit longer or you going home?"

"I'm staying." Anything I could want to do at my place, I could easily do here, and I want to be here in case my mother needs something given that my father is out hitting the links.

Oliver jangles his keys and ducks out the side door. A minute later his Aston Martin roars to life in the circle drive before peeling out in a cloud of burnt rubber and dust. Never mind that my mother is trying to rest …

I fix myself another drink and pad towards the primary suite, listening from my side of the closed door, though for what, I'm not sure.

I hate that she won't let me help her.

The only thing she's ever let me do is just … be there for her in presence. Nothing more, nothing less.

Settling into the family room, I attempt to distract myself with some mind-numbing TV. My parents have every streaming service under the sun, but for some unknown reason I select Netflix. I'm browsing the new releases when Mr. Perfect pops up. The preview begins to play and I find myself chuckling at how ridiculous that movie was. It was almost satire or a parody of every romcom ever made.

I zone out while the preview loops, my thoughts drifting until they land on Campbell. While we may not be marrying by choice, there's no denying there's some kind of chemistry between us with our nonstop bantering. I'm not sure if I'd call it flirting, but it's … *something*.

I wish I loved her the way my mother imagines I do.

I wish our marriage wasn't a bona fide business transaction, a deal sealed only to safeguard our respective legacies.

Yet everything aside, I can't help but wonder about the woman I'm about to marry. An unfamiliar sensation stirs inside me. Curiosity, perhaps? A desire to know more about her? To understand her? In all the years I've known her, I've never once felt anything like this. In fact, I've done everything I could to bury my head in the sand and not make an effort to get to know her—an act of rebellion, I suppose. But my efforts —or lack thereof—were in vain because the wedding is moving full speed ahead and nothing can stop this train.

I shake my head, trying to clear these unfamiliar thoughts. I have a mission to complete, a future to secure. I can't afford to let my feelings, or my curiosity, get in the way. It's imperative that I treat this like the thing that it is—a loveless arranged marriage—and not waste a single second thinking it could ever be anything else.

I browse more new releases before settling on some space documentary narrated by Neil deGrasse Tyson.

I've had enough emotions for one long weekend.

I need facts and figures.

One hour and fifty-four minutes later later, I make sure Mom is still resting comfortably, kiss her forehead, and head out.

Climbing into my car, I recall the way Mom's face lit up when she talked about seeing Campbell again.

I need to fly her out here—sooner than later for obvious reasons.

Pulling up my phone, I pick a wistful, sullen playlist that fits my mood perfectly. Listening to other people sing about their woes has always helped me feel less alone in this world and more understood.

Tonight, I've lied to my dying mother, pretended to be in love, and discovered an inexplicable curiosity about my soon-to-be wife.

It's been a strange day, and as I drive off into the night, I can't shake the feeling that things are about to get a whole lot stranger.

Slade—
Last week was our junior high winter formal.
My mom is insisting that I send you a picture of
me with my date, Jake. She also insists that I
tell you Jake is <u>just a friend</u>. She says honesty is
the best policy. I'm sure once you get this
picture you'll rip it up anyway. But whatever.
Here's some food for your paper shredder.
Campbell (*age 13*)

Campbell—
Jake looks like a tool. And why is your dress
light purple? You look like an Easter egg.
Slade (*age 14*)

Slade—
My mom picked the dress. She says it's my
color. I'd have gone with blue. My dad says blue

brings out my eyes. Do you have winter formals
at your school?
Campbell (*age 13*)

Campbell—
Yes. And I was forced to go. Dances are stupid
and awkward. Anyway my mom is making me
include a picture of me with my dates—Tabitha
and Greer. Yes, they're twins. Yes, they both like
me. Yes, it's weird. Please don't reply because
this exchange is already boring me to tears.
Going forward, I'd appreciate if you only sent
me letters when you have something interesting
to say.
Slade (*age 14*)

Slade—
Did you know that during adolescence, a boy's
reward system in his brain is wired to seek
more novel and exciting experiences? That's
probably why you took two girls to the dance
instead of just one. Also, increased sensitivity
to peer influence at your age can make you feel
you have to conform to societal expectations in
order to fit in—which is probably why you went
to the dance even though you think they're
"stupid and awkward."
I don't know about you, but I found those facts
interesting enough to warrant writing you
another letter.
Campbell (age 13)

Campbell—
Please cite your sources. No one likes a plagiarist.
Slade (*age 1 4*)

Slade—
I haven't learned how to do citations yet. Please find enclosed photocopies of the articles from Psychology Today that support my previous letter.
Campbell (*age 1 3*)

11

Campbell

"Ms. Wakemont, welcome." Slade's housekeeper, Fiona, greets me at the door when I arrive. A few days after he left Sapphire Shores, he texted me saying I should come to Palm Beach soon to iron out a few household things as well as spend time with his mother. I wasn't able to see her last time as she was out of town, but apparently she's beyond excited about our impending nuptials and has been wanting to spend some one-on-one time with me.

Delia has always been a delight to be around. Effervescent and filter-free, her smile can light an entire room and instantly puts even the sourest of souls in a good mood.

They say the apple doesn't fall far from the tree, but if it weren't for their uncanny resemblance, I'd wonder if Slade fell from Delia's tree at all.

I suppose he has his mother's dark and angular features and his father's, uh, winning personality.

Victor is as straight-laced and serious as they come.

Minimal sense of humor.

Always in work mode.

I wheel my suitcase in. I brought a big one this time seeing how I'll be here for an entire week. It's warmer here than I expected. The weather called for highs in the upper seventies but the balmy atmosphere makes it feel much warmer.

"Please," Fiona reaches for my suitcase. "I'll take this to your room for you. Make yourself at home. Mr. Delacorte should be home from work any minute."

"Thank you, Fiona." I remain planted in his white-on-white foyer while she wheels it down the hallway, disappearing around the corner. Arms folded, I kick off my shoes and set them neatly on the rug. Everything here is so ... perfect.

With nothing else to do, I take a self-guided tour, seeing if I can remember where everything is.

To my left is the living room, looking just like I remember from last time—magazine worthy and untouched. A shiny black grand piano takes the spotlight in the far corner, leading off a wall of arched windows with an unblocked view of the ocean.

To my right? The dining room. Black table with upholstered chairs. Crystal chandelier. Oversized potted ficus trees framing the wall of windows.

Beyond that is a butler's pantry with floor-to-ceiling cabinetry on one side and a sink, hidden dishwasher, and shelves full of pristine drink ware on the other. Passing through, I end up in the kitchen with its restaurant-grade appliances, double islands, plethora of marble and stainless steel and modern black everything else. Towards the seating area is a wall of windows that I distinctly recall from the last time—they fold into the wall, somehow vanishing and making the space open up to the courtyard, where Slade can enjoy his meals next to a bubbling marble fountain and neatly trimmed topiaries imported from Sardinia.

Making my way around his U-shaped main floor, I pass the spiral staircase and end up in his study. I know from the last time I visited, he splits his work time between here and the office, and he's religious about maintaining his strict schedule ...

If I recall from last time, Slade wakes up at 5:30 or 6 AM, goes for an outdoor run for at least an hour—rain or shine—returns home, showers, drinks his coffee at 7:30, then takes a handful of supplements before putting in a few hours of work. At noon, his chef prepares him a macro-specified meal subsisting of zero processed food. After lunch, he heads to the office for the rest of the afternoon.

All things aside, I admire Slade's dedication to his health and his commitment to his routine. No one could ever accuse the man of being lazy or unmotivated. My father has always said the most successful people in this world have mastered the challenging art of self-discipline.

I've always been more of a go-with-the-flow type, though, much to my parents' dismay.

I think it stems from having every millisecond of my life scheduled for me.

Whenever I have true free time, I tend to go where the wind blows me and do whatever I feel like doing in that moment.

It's all about balance.

Trekking up the spiral stairs, I pass Slade's home gym at the top—warmed by sunshine and filled with natural light and expensive-looking equipment I couldn't begin to know how to use. Next is the guest room I stayed in last time. I peek my head in, only to find it filled with boxes, and not in any kind of useful state. Quietly, I shut the door. Maybe he's putting me in a different room this time?

The next room is a hall bath. Then a linen closet. After that is another guest room, only this one is missing a bed. The double doors at the end of the hall lead to Slade's suite. I remember that from before as well, only I've never set foot in there. Last time, he never invited me in and I never asked.

The doors swing open, sending a start to my heart.

But it's only Fiona.

"Hi." She smiles. "I was just putting your luggage in here. I unpacked your things as well. Mr. Delacorte designated half of his dresser and a portion of his closet for your use. He'll clear out more space for you once you're here full-time."

So ... I'm sleeping in his room this time?

That's news to me.

Guess I'll have to get used to it sooner or later—I just hope he leaves his expectations at the double doors before he climbs under the covers beside me tonight.

"Thank you," I tell her. I wait for her to pass by before heading in to check out the mystery room where my *beloved* lays his heavy head at night.

One step in and my foot sinks into the plushest, lushest carpet I've ever felt in my life. Soft as cashmere, fine as rabbit fur. I'm not sure what this is, but holy shit. I resist the urge to lie down and do a series of snow angels right then and there.

In the center of the main wall is a modern-looking four poster king-sized bed. Or perhaps it's a California king? The perspectives of this space with its sweeping ceiling and oversized doors and furnishings are throwing me off. It's truly a space built for royalty.

A remote rests beside the lamp on one of the nightstands. The thing must have a hundred buttons if not more. I press one and the curtains float down, turning the room pitch black and drowning out the ocean noise from outside.

"Shit," I whisper. It's too dark to see which button makes them go up, so I flip on the lamp so I can see what I'm doing. Only none of the buttons are labeled. They're all color-coded. Carefully I put the remote back where I found it and make my way to the en suite ... which does not disappoint.

In the center of the space is a glass-encased steam shower, complete with nine body jets and an overhead rain shower fixture. Nestled along the neighboring wall is a sunken tub, big enough for two if not three people. Overhead is a crystal chandelier with modern, clean lines that complement the black and white aesthetic and provide a bit of character in a space that might otherwise feel sterile and futuristic.

Every inch of this room is as clean as a five-star resort bathroom. In fact, there's no sign of Slade anywhere in here. Not an out-of-place razor. Not a single speck of beard trimmings in the sink. No toothbrush forgotten and left on the counter. I've always considered myself a neat and tidy person but if this is how he lives, I'm going to have to step up my game a tad.

Curiosity gnaws at my insides, prodding me to check out the drawers to see if he's cleared any space for my things. Sliding out the top left drawer first, I'm met with toothpaste, aftershave, floss, and a handful of other things all stored in clear plastic organizers. This is clearly his side, so I move to the right.

The top drawer is empty.

"Find anything interesting?" A man's voice sends my heart jumping up my throat.

Gasping, I spin around and find Slade in the doorway. He's unfastening the knot of his navy blue tie. With a single tug, it slides off. He wraps it around his fist, his eyes homing in on me the entire time.

"I had no idea you were so ... organized," I say. "I'm impressed."

He disappears into a doorway to the right—a walk-in closet, I presume.

The clink of his belt buckle follows.

I swallow the stubborn knot that has suddenly taken residence in my throat.

"Wish I could take the credit." He returns, sans tie and belt. Unbuttoning the top three buttons of his white dress shirt, he stops. "Not used to having an audience."

I'm about ready to apologize and see myself out when something comes over me.

"Are you always this shy?" I say, meeting his snark with my own.

"Shy isn't in my vocabulary." He unfastens two more buttons.

Is he testing me?

It takes every ounce of strength I have to maintain a poker face as he gets to the last button and shrugs out of his shirt completely—revealing a smooth, taut, tanned chest and a rippling eight-pack.

Of course *Mr. Tall-Dark-and-Handsome-and-he-knows-it* has an eight-pack ...

The man never misses a jog and rarely lets a single processed calorie pass his lips.

He slides his zipper down next, his dark eyes locked on mine and the faintest hint of a smirk on his face. He's enjoying this, trying to get a reaction out of me. But I can't give him the pleasure. Not yet. He's gorgeous and he's technically mine, but I still want him to work for me.

"You finish doing ... *that* ..." I let my eyes drift to his pants for a moment, feigning disinterest. "I'm going to check out our *marital* bed." I turn to leave, realizing what I just said and how it could easily be misinterpreted. Spinning around, I point at him. "That's not an invitation, by the way."

"Wouldn't dream of one," he counters without missing a beat.

With that, I leave him in the en suite, closing the double doors behind me.

The room is still pitch black from before, so I have to feel around for the bed. In the process, my feet get caught on a rug and I nearly trip, tumbling forward and catching myself on one of the nightstands. I've never been the most elegant person, but I'm grateful that no one saw that.

"Everything okay out there?" he calls out. The man must have supersonic hearing from all those expensive supplements he downs every morning.

I find the bed and take a seat on the edge, my body sinking into downy soft plushness. Last time I visited, I slept in the guest room on a mattress harder than Mount Rushmore.

Closing my eyes, I lie back and let my body relax for the first time all day. Despite having flown all over the world since infanthood and having a generally laid-back personality, flying is the one thing that has always made me tense.

A couple of minutes pass in this dark silence before Slade emerges from the bathroom. The natural light filtering in from behind him illuminates the man like he's some heaven-sent angel—in low-slung sweats and a white t-shirt.

"Don't get too comfortable," he says, making a grab for the remote. He presses a button and the curtains rise, letting the remaining daylight spill in as the ocean view comes into focus. "Dinner's in ten."

"Oh." I sit up. "Should I dress down, too?"

He sniffs a laugh. "Forgive me for wanting to be comfortable in my own home after a long day at the office."

I lift my palms. "It was only a question. Not passing judgement. I just didn't know if there was some kind of dress code I needed to adhere to about here."

"Only a question," he chuffs. "Everything that comes out of your mouth is a double entendre of some kind."

"Rich coming from you."

He moves for the exit. I rise, following him to the hall.

"So I was thinking," I say as we walk side by side. He glances at me through his periphery. "My porcelain dolls would look amazing in the southeast corner of the primary suite ..."

"We both know your mother would never let those dolls leave the great state of Maine. They're practically her pride and joy. Other than you, of course."

"You don't miss a thing."

"You're right," he says as we descend the sweeping staircase that deposits us in the marble foyer. "And one of these days, you might realize it's both the best and the worst thing about me."

Slade—
Happy birthday. I hope you did something fun.
Okay, I'm lying. I hope it felt like any other
Thursday, but knowing your mom, she probably
made it feel like some kind of presidential
inauguration. No offense to your mom. She's
actually pretty great. I just worry that she's
giving you the impression that you're the center
of the universe.
Best,
Campbell (*age 14*)

Campbell—
Who the hell signs their letter with "best?" How
old are you? I told my mom what you said. She
wasn't very happy. Just kidding … I would never
tell her that because she's a saint of a woman
and who are you to criticize how she raises her

only child. If that's any indication of what kind of mother you're going to be, then our future kids are screwed.
Worst,
Slade (*age 15*)

Slade—
I've gone fourteen whole years without thinking about having kids with you. Thanks a lot for the reminder.
Best, best, best,
Campbell (*age 14*)
PS—I'm going to be the BEST mom someday … just wait.

Campbell—
Just so you know, there's a difference between confidence and delusion. I hope our children inherit my sensibility.
Slade (*age 15*)

12

Slade

"Campbell!" My mother squeals when she sees my fiancée. Literally squeals. "It's absolutely wonderful to see you, darling."

She rises from her chair, dressed in her usual uniform of a Pucci house dress and coordinating head scarf. From the looks of it, she took the time to put on some makeup today as well, adding some color to her complexion and making her appear healthier than she actually is.

The two of them embrace, and it's strangely like seeing my past and my future collide.

"How was your flight yesterday?" Mom asks, cupping Campbell's face the way she used to when we were kids. She always used to fawn over Campbell, lavishing the Wakemonts with compliment after compliment about how sweet-natured and lovely Campbell was and how if she had ever had a daughter, she'd have wanted her to be just like Campbell.

I always thought she was blowing smoke, saying things that people say out of politeness.

But over the years, I came to realize she meant every word.

"It was great," Campbell tells her with more enthusiasm than I'm used to from her. "How have you been? Feels like haven't seen you in ages."

Mom takes Campbell by the hand, leading her to the living room where a plate of pastel macarons and her favorite Baccarat tea set—which she always reserves for her favorite visitors—wait for us.

While the two of them catch up, I excuse myself to take a work call in my father's study. My mother would think it's in poor taste, but right now she's so caught up in all things Campbell that I doubt she notices my absence.

"Slade." Oliver scares the shit out of me when I hang up.

"Jesus Christ. How long have you been sitting here in the dark?" I click on the lamp next to the leather Chesterfield. "You look like ass." The scent of stale cigar smoke and yesterday's liquor fills my nostrils. "You smell like ass too."

"I might have partied a little too hard last night." He yanks the folded sunglasses off his shirt collar and slides them over his nose before slinking back against the sofa.

"What the hell are you doing here? Clean yourself up before you come around my mother with this shit."

Oliver has always been a life-of-the-party type, but ever since Mom's condition worsened, he's been taking it to a whole new level. It's tough watching someone I've always looked up to fall apart at the seams, but the more he falls apart, the more I'm compelled to keep it together. Not for me, but for Mom.

"I would never insult Delia by pretending to be someone I'm not," he says.

"It's not about insulting her, it's about having some respect. For her. And for yourself."

"Hey, hey, hey," he splays a hand. "Keep it down, alright?"

"I'm practically whispering."

Oliver massages his temples. "Can you hand me that Hermes blanket over there. I need a little catnap. Maybe I can sleep this off before dinner."

I check my watch. It's 2 PM and Oliver has never been able to nap in his life. If this clown passes out, he won't wake up until dark.

"Campbell's here," I tell him as I yank the blanket off the back of a nearby chair. Folding it in my arms, I make no attempt to hand it to him because this thing is stupid expensive and cashmere deserves more than to be comfort for some thirty-five-year-old man child's hangover. "You should think about cleaning yourself up and making an appearance."

"Shit. That's today?" He makes no attempt to move from his reclined position. "Tell her I'll raincheck her visit. How long is she in town? Maybe I can take her out on the water later this week?"

"Her schedule is spoken for."

"Ah. Of course. You've probably scheduled every minute of her time here right down to her bathroom breaks."

He's giving me shit, but he's not entirely wrong. I've maximized her time here, but only in the name of efficiency. Nothing wrong with that. Besides, I doubt she wants to be here a day longer than necessary.

"Hey, can you turn off the lamp on your way out?" Oliver asks.

I shouldn't.

But I do.

He's a sorry bastard sometimes, but he's my sorry bastard.

If filling his nights with liquor and beautiful women helps him forget what we're going through, so be it.

If things were different, I'd probably be doing the same.

I return to the living room, where Mom and Campbell are knee-deep in some discussion about some charitable foundation Campbell plans to start after we're married. From what I can tell, Mom is delighted, doling out advice as Campbell nods and listens intently.

I take a seat next to my bride, though the two of them haven't so much as acknowledged my return.

"Slade, my love," Mom finally says after a few minutes. "I was going to see if I could borrow Campbell tomorrow? I thought maybe we could have a girls' day? Brunch? Spa? Shopping? Girl talk?"

I've already moved some meetings around so Campbell and I could tackle a few of the items on our to-do list, but I yield.

"Of course," I say.

Mom gathers Campbell's hands in hers, her eyes gleaming as if she's been given the greatest gift in the world. I try not to take it personally that I'm suddenly chopped liver. There are worse things in the world than your mother wanting to spend quality time with the woman you're marrying.

"We're going to have the best time together," she tells Campbell. "Slade, drop her off first thing in the morning. I'll have Broderick take her home when we're done."

My schedule for tomorrow now has a gaping hole in it that Campbell was supposed to fill.

"Can't wait," Campbell tells her. I imagine part of her is relieved to have a respite from me. After dinner last night, she curled up on the veranda reading a book and didn't come in until almost midnight. She claimed she couldn't sleep, but I couldn't help but wonder if she was avoiding having to lie next to me in bed longer than necessary.

We'd been flirting since the second I found her rifling through my bathroom drawers.

The tension between us is ripe.

And while I've never been a fan of mind games, the harder she is to catch, the more I find myself in the unexpected position of wanting to catch her.

Slade—
Your mom sent us your junior prom photos. You actually clean up nicely. I was shocked. The girl on your arm looked like she didn't want to be there though. What's up with that?
Campbell (*age 15*)

Campbell—
Her name is Claudia Berenson and she actually passed away last week. It was a Make-a-Wish type of thing. She wanted me to take her to prom before she died.
Slade (*age 16*)

Slade—
You need to work on your dark humor. It's ... I don't know ... off? That wasn't remotely funny. Why did she look so miserable though? I'm curious.

Campbell (*age 15*)

Campbell—
I don't know? Maybe you can ask her yourself?
I don't give a flying fuck. She was lucky I took
her at all. I had to turn down at least eight other
girls and two of them don't even go to my
school. Anyway, her number is 561-555-7583 if
you want to be a weirdo and stick your nose
where it doesn't belong.
Slade (*age 16*)

Slade—
WOW. You actually gave me her real number. I
thought it was going to be some pizza place or
something. She's actually really sweet. And she
told me what a douche you were to her all night.
Congratulations on ruining a nice girl's junior
prom by showing up plastered off liquor you
stole from your parents and then puking on her
shoes. Hope it was worth it.
Campbell (*age 15*)

Campbell—
WOW. You actually called her? And you'd drink
too if you had to marry you in nine years.
Slade (*age 16*)

Slade—
I hope you didn't strain that big beautiful brain

**of yours too hard coming up with that lame
response.**
Campbell (*age 1 5*)

13

Campbell

"I hope you don't mind if we make one more stop?" Delia rests a delicate hand over her décolletage in the back of her chauffeured Rolls. We've been going nonstop since she picked me up this morning ... starting with manicures and pedicures then a massage and facial and the most heavenly lunch at The Breakers. I'm smooth and shiny and full and ready for a nap and I have no idea how this woman is still going, but I'm not ready for this day to end either.

"Of course not," I say. "I'm still in if you are."

She squeezes my hand and smiles. "That's the spirit. Broderick, can you please take us to Worth Avenue?"

Her driver nods and switches lanes.

"I should text Slade and let him know you'll be home a little later than expected," she says.

"I don't think he'll care either way ..."

Delia cocks her head. "Really?"

I laugh. "Yeah. Why would he?"

She squints, as if she's confused. "Because the man adores you, that's why. I feel awful stealing you away from him when you're only in town for a few days."

Slade ... *adores* ... me?

I swallow my shock and put on my best poker face.

The Slade I know—the only Slade I've ever known —*loathes* me.

The man sent me literal hate mail for almost twenty years straight ...

Delia fires off a text, her glossy red nails clicking against her screen, before sliding her phone back in her crocodile Birkin.

"Communication is key," she tells me. "That's the secret to a successful marriage. That and being able to apologize when you're wrong."

Broderick slows to a stop as we approach a row of shops with colorful awnings and chic window displays. He parks in front of the one with the baby blue door and the cursive font on the glass that spells out the phrase *All Things Precious* but in French.

"I realize I'm a little bit ahead of the ball here, but I thought since we were out, we could pick out a few baby things?" Delia says as Broderick opens her door.

Slade and I haven't even held hands and she's wanting to go baby shopping?

I don't want to ruin this lovely day, so I smile and pretend to be enthused as we head inside.

We're greeted with a blast of ice-cold air that smells faintly of baby powder and lavender. Racks of tiny clothes and shelves of books and stuffed animals fill every square inch of the space while music box lullabies play on low volume.

Delia makes a beeline for the newborn rack, immediately reaching for a white linen onesie covered in tiny giraffes.

"Isn't this darling?" She grabs another one. "They have it in pink and blue, too."

"Y-yeah," I stammer. "You don't think we should wait? I don't want to jinx anything ..."

"Sweetheart, the two of you are going to have a baby at some point—naturally or otherwise. And baby clothes don't expire," she says with an amused chuckle. "No harm in putting a few little things in your proverbial hope chest."

Making her way to another newborn rack, she selects a floral pajama set as well as a blue gingham button down and a yellow polka dot sleep sack.

"Ah," she squeals. "I feel like I've been waiting my whole life to shop for a grandbaby. I just can't wait a second longer. I hope you don't mind ..."

"Not at all." I force a smile, following her around like a lost puppy. I can't bring myself to touch anything here. Not yet. It doesn't feel right. It feels too soon, which is ironic since there's a very real chance that this time next year I could be pregnant.

"Is anything catching your eye, darling?" she asks after handing an armful of clothes to the shop attendant to set aside. "Whatever you like, just place it in the pile by the register. It's my treat."

Out of politeness, I peruse a rack labeled 9-12 months and I manage to select a handful of outfits despite not knowing what season my future child will be born in or if these clothes will ever be put to use.

"Think layers," she tells me. "Babies need layers, no matter the time of year. They can't regulate their body temperature like we can."

I nod. The number of babies I've ever actually held I

could easily count on one hand. Growing up, I never babysat because I was too busy with tutors, riding lessons, extracurriculars, camps, and travel. All of my cousins were my age. And so far, none of my friends have had babies. If someone handed me a screaming infant right now, I wouldn't know the first thing about soothing them.

"I think we've done enough damage for the day," Delia announces after handing off another armful of clothes to the saleswoman. "I can't wait for Slade to see this. He's going to be tickled about that adorable little suit I picked out. Looks just like a miniature version of something he'd wear to the office."

I've never heard or seen Slade utter a single word about babies.

Ever.

If he gets "tickled" at the sight of these baby clothes, I'll eat my fist.

We're halfway to Slade's, her trunk filled with two grand worth of baby clothes and accessories, when Delia falls asleep next to me.

"Maybe she's had too much excitement for one day," I say to Broderick, keeping my voice low.

He smiles and nods in the rearview before returning his gaze to the traffic ahead.

It isn't long before the houses we pass grow familiar, and he turns onto the gated road that leads to Slade's street. For the first time, I attempt to picture the two of us raising a family together, in that three-level monstrosity of a house where the pool and cabana take up so much room in the back yard that there'd be no place for a swing set. Not to mention the proximity to the ocean, which can't be safe. And all the white. White everywhere. A toddler would ruin that house in an hour, tops.

Broderick pulls into Slade's circle drive.

I'd say bye to Delia and thank her for the millionth time today if she weren't sleeping so peacefully.

"Thank you," I tell him as I let myself out. Heading in, I pass through the front door of my future home, stride across my future foyer, and find my future husband waiting for me in his study because he's never not working. "Hey."

"You're back," he says without looking up. "How was it?"

"It was nice," I say. He glances up, drinking me in. At least I think he is? It's hard to tell in this dim lighting. Also, I'm exhausted. I could be imagining it. I'm tempted to ask him why his mother is under the impression that he adores me—but something stops me. "Think I'm going to head upstairs and crash for the night."

I'll bring it up another time …

Slade—
I'm studying abroad in Paris this semester, so
if you don't hear from me for a while, please
know that I'm having the time of my life
reading all the Sarraute, Queneau, and Herbart
I can get my hands on instead of your hate
mail.
Campbell (*age 16*)

Campbell—
Please know that in your absence, I sincerely
look forward to not receiving your obnoxious
excuse for letters.
Slade (*age 17*)

14

Slade

"Thanks for showing me around," Campbell says the next evening when we get home. We'd just finished dinner a few hours ago when she requested a tour of Palm Beach. "Just don't quit your day job anytime soon."

"What are you talking about?" I kill the engine of my Aston Martin.

"This is the slip where we keep our family yacht," she says in a deep, monotone voice, mocking me. "We have boathouse privileges in the south marina. And here's my gym. Happy to add you to the membership. That's my favorite restaurant. I have standing reservations there on Thursdays. My uncle Oliver lives up that road over there ..."

"That's not what I sound like."

"Mm hm," she teases as she follows me into the house. "As much as you claim to love living here, you showed zero enthusiasm while showing me around. I thought you'd be more, I don't know, excited? Like ... this is where our yacht almost capsized three winters ago and this restaurant has the most melt-in-your-mouth caviar this side of the Atlantic and Oliver bought his house from the guy who invented Pop Tarts. Those are just hypothetical examples obviously."

"I wasn't aware I was supposed to be entertaining?" I place my keys on the leather tray by the entry table. "And caviar shouldn't melt in your mouth. It should burst."

Turning to me, she cocks her head sideways, her full lips bunching at one side.

"I don't love you," she says, "but I absolutely love giving you shit sometimes."

I roll my eyes.

"Don't you ever get tired of taking life so seriously all the time?" She steps out of her leather sandals and loops them over her finger. "Do you ever laugh? Do you ever joke? Do you ever stop jogging and working and supplementing long enough to actually enjoy yourself?"

"Do you care?"

"Obviously or I wouldn't be asking ..." She eyes the hall. "Want to watch a movie? I feel like we could use something funny to lighten the mood. You have TVs here, right? I'm pretty sure some of the art hanging up around here are actually TVs, but it's hard to tell which ones."

"Of course I have TVs." My family made their billions by owning one of the largest media conglomerates in the world. Aside from running various newspapers and magazines, we've got a plethora of news stations as well—all details that Campbell is well aware of. "But it's too late to watch something anyway."

She blows a breath between pursed lips. "It's eight thirty. There are kids who stay up later than you."

"I go to bed at nine every night. You know that."

"I thought you weren't working tomorrow? Aren't we having brunch with your parents and Oliver?"

"Nothing wrong with staying on schedule." I climb the stairs, heading to our room, and she follows. "Do you even have a schedule? What do you do with all your free time?"

"Fair question." She grabs a cerulean blue satin pajama set from the dresser drawer I designated for her and I head into my closet to change. When I return, she adjusts her pajama top and skillfully maneuvers herself out of her bra without revealing a thing. "Seeing how I just graduated from grad school a couple of months ago and our wedding is in less than six months and I'll be moving here, it's pointless for me to get a job. I stay busy with volunteer work and helping my parents' staff with some projects around the house. I spend quality time with friends and family. I read. I watch movies. I don't know if you're insinuating that I'm lazy or unmotivated because I don't have a schedule, but I'm just playing the hand I've been dealt."

"I insinuated nothing."

We meet by the sinks next.

"What are you going to do when we have kids and they're not on your schedule?" she asks as she lathers a pump of face wash between her palms. "Don't kids have their own schedules?"

"We'll cross that bridge when we get there." I run my toothbrush under the water before squeezing a minty stripe across the bristles.

"Do you want babies?"

Her question almost makes me choke on my toothpaste.

"Or is it just an obligation you have to fulfill?" She splashes water on her face, eyes squeezed tight as she feels around for a towel. I retrieve one from the drawer and place it in her hand. "Thank you."

"I can imagine myself as a father."

She dries her face. "That's not what I asked."

"Does it matter?"

Campbell rolls her blue eyes to the back of her head. "Every time I ask you a question, you either deflect it with another question or act like my question wasn't important. If it wasn't important, I wouldn't ask. I'm trying to get to know you here."

She's not wrong.

My whole life I've never had to answer these kinds of questions. It's a luxury I've taken for granted, I suppose.

"It's intimate," I tell her after spitting out my toothpaste and rinsing the sink, "having access to someone's innermost thoughts and feelings. I don't think we're there yet."

"We have to start somewhere."

Campbell folds her used towel and sits it on the counter before angling her body to me. Her nipples are standing at full attention, all but poking through her thin top thanks to the icy blast of AC and chilled marble floors cooling the room. I do my best to keep my eyes on hers, but I'd be lying if I said I wasn't sorely distracted.

"We've had twenty-four years," she says, grabbing her toothbrush. "And I still feel like we're strangers."

I cross my arms, waiting as she brushes her teeth and proceeds to talk to me with white foam around her mouth like a rabid animal—except it's kind of ... cute.

The women I've been with in the past, although it was always in a casual sense, were always so self-conscious and insecure. One would always wake up earlier than me, run to the bathroom to fix her hair and makeup and gargle a capful of mouthwash, and then climb back under the covers thinking I didn't notice.

Another woman was so embarrassed that she started her

period and bled through her white jeans while we were out dancing that she blocked my number afterwards. When I ran into her a month or so later, she pretended like we'd never met.

The last woman I hooked up with would constantly criticize other women in front of me, tearing them down for having fake breasts, lip injections, hair extensions, or anything else she deemed unnatural because it made her feel better for having her own perceived imperfections.

Campbell, in comparison, is a breath of fresh air.

I wait for her to finish up before flicking off the lights and heading to bed.

She climbs in beside me. "We still have twenty minutes until your bedtime."

"And?"

Lying on her side, she faces me, her head cradled on the top of her hand. "We should talk. Really talk for once. Get to know each other better. None of this bickering, bantering, flirting stuff."

"What could you possibly need to know about me that you don't already know?" I ask. "And I don't know if you understand what flirting is ..."

"You're going to have to let your guard down at some point. You can't be like this forever." Campbell sighs. "God, it must be exhausting being you."

If she only knew.

Slade—
I had an epiphany today. What if you secretly <u>do</u> like me? What if you're only being mean because you're like the playground bully who doesn't want anyone to know he has a crush on a girl? I don't know why that just occurred to me today, but I was thinking about how you can't really hate someone if you don't know them. And you don't know me at all.
Campbell (*age 17*)

Campbell—
That's not so much an epiphany as it is wishful thinking. Plenty of people hate other people without knowing them. Maybe open a history book at some point and enlighten yourself.
Slade (*age 18*)

Slade—

Are you putting yourself in the same category as Nazis? KKK members? Hating people without knowing them is pretty evil.
Campbell (*age 17*)

Campbell—
When have I ever said I hated you?
Slade (*age 18*)

Slade—
The first letter you ever sent me. You literally said you hated me ...
Campbell (*age 17*)

Campbell—
That's right. Forgot about that. Anyway, I don't hate you. But I don't like you either. Hope that clears everything up for you.
Slade (*age 18*)

Slade—
Can I ask why you don't like me? Not that I care. Just curious.
Campbell (*age 17*)

Campbell—
No you may not.
Slade (*age 18*)

15

Campbell

I wake with a pounding headache the next morning as a thunderstorm rolls through the area. Fluxing barometric pressure always does this to me and Florida is the thunderstorm capital of the country, but of course I left my migraine medicine at home.

The clock on the nightstand reads 6 AM and Slade's half of the bed is empty, the covers pulled up to his pillow and smoothed out. He's probably out doing his daily half marathon. I'm usually a light sleeper, but all week he's managed to impressively get out the door without waking me. Whether it's intentional or not remains to be seen. Maybe I'm just sleeping harder here because of the plush bedding and blackout curtains? With the exception of today's headache, I've been waking up feeling unusually refreshed all week.

Shuffling to the bathroom, I rifle through a few drawers in search of Advil, Tylenol, or aspirin only to come up empty-handed. Heading down to the kitchen, I open every cupboard until I find a shelf with bottles upon bottles of vitamins and protein powders.

"Can I help you find something?" A man's voice startles the breath from my lungs. But it isn't Slade.

"Oliver, you scared me," I say. "What are you doing here? The sun isn't even out yet ..."

"Slept here last night. My house is getting renovated." He grabs a coffee mug from a cupboard. "Been going between here and Delia's."

"Oh." I had no idea.

"You want coffee?" he offers.

"Sure."

He grabs a second mug and heads to the built-in espresso machine.

"How have you been?" I ask when we settle into two stools at the island closest to the windows. The sun should be rising any minute now and the sky is already painted dreamy shades of peach and lavender and baby blue. I've watched the sun rise back home more times than I can count, but something about the swaying palm trees gives it a whole new vibe.

"Just living the dream," he says with a chuckle as he sips his coffee.

"How's the yacht business?"

"A little slow this time of year, but our calendar's getting full for the upcoming season. How's being a stay-at-home person going?" He winks.

I laugh, nearly spitting out my coffee.

The thing I've always loved about Oliver is that he can give me a hard time without coming off like an asshole.

"I'm going to tell my mom to use that term when people ask her what I'm up to from now on," I say, though Blythe

Wakemont would *never*. "Half the time she trips over her words and gets all embarrassed, like it's somehow shameful to her that I'm not doing anything remarkable or bragworthy right now—never mind that she's the reason for that. Well, her and my father."

"What would you be doing if you weren't ... betrothed?"

I cup my chin on the top of my hand, contemplating my response. "I just finished my Masters degree in social work. Maybe I'd be a counselor or something?"

"Wait, how did I not know this about you?"

I shrug. "You've never asked."

"Why'd you go to grad school anyway? Seems like a waste of time and money."

"I'm infinitely curious. And I like to help people," I say. "After the wedding, I plan to start some organizations, use my privilege to help people. That degree taught me a lot about the injustices of the world and opened my eyes to experiences I never would've had otherwise. It wasn't a waste. If anything, it was the exact opposite."

He straightens his spine, lifts his brows, and gives an approving nod. "Well, then. I stand corrected."

Somewhere in the house, a door opens. Shoes pad across hardwood. Keys jangle.

"Your prince charming is back from his run," Oliver says before shouting, "In the kitchen."

A few seconds later, Slade appears.

Shirtless.

Abs glistening.

A gray sweatband shoves his dark hair off his forehead.

"Morning," I say.

"Morning," he mutters as he heads to the cabinet with all of his supplements. His forearm veins are particularly prominent as he mixes various powders and potions. There must be at least a dozen of them.

"Do you have any Tylenol, by chance?" I ask. "My head is pounding."

"Acetaminophen is toxic." He scoops some off-white powder into a shaker bottle. "It destroys your liver."

"Um, okay, then how about Advil?"

He twists the cap onto the bottle and gives it a few good shakes. "Ibuprofen destroys your stomach lining."

Oliver chuckles under his breath.

"So what do you take when you're in pain?" I ask. "Or do you just suffer through it like a martyr?"

"I don't get headaches," he says, sipping his concoction. "And when I'm in pain, I use heat, ice, massage, CBD oil sometimes."

Oliver and I exchange looks.

"Welcome to the rest of your life, Campbell," Oliver quips. "For the record, I have plenty of Advil and Tylenol at my place."

Slade shoots him a glare—though I'm not sure why. Does he feel possessive of me? Surely not ...

"When I move in this summer, the first thing I'm doing is stocking your medicine cabinet with things that actually work," I declare.

"Try running your head under cold water." Slade tugs the sweatband off his head, leaving his hair mussed in the process. "That should help your headache. Or I've got a cold plunge tub you can try."

"Of course you have a cold plunge tub..." I say. "Besides, you keep your house at a frigid sixty-seven degrees. If a little bit of coldness is all it takes to get rid of a headache, I wouldn't have gotten one in the first place."

Slade chugs the rest of his shake before pouring a glass

of filtered water and swallowing a handful of earth-toned capsules.

"Going to hit the shower. Brunch is in two hours," he says before leaving the room.

"You're coming, right?" I turn to Oliver.

"I wouldn't miss this shit show for the world." He takes another sip of coffee, smirking over the rim. "No offense."

I laugh. It feels good to have someone else to talk to about this, especially when that person has a decent sense of humor.

"Go on any hot dates lately?" I ask. Last time I was here, Oliver entertained me for hours with nice wine and humorous tales of his bachelorhood. I've never known someone who was both obsessed with women and obsessed with his freedom at the same time. He tends to waffle between the two states, depending on the day, and that always gets him in trouble. The man strikes me as complicated, then again, who isn't?

My parents mentioned years ago that Oliver moved in with Delia and Victor when he was in high school because he was getting into trouble at home and his father (who was never around anyway) thought that pushing him off onto Victor and his family could provide him with some semblance of a stable home life.

While I have no doubt that it was all for the best, I imagine Oliver is probably dealing with some abandonment issues? If that's the case, it makes perfect sense why he is the way he is.

Supposedly he was the product of an affair between Victor's father and some college intern who signed away her rights to Oliver the second she pushed him out of her body, though knowing the Delacortes, I'd be willing to bet there was an exchange of money involved in that whole situation.

"None worth mentioning," Oliver says. "They can't all be Campbell Wakemont."

I swat at him. "Whatever."

"You should come out on the water sometime."

"You know how I feel about boats." We've had this talk before. Growing up, everyone in Sapphire Shores had boats, but my grandfather died in a freak boating accident when I was a toddler and my parents forbade me from stepping foot on one after that. Not only that, but they took it a step further by instilling the fear of God into me when it came to all things boats.

"One day with me and you'll wonder why you were ever scared of them in the first place. I promise you'll be a convert when I'm done with you."

"I don't know ..." I wrap my palms around my lukewarm mug.

"Think about it." Oliver rises from his bar stool. "No pressure. Just consider it."

"How safe is it though?"

"You won't find safer boats than mine. I've got everything. Life jackets. Inflatable rafts. Flares. Satellite cell phones. Radio. Emergency food and water. Navigation. First aid kit. Weather monitor. Anchors. Do you want me to go on?"

Exhaling, I study the eagerness washing over his face. If I squint, he almost looks like a one-off of Slade but with fewer muscles, slightly lighter hair, and a hint of crow's feet at the corners of his chocolate-brown eyes.

"We won't go more than twenty, thirty miles out," he adds. "We can stay close to the shore if that makes you feel better."

"I get seasick sometimes ..."

"Dramamine. I have Dramamine in all of my first aid

kits." Oliver chuckles. "Your excuses won't work on me. They might buy you some time, but one of these days I'm going to get you on one of my boats."

"Sounds like you're not going to take 'no' for an answer."

"I'm a Delacorte." He places his mug in the dishwasher. "What do you expect?"

"True."

"I promise I'll get you home safely and you'll have the time of your life." Oliver lifts a hand, making a Scout's Honor sign with his fingers.

"What kind of promises are you making now?" Slade appears in the arched doorway to the kitchen, his hair slicked wet from his shower, donning a slim fit white polo and navy slacks that show off his taut runner's build.

"He wants to take me yachting," I tell him.

"Did you tell him not everyone's as obsessed with boats as he is?" Slade asks.

I offer Oliver a warm smile. Slade can be cruel sometimes. I'm sure he's used to it, but I hate for anyone's passions to be insulted.

"He thinks he can get me over my fear of boating," I say.

"I don't think I can—I know I can." Oliver squeezes my shoulder on his way past. "I should head out, check on my contractors. I'll just meet up with you guys at the restaurant." As he passes Slade, he taps him on the arm. "Your mom showed me all the baby stuff they got the other day."

"What are you talking about?" Slade's brows lift and his gaze travels from Oliver to me and back.

"I forgot to tell you ... your mom wanted to get a few baby things when we spent that day together," I say. I hadn't forgotten so much as it hadn't come up in conversation and I didn't want to blurt it out with no context or warning.

Slade's expression turns blank.

I was expecting a reaction, but not … *that*.

Not … nothing.

"She's really excited to be a grandma someday," I tell him. "I know we're quite a ways from that, but she was having so much fun, I didn't want to take that from her."

"Can I be honest? I cannot begin to imagine the two of you with a baby," Oliver interjects. "If you can't stand each other now, wait until you're arguing over who has to get up for the third time in the middle of the night with a screaming baby. Wait. Never mind. Slade will probably hire a night nurse. He outsources everything."

"It's called being efficient," Slade shoots back.

I wrinkle my nose. "We don't need a nanny. I had several growing up and they were great, but I always missed my mom. I always wished I was doing all of those childhood things with her instead of someone who was paid to do them with me. I want to be as hands on as possible with my children."

"You say that now," Oliver chuckles. "Talk to me when you're on baby number two and you're going on three years of sleep deprivation."

"You're quite the parenting expert over there for someone who's never held a baby in his life," Slade says to Oliver.

Despite being Slade's half-uncle, the two have always acted more like brothers, with Slade being the serious one and Oliver providing the wisecracks. In an offbeat way, I consider Oliver one of the perks of marrying into this family. There's never a dull moment when he's around.

"You're not going to fit in out here if you don't have a nanny," Oliver says, though the glint in his eyes tells me he's only half joking. "Just so you're aware."

"Good thing I've never cared about fitting in," I say. "Anyway, I should start getting ready for brunch."

Coffee mug in hand, I head upstairs, only I'm not quite to the foyer when Oliver's voice trails from the kitchen.

"I can't believe you're not more jazzed about marrying this woman," Oliver says. "She's perfection and you can't even see it."

"Forgive me for not getting on my hands and knees and worshipping the ground she walks on," Slade says.

I pause in my tracks. I'm not normally one to eavesdrop, but I'm curious to hear what Slade truly thinks of me.

"Psh. I would," I hear Oliver tell him. "If I were you, I'd be acting a hell of a lot more excited about this whole thing, that's all I know."

"Well, you're not," Slade snips back. "And I'd appreciate it if you'd dial down your ... crush or whatever the hell is going on. It makes me cringe seeing the way you light up around her. Plus it's disrespectful."

"Makes you cringe?" Oliver asks. "Or makes you jealous?"

"Don't you have somewhere to be? A boat to polish or something?"

"I have people who do that for me, but yeah," Oliver says. "I'll get out of your hair. But I meant what I said. You should be more excited. She's a great girl."

Slade (AKA BMOC)—
How's college life? Your dad said you joined a frat. Little cliché, don't you think? What's next? Keg stands and toga parties?
Campbell (*age 18*)

Campbell—
It's called networking.
Slade (*age 19*)

16

Slade

"What are we doing?" I ask when Campbell pulls into a gravel parking lot. In the distance is a stony path that cuts between sky-scraping evergreens.

I'm back in Sapphire Shores for a quick weekend. At this point, Blythe has all the wedding planning under control. The only thing left to do is bond with Campbell, I suppose. Coming here was easier when we had a schedule, an agenda, a purpose. This whole going-with-the-flow and trying to connect makes me feel like I'm out of my element —and out of control. Not ideal.

"Stargazing." She kills the engine of her little silver Audi and grabs a bag out of the backseat.

"Is this something you do here ... for *fun?*" I follow her down the trail until we reach an open field of grass with a stretch of fence along the east section where it turns into a cliff. Below, waves crash. Above the full moon casts a glow across an otherwise pitch black sky. Scenery aside, there's nothing worse than being forced to be alone with my thoughts.

We're the only two souls here, likely because it's mid-March and all the locals have jetted off to warmer climates for spring break.

Smart move.

"It's something I do to relax," she says. "Isn't it so peaceful out here?"

Crickets chirp and somewhere behind us, an owl hoots. We might as well be in a scene from The Notebook or Where the Crawdads Sing.

Campbell spreads a red flannel blanket on the ground before producing a bottle of pinot noir, a corkscrew, and two stemless glasses.

"Not trying to be romantic or anything," she says as she opens the wine. "Just thought this might help take the edge off."

"What edge?"

She shrugs as she pulls the cork. "You're always so tense around me. And I never know how to act around you. We've got to get over this."

"Wasn't aware I was tense."

"Oh." Her bright blue eyes flick to mine. "So that's just how you always are? Frowning? Stiff? Formal? Serious?"

"You've known me for twenty-four years," I remind her. "Have you ever known me to be any other way?"

"To be fair, I've known you for twenty-four years, but only as an acquaintance and a poor excuse for a pen pal. We've never actually even tried to get to know each other on a personal level."

"Why start now?" I take the glass she hands me and offer her a wink in exchange.

"Because we don't want to be miserable for the next

twenty years," she says before taking a sip. "That's why. Now lay back and relax."

She lies down, nestling her glass in a grassy patch beside the blanket and slipping her hands behind her head. Drawing in a long breath, she releases a yawn. All afternoon, she drove me around Sapphire Shores, showing me every square inch of the fairytale town. The woman had a story or informational side note for everything.

The time she volunteered at the animal shelter and came home with a mama dog and four foster puppies.

The time she tee-pee'd the principal's house on Sherwood Hill, got caught, and received detention for a week and almost had to miss the homecoming dance ...

The time she snuck out to go to a party at the Mansfield Mansion with her best friend, Stassi, and the cops were called, but they let her go because her father donated money to the local police department each year ...

The time she fell asleep in her car outside the public library because she'd been studying for twelve hours straight and someone woke her up by tapping on the window and it was the same principal whose home she had tee-pee'd the year before ...

The horse stables where she learned to ride for the first time ...

The "boring" country club where her parents spend seventy percent of their free time ...

The park where she had her first kiss in seventh grade and the boy's bubble gum got stuck in her braces ...

Campbell gasps. "Did you see that shooting star?"

"Must have missed it."

She swats my arm. "Lay down then."

I swallow a mouthful of wine and lean back on my elbows.

"All the way," she says.

Groaning, I do it, but only so she'll stop hounding me. The earth beneath us is hard, littered with small twigs and rocks and who knows how many bugs. Nothing about this is comfortable or relaxing, nor am I dressed for it in my gray slacks and pristine white button down. Had she told me we were going to be spending time outdoors, I'd have come prepared.

From the corner of my eye, I watch my future wife gaze at the sky with sheer awe. Her chest rises and falls, slow and gentle, and her eyes shine with the reflection of a million stars.

What I wouldn't give to be so carefree and in the moment sometimes ...

"Do you think if we'd have met in, I don't know, college, as complete strangers, we'd have hit it off?" she asks.

"Impossible to know."

"If you didn't know me right now and you saw me at a party, would you come up and talk to me?" She turns to me, a half-smile curling her full lips. "And don't say it doesn't even matter, because it does or I wouldn't be asking."

"Like I said, impossible to know." I don't like thinking about what ifs, only certainties.

I know for certain, I've been engaged to this woman my entire life.

I know for certain, we're getting married in August.

I know for certain, my mother is dying.

I don't waste time living in alternate realities.

"Do you ever wonder what your life would be like if it wasn't all predestined?" she asks. "Like maybe you'd have met the love of your life somewhere random, like at the supermarket. Maybe you both reach for the same baguette and your hands brush and you smile and somehow that turns into the two of you deciding to split it and that turns into a date."

"I think you think too much."

"I'd rather think too much than not think at all," she says.

"You don't have to share every thought you think."

"Is it bad?" she asks. "Wearing your thoughts on the outside instead of making people guess and assume all the time?"

"Aren't you tired?" I check my watch. It's past nine. If we were at her parents' home, I'd be in bed by now.

"A little." She adjusts her arms behind her head, breathes in, and closes her eyes. She's been up with me since 6 AM, when she randomly decided to join me on my run—which necessitated me to run at half speed so she could keep up.

When it was over, she insisted on taking all the same supplements as me. Said she was curious to see if she'd feel any different. I told her it'd take more than a day to get the full effects, but she was adamant about trying anyway.

As annoying as it's been not having an ounce of alone time today, I have to give her credit for making an effort. It's more than I can say. I've never once attempted to show interest in her hobbies, a move more intentional than she could possibly know.

The last thing I want is to get attached. Not just to her. To anyone.

I watch her for a few more minutes, noting when her breath steadies to an even pace and her expression turns fully relaxed.

She's out cold, looking like a real life Sleeping Beauty.

The idea of kissing her crosses my mind like an intrusive thought. I won't do it as it would be random and out of context, but I can still imagine the way her lips would feel pressed against mine.

Warm, soft, inviting.

I've spent my entire life intentionally pushing her away. It's become such an essential part of our dynamic now that I don't know how to change it without coming off like some kind of psychopath. If we woke up tomorrow and I was suddenly buying her flowers, holding her hand, and having genuine conversations with her, she'd probably take me to the doctor and get my head checked.

Sometimes I'm certain I've sabotaged any chances we have at ever truly being happy together.

Everyone who has ever met this woman loves her—everyone except me.

And god damn it, I should.

She's beautiful inside and out. Funny. Genuine. Intelligent. Serene. Generous.

I want to change ... I do.

I want to be the lovestruck moron who can't stop grinning because five months from now he's going to be the luckiest man on earth.

I just can't bring myself to do that.

But I'm going to try.

For her.

For me.

For *us*.

My phone vibrates in my pocket, distracting me from this rabbit hole of uncomfortable self-awareness.

It's Oliver.

"Hey," I answer, keeping my voice low. Oliver calling this time of night on a Friday isn't normal. He's usually at the boathouse bar, working on his third Tom Collins of the evening as he mentally calls dibs on all of the beautiful women walking in. "What's going on?"

"I don't want you to panic," he says, breathless, "but your mother was just rushed to the hospital."

Slade—
Wellesley is no joke. I wish I had something
more riveting to say but I've been buried in
mid-terms, study groups, and research papers.
My brain is basically scrambled eggs. I don't
think I could come up with a passive-aggressive
insult if I tried.
Campbell (*age 19*)

Campbell—
Thanks for wasting a postage stamp and fifteen
seconds of time I'll never get back.
Slade (*age 20*)

Slade—
Wow, okay. You want to be entertained? Fine.
Let me tell you a little story. Last month I went
to a party in another town with my roommate. I
met this guy. His name was Seth. He was funny

—life-of-the-party type. Hot lumberjack looking guy with muscles for days and the most emerald-green eyes I've ever seen. I'll spare you the details beyond how sparks literally flew through the air the second our gazes intersected, but let's just say the night ended with a hardcore make-out session and him asking for my number. Do you realize how badly I wanted to give him my number?! But I didn't. I can't. I don't have that luxury. I can't even casually date anyone because I'm afraid I'll get attached and I'll have to break it off because, well, you know. The end.
Campbell (*age 19*)

Campbell—
Sucks to be us.
Slade (*age 20*)

17

Campbell

Rain beads down the arched glass windows that separate the primary suite from its sweeping terrace. The mid-day sky is ominously dark and flashes of lightening intermingle with rumbles of thunder. Fiona met me with an umbrella when I arrived in the circle drive hour ago, ushering me inside as she told me April is one of the rainiest months here.

I haven't seen or talked to Slade since he cut our visit short last month.

We were laying on a blanket under the stars after spending a full day ambling around together and attempting to connect when he suddenly announced he had a work emergency and had to leave early. I assumed he meant he'd fly out the next day, except he flew out that night. The second we returned to my parents' home, he packed his things, called his pilot, and left for the airport.

What's curious to me is that all of that came on the

heels of me asking him a couple of deep questions … would he have liked me if we'd met by chance? Does he ever wonder how his life would've turned out if it weren't already planned for him? Of course he didn't answer me. I ended up falling asleep thanks to the quiet and the lull of the ocean in the distance. Then I woke up to him saying we had to leave immediately.

Abandoning the window and the despondent gray-blue view outside, I attend to my suitcase, unpacking my things for the week. Except I'm halfway done when I realize a bottle of facial cleansing oil somehow became uncapped during the flight and spilled over half of my clothes.

Taking the armful of stained garments, I trot downstairs to the laundry room.

"Need something washed?" Fiona asks as she folds a stack of crisp white towels.

"My face wash spilled. Do you have any stain remover?" At home, my mother never taught me how to do laundry. We always had someone to do those types of things for us. It wasn't until I went to Wellesley that I figured out the basics.

Fiona shoves her wiry glasses on the top of her head, examining one of my shirts. She runs her finger across the dark splotches.

"You said this is face wash? Why is it slick?"

"It's oil based."

Her thin lips press flat. "You can't use ordinary stain remover for this. We'll have to use dish soap. And it'll have to soak. It'll be a whole process, but I've never met a stain I couldn't get out."

She takes the shirt from me and motions for me to place the rest of the items on the counter.

"Oh, you don't have to do that for me," I say.

Waving her hands she says, "I insist. Besides, Mr. Delacorte is such a clean freak. I love a good challenge when I can get one."

"Are you sure?"

"Go," she shoos me towards the doorway. "I've got this. I'll have these washed and folded for you by the end of the afternoon."

"Thank you so much." I head out, feeling both guilty and grateful. I know Fiona's job is to manage the house and everything in it and I'm no stranger to having help, but it's not like I'm doing anything anyway.

I'm rounding the corner in the hallway when I bump into Oliver. I didn't even know he was here.

"You again," he teases, pretending to be annoyed. "Back so soon? Weren't you just here a month ago?"

"Two months ago," I say. I was supposed to come back with Slade after last time, but then his whole work emergency happened and he told me he'd figure everything out when he got back. By the time that happened, it was already April and now here we are. "What are you doing here? Come to borrow another car?"

"You know me too well." He jangles a set of keys.

"Which one are you taking this time?"

"The Bugatti, obviously." He puffs his chest.

"The Divo?" I ask. I only know what it's called because last time I was here, I was bored one day and gave myself a tour of Slade's car collection while he was at work. His ten-car underground garage is like a middle-aged man's wet dream. Why one person needs that many vehicles is beyond me, especially when he works so much he hardly has time to drive them.

"That'd be the one."

"Hot date?"

"Lukewarm date. They can't all be like you," he says with a wink.

"Pretty sure you've used that line before."

"I guess it's worth repeating then."

I can't tell if Oliver is just being Oliver … or if he's trying to flirt with me. Last time I was here, he made a comment about me being 'perfection' when he thought I was out of earshot. But he's never touched me, made a move, or made me feel uncomfortable, so I didn't give it another thought.

"If she's nothing special why go to the effort of borrowing Slade's favorite car?" I lift a brow, ignoring his compliment. I can't be certain, but I'm pretty sure Slade would kill him if something happened to that one.

"Because it's cool as hell, that's why," he says. "And Slade says I've been putting too many miles on the Portofino. I guess he plans to trade it in soon. Maybe for a minivan or something."

"Really?" I can't tell when Oliver is kidding half the time. "A minivan?"

"No." He chuckles. "He'll probably trade it in for a newer model."

"Do you ever think about buying your own cars?"

"Why do that when I can buy boats and drive his cars instead?" He taps me on the shoulder. "Speaking of, you coming out on the water this week? It should warm up … if it ever stops raining."

"Not this time."

"Wow, you didn't even hesitate. Not even an ounce of false hope this time."

"Thought I'd be more direct," I say. "Maybe Slade's rubbing off on me a little."

Oliver rolls his eyes. "You say that like it's a good thing."

"Say what you will about it, at least we all know where he stands."

"You sure about that?" he cocks his head. "I've always thought of the guy as more of a cryptograph."

"It's not like he speaks in riddles," I say. "I'm never confused about where I stand with him. I'm just some woman he has to marry, nothing more, nothing less."

"Hm," the tone of Oliver's voice is neutral, as if he doesn't agree nor disagree.

"What?"

"I hope one day he realizes how good he has it," Oliver says before lifting a palm. "And I don't say that in a creepy young uncle hitting on you kind of way."

I chuckle. "Good. Because I like you and I don't want things to get weird between us."

"Same," Oliver says. "Anyway, Slade's a stubborn bastard. Always has been. I have a feeling he'll come around on his own terms."

"Maybe, maybe not. We'll see."

"At least he's making an effort to spend time with you, especially with everything going on."

"What do you mean? What's going on?" I ask. "Besides work, which is always going on ..."

"I just mean, with the wedding and the stuff at the office. You might not be his number one priority, but you're on the list. That's huge for him." Oliver points the keys at me. "You know how many people would love to be on his list?"

"And what list might that be?" Slade appears behind Oliver. I hadn't heard him come home.

Oliver whips around. "We were discussing your busy schedule."

Slade squints, like he's trying to have some silent conversation with his uncle.

"Anyway, just here to grab the Divo," Oliver says on his way out. "I'll have it back tomorrow, freshly washed and waxed per usual."

"Mm hm," Slade says as he strides towards me. The vision of Mr. Tall, Dark, and Moody in his all black dress shirt and slacks and the glinting white-gold Rolex on his wrist sends a flutter to my heart as I forget, momentarily, that he's my future husband and not some handsome rando.

"Hi." I offer a tepid smile, unsure of his mood or the reason behind his hasty exit and radio silence last month.

"Hi." He unfastens his watch and slips it into his pocket before unbuttoning his cuffs and rolling his sleeves up his forearms.

"How was work? Oliver said you've been dealing with a lot lately?" I ask. "You left so fast last time and we never talked about it ..."

"Work is work."

I follow him to his study, where he pours himself a drink before standing in front of an arched window with a million-dollar view of the bay. The rain has let up somewhat, and a hint of sun peeks from behind dark clouds, but the thunder remains.

"Well if you ever need to vent," I say, "I'm happy to listen—"

"You don't have to be kind to me just because we're getting married." His voice is stony and unfeeling, everything about him is ice cold. More than usual—more, even, than last time. "It's insulting, honestly."

Slade tosses back his Scotch with a single unflinching gulp.

"I'm confused," I say. "Are you mad because I'm trying to be nice?"

"Not mad. It's just not what we do. It's not what we've ever done. It feels disingenuous." He runs his hand through his chocolate-brown hair, his gaze growing unfocused as he studies the storm.

I've only been here a couple of hours and this is how we're kicking off the week?

I turn to leave, to give him the space he clearly needs.

"Where are you going?" He's staring outside but speaking to me.

"I've never been called disingenuous in my life," I say. He turns around and our eyes catch. I search for any signs in his that he knows he's wrong, that he regrets his words or his off-key treatment of me, only he's as unreadable as always. "I'm going for a walk."

"It's raining." He pours another finger of Scotch from his decanter. "And you don't know your way around."

"I'll bring an umbrella," I tell him. "And I'll figure it out."

Slade—
So the funniest thing happened. I was in Kennebunkport last weekend with my mother and my aunt, and I saw this guy sitting at this sidewalk cafe who looked <u>exactly</u> like you. I pointed him out to my mom, who of course had to point him out to my aunt. Only with all the pointing and whispering going on, the guy noticed. Mom apologized and explained to him that he looked like someone we knew. Then, of course, my aunt started chatting him up about random things because she's never not talking. In the end, he added me on Instagram, and by the time I got home, he had slid into my DMs and asked me on a date. Anyway, his handle is @AlexStone91857 if you want to check out your doppelganger.
Campbell (*age 20*)

Campbell—
What was your intention with that story? Were you trying to make me jealous?
Also, he looks nothing like me. Not even close.
I'm actually kind of insulted that you think that's what I look like.
Slade (*age 21*)

Slade—
I don't have the time or energy to worry about making you jealous.
The fact that you're even mentioning the feeling of jealousy suggests you might have felt a twinge of it? I think Freud would agree.
Campbell (*age 20*)

Campbell—
Freud also believed that young boys develop sexual feelings towards their mothers and that little girls experience "penis envy". Get out of here with that psychoanalytical bullshit.
Slade (*age 21*)

18

Slade

"Can I get you anything before I go?" I'm seated next to my parents' bed after a long day of getting Mom settled at home. She's spent the past week in the hospital, but her doctors finally discharged her after having exhausted every treatment option under the sun. The last thing they said was that all we could do was keep her comfortable.

"I'm fine, sweetheart." The wince on her face contradicts her words. "Though maybe if you stop by tomorrow, you could bring some daffodils? I could use a little sunshine."

"Of course." It's May so I should be able to find some somewhere. If not, I'll have them flown in. I'll fill her entire room with them if it means putting a smile on her face and a little joy in her day.

"Aren't you leaving for Maine soon?" Her voice is cracked and her eyes are closed. The medication she's on makes her groggy. But despite how exhausted her body gets, her mind always tries to fight it, to have one more conversation, one more deep breath, one more foot in amongst the living.

I'd do the same.

"I cancelled it," I say.

"Hopefully not for my sake."

"I'm not leaving when you're ..." I can't bring myself to finish my sentence. "Campbell's actually here now. At my house."

When Campbell visited last month, I wasn't the easiest person to be around. I was short and curt and I spent as little time with her as possible, blaming work when I was mostly keeping watch over my mother at my parents' house. I hated lying, but I didn't have a choice.

Every night when I'd come home, I'd walk through the doors and tell myself I was going to be kinder to her this time, but it never happened.

I took my anger out on her ... and I couldn't apologize or explain, which only made it worse. She kept asking if I wanted to "vent" about work. One day she and Fiona baked cookies, thinking it would cheer me up. Another night, I came home and she'd set up a bunch of board games in the dining room. I bypassed the scene, telling her I wasn't in the mood to *play*.

After a few days, she gave up trying at all.

I didn't blame her.

"You haven't gone up there for a while. I feel awful if I'm keeping you from them," Mom says, scratching her nose with a crumpled Kleenex.

I'm about to say I have the rest of my life to travel to Maine, but I keep it to myself. No sense in reminding her of the one thing she doesn't have: time.

"Campbell really wanted to see you last time she was here," I say. "She keeps asking about you."

"I wish I could spend time with her. We had the best time together that day." She turns towards my voice, her eyes forming thin slits as she tries to look at me. "You haven't told her anything, have you?"

"Of course not." I wish I could, but my mother won't have it. She's afraid Campbell will make a fuss over it or mention it to her parents. Once Cedric and Blythe catch wind, it'll be game over. The entire world (at least their entire social circle, which is essentially their entire world) will know my mother is dying by the end of the next business day, and that's the antithesis of what she wants.

We've known this moment was coming for a while now and she's never wavered in her wishes to go out on her own terms: privately and surrounded by me, my father, and Oliver.

The least I can do is honor that.

"Send her my love, will you?" Mom asks, her eyelids floating closed. Her words are breathy and forced.

"Of course." I give her hand a squeeze before dimming the lamp beside her, adjusting her covers, and ensuring her water bottle is full. It's late and she needs to rest and she won't do that if I'm here. She'll want to keep talking, even if it takes all the strength she has to form a single sentence. "Get some sleep, okay? I'll be back first thing in the morning."

I arrive home a short while later, following the trail of laughter and conversation to the family room where Campbell and Oliver are feasting on junk food and marathoning Below Deck. Oliver spent most of the day with my mom, but my father told him to take a breather. He told me the same thing, but unlike Oliver, I stood my ground.

"See, that's what I'm talking about," Oliver points at something on the TV.

Campbell wrinkles her nose. "Is that something that really happens?"

"Sometimes." Oliver reaches for a green glass beer bottle and takes a swig, beaming. I've never known anyone who loves anything more than Oliver loves boats. I've always likened it to the fact that when my grandfather, Oliver's father, was still around, boating was the only quality time he'd ever spend with his bastard son.

God, now I sound like Campbell and her psychoanalytical bullshit.

"Oh, Slade—didn't see you standing there," Campbell says when she spots me from the corner of her eye. The carefree smile painted on her pretty face a moment ago has disappeared, like I've suddenly sucked all the fun from the room. "How long have you been home?"

"A few minutes," I say.

Oliver pauses the show. "Everything okay at the office?"

"It's about the same." I shoot him a knowing look.

"Dinner's almost ready," I say. "I had Fiona order out tonight—sushi."

"Oh." Campbell looks to Oliver. "We didn't know you were going to do that. My flight got in early and Oliver was here, so we already ate. I should have texted you. I can sit with you while you eat if you want?"

"No need." I yank off my tie and head upstairs to change.

I'm halfway to my room when the echoes of laughter and animated conversation resumes, trailing down hallways and filling the empty space in this home.

Oliver would never steal her out from under me. For

starters, he can't. My father would straight up murder him or at the very least, find a way to sabotage his financials with a devastating lawsuit or "mishandling" of investments. I've seen him bring other powerful men to their knees, and I don't believe for one second that he'd make an exception for his half-brother. It's amazing the things people are willing to do if you wave a thick stack of cash in their face. Second, Campbell's aware of Oliver's playboy reputation. On top of that, she'd forfeit her entire inheritance—if her parents are truly that heartless.

Ironically, though, the two of them would be a much better match. I'd have to be blind not to notice it. And Oliver is exceedingly aware. I seat in his eyes every time he looks her way.

I shake my head.

I'm getting ahead of myself, conjuring up worst-case scenarios. My mind hasn't been in the best place lately. It's hard to see the sun behind all of those dark clouds.

When I spoke with my mother's doctor earlier today, he told me she'd be lucky to make it until next month and that we should be looking into ways to make her more comfortable as she "transitions."

He can call death a transition all he wants, but it doesn't make it any easier to swallow.

I eat my sushi alone, in a quiet house occasionally peppered with merriment from the TV room. Once I'm finished, I return upstairs, grab my iPad, and catch up on the Wall Street Journal in bed. Grand Venture Media Group has been trying to buy up every small media firm they can get their hands on ahead of the next election cycle for reasons obvious to anyone with half a brain cell. They've made laughably small offers to us more times than I can count, but lately they've had their sights set on procuring

Franklin and Dodd out of Massachusetts—a purchase I've been negotiating for the bulk of this year.

For the two hours that follow, I go down a work-related rabbit hole. It's the only escape I have these days.

"Sorry. I know it's late," Campbell says when she strolls in. "That show is really addictive. I wasn't paying attention to the time and—"

"—don't worry about it." I don't glance up from my screen.

"Oliver left, by the way. He said he was staying at your parents' tonight. Oh, and he said he needs to borrow your Phantom tomorrow."

I tap the messages app on my iPad and fire off a text to my uncle, telling him to stop spending his trust fund money on yachts and start buying his own damn cars. Meanwhile, Campbell grabs her pajamas and heads into the bathroom.

The room is quiet save for the sound of running water on the other side of the closed door, and a short while later, she emerges smelling of spearmint and roses as she climbs into bed.

"Is everything okay?" she asks. "I just ... the last couple times I've seen you, you've been ... different."

I lift a brow, playing dumb. "Different how?"

"Colder. More distant," she says, fussing with the blankets. "I thought we were finally turning a page and then ... I don't know what happened. If you want to call the wedding off just—"

"—work has been stressful," I cut her off. "The wedding is on. I apologize if I've been checked out. I've got a lot going on right now."

"I'm sorry to hear that. I'd ask if you want to talk about it, but I already know what you'll say." There's a bit of pity in her voice for some reason, almost like she feels sorry for me for being such a curmudgeon.

But I don't need her sympathy.

The only thing I truly could use right now is a miracle.

"You know me well," I say, paging to a new article on my tablet.

"What's on the docket for the week? Are we going to visit your parents?"

"They're unavailable this week."

"Oh." I can tell she wants to ask why, but for whatever reason, she doesn't. "So, what's the plan?"

"What's with you wanting a plan? You're never like this."

"I just figured you had the entire week all mapped out. Sorry for asking." She rolls to her side, reaching to turn off the lamp on her side of the bed. As a night owl, it's unusually early for her to be calling it a day.

I imagine her lying there for the coming hours, pretending to be asleep. Maybe she feels guilty for spending her evening with Oliver instead of me, though she shouldn't. I'd rather she enjoy herself than hate every second she spends under my roof.

Without a word, I reach into my nightstand drawer and retrieve a white remote. With the press of a button, a TV lowers from a hidden section in the ceiling. I power it on, pull up the streaming menu, and cue Below Deck for her.

It's the least I can do.

Slade—
What do you think we'll be doing ten years
from now?
Campbell (*age 21*)

Campbell—
I try not to think about that if I can help it.
Slade (*age 22*)

19

Campbell

I plug my AirPods in, cue my music to a nineties station, and fan myself with the latest Taylor Jenkins Reid paperback. Despite it only being 8 AM, the Palm Beach sun is radiating in full force and I'm pretty sure I've got roughly thirty more minutes before I melt into a pile of sunscreen on this lounge chair, but I persist.

It's June and I need to acclimate myself to the summer climate. Fiona said July and August are even worse, which I can't imagine. Maybe I'll have to be someone who goes north for the summer.

Alaska is sounding like a dream right now.

Grabbing my phone, I fire off a text to Tinley, Elise, and Stassi, asking what everyone is up to. I follow it up with a few pictures of my current situation along with half a dozen sun emojis. Once the dust settles, I can't wait to have them down for regular visits. Lord knows we have more than enough guest rooms, and Slade's house, while immaculate, is missing things like laughter and warmth and good memories.

An angsty Fiona Apple tune croons in my ear as I flick to a dogeared page in my book. It's so hot, I can hardly concentrate, and a cocktail of sweat and sunblock burns my eyes and blurs my vision. Wiping my face with a clean beach towel, I manage to get my vision back in time for Fiona to appear with a breakfast tray.

"You didn't have to do that," I tell her as she places my usual favorites on the side table. "But thank you."

She smiles. "Let me know if you need anything else."

I'm halfway through my avocado toast when Slade steps out onto the terrace, his sweat-glistened torso glimmering in the sunlight as he shoves his sweatband up his forehead.

"Have a good run?" I ask between bites. Lately this is what we do—small talk. Neutral conversations. Non-sations as I like to refer to them. As long as I don't ask him if he's okay or if he wants to do anything fun, he doesn't snap at me. Every once in a while, he'll throw me a bone by doing something unexpectedly or randomly nice. Most of the time, though, I'm walking on eggshells around him.

He says it's work, but the closer we get to the wedding, the worse his moods get. Correlation doesn't always equal causation, but I can't imagine what else it could be?

"The keys to the Tesla are on the dresser," he says. "I'm grabbing a shower and heading out."

The plan for the day is for me to drive around the city—solo—to learn my way around. Slade gave me a list of all the places we'll likely frequent after we're married as well as a few places he thinks I might like—various restaurants and shops, his parents' house, Oliver's house, the family's country club, fitness centers ... I have my own list of places too. Mostly charities and animal rescue organizations I'd like to volunteer at when I'm here full-time. I imagine cruising around is going to take up all of my day, which is exciting because lazing around Slade's ice-cold mansion gets old after a day or two.

"Thanks," I tell him, cupping my hand over my eyes to block the angry sun. It's hard to believe I'll be living here full-time two months from now. Despite having over two decades to prepare, it still doesn't feel real. "Oh, I was going to see if we could visit your parents sometime? I haven't seen them in months."

It feels rude being in town and not seeing my future in-laws, even if they're the ones who have been busy. Even if they're not free this week, I at least want to make an effort.

Slade rakes his hand along his jaw, engrossed in the ocean view as he appears lost in thought.

"I'll see what they're up to and let you know." His voice is monotone, disinterested. Maybe he had a falling out with them? Though I can't imagine that given that they're forcing his hand in this marriage and he's doing exactly what they want. I make a mental note to ask Oliver when I see him next. I'm not usually one for gossip, but if he could fill in any of these missing puzzle pieces, I'd appreciate it.

As soon as Slade leaves to do his thing, I decide I shouldn't have to wait for him to orchestrate anything when we're all practically family already. Shooting off a text to Delia, I let her know I'm in town and I'd love to see her if she's free.

Phone in hand, I wait for her reply. Any time I've ever messaged her, she responds within seconds, and whenever I've been around her, I've noticed her phone is basically glued to her hand. Only a few minutes pass and my message remains on delivered status, never changing to read.

A few hours later, I'm cruising around, going from stop

to stop, basking in the vibrancy of this crazy little city. So far I've seen pretty much every sports car known to man in just about every color under the Florida sun—tangerine, iridescent purple, turquoise blue, lime green, gunmetal gray, and Barbie pink to name a few. Even the people dress in joyful hues that play off their suntans and blinding white smiles.

With a mix of locals, vacationers, and retirees, the fast-paced city is teeming with life at every turn. In Sapphire Shores, no one is ever in a hurry to get anywhere unless it's an emergency.

It's a little after one by the time I pull into the parking lot of a little Asian fusion bistro to grab a quick lunch. Before I head in, I check my phone. Still nothing from Delia.

I snap a picture of the awning and sign and send it to Slade, asking if this place is any good.

He replies with a thumbs up.

I ask him if he wants to join me?

He says he can't—he's busy.

It was worth a try.

I'm seated at a small table for two a few minutes later, when I text him again, asking if he wants me to grab anything while I'm out and about. Chuckling to myself, I realize it's such a "wife" thing to do and I don't know that we'll ever have that dynamic.

A few minutes later, Slade finally gets back to me, and rather than giving me a simple yes or no, he tells me if there's ever anything I need to let Fiona know and she'll handle it.

Exhaling, I sip my ice water and do a bit of people watching.

Beside me, a couple my age are sharing dim sum. Between bites of dumplings and steamed buns, they're nothing but smiles and sweet conversation. There's a tenderness between them as they take their time enjoying their meals and each other's company. When they're finished, they hold hands across the table and talk about what they should do after this.

What I wouldn't give for even an ounce of that from Slade ...

Growing up, I was always indifferent about him. I didn't care that he hated me or that he never made an effort. I mirrored his energy and figured he'd eventually come around the closer we got to the Big Day.

Wishful thinking is the plight of an eternal optimist.

I never took his distant personality personally before. But now? Now I'm not sure.

I used to tell myself that things would change some day when I least expected it, that there might even be love on the other side of all his resentment. But who am I kidding? Heartless men, by their very nature, are incapable of love.

Slade—
Haven't heard from you in a while. Just
checking to make sure you're still alive and that
I'm not a pre-widow.
Campbell (*age* 22)

Campbell—
If I died, you'd know because my parents would
nationally televise my funeral on every network
they own.
Sorry to disappoint you.
Slade (*age* 23)

20

Slade

"Maybe you should slow down on those." I move for Oliver's tumbler and the near-empty bottle of Macallan and slide them out of his reach.

Mom took her last breath six hours ago. She passed warm in her bed, myself, Oliver, and my father at her side, just like she wanted. In May, the doctors told us we'd be lucky if she made it to June. In June, they told us it was a miracle she'd made it that far. When July rolled around, we were quietly hopeful that she might make it long enough to get to witness the wedding. Deep down, we all knew that's what she was holding on for. She might have lost her battle, but she put up one hell of a fight.

Somewhere in the depths of this never-ending home, my father is processing his loss alone. He's never been one to show emotions in front of others. Looking weak isn't the Delacorte way, he's always told me.

Oliver copes by drinking until he can't feel his face—or his feelings.

I'm numb. I imagine everything will hit me when I least expect it, but for now, someone's got to hold this family together.

I sat by Mom's bedside while the home nurses came in and did their thing, and then I locked myself in my father's study, making all the necessary phone calls. When I came out, Oliver was stumbling around the bar, tears in his eyes, mumbling to himself.

My phone vibrates with call after call. I let them all go to my voicemail, where a freshly recorded greeting gives them the funeral details and directs them to my family's public relations contact for any comments or questions. My mother wasn't a celebrity by any means, but as the wife of one of the wealthiest men in the world, her death is going to make headlines.

"It's bullshit," Oliver slurs. His eyes are unfocused and I'm certain he's talking to the universe and not me. "Why her? Couldn't it have been anyone else?"

He slumps into an oversized leather chair, burying his head in his hands.

Glancing at my phone, I'm tempted to put it in do not disturb mode, but I don't in case the funeral home calls. I easily could have outsourced this task to someone on my father's payroll, but I want to personally ensure every last detail is exactly how she wanted it. They're supposed to be sourcing daffodils and working on getting her favorite opera singer to fly in to perform *Ave Maria* and *In Paradisum*.

I lie down on the Chesterfield sofa, next to a sobbing Oliver, and close my eyes. I keep expecting something to wash over me, a flood of grief, but my insides are still a void of nothingness.

"You two doing okay?" My father's broken voice breaks the silence after a while, and I find him standing in the doorway. His silver hair is ragged, like he's been running his hands through as he agonized over the past several hours.

Oliver mutters something neither of us can hear.

"You should go home, Slade, get some rest." Dad takes a seat next to me. "It's been a long day."

"I'm not leaving you two here alone."

"We'll be fine." He speaks with conviction, though his eyes are laced with a desolate heaviness unlike I've ever seen. My entire life, this man has never shed a single tear. I realize now he's been holding them back all day, waiting to be alone so he can finally let it all out. He doesn't just want me to go, he needs me to.

"As long as you're sure," I say.

His lips turn into a hard line. "I'll let you know if we need anything."

"Keep this one away from the liquor cabinet." I point at Oliver. "Not trying to bury two family members in one week."

Dad nods.

I show myself out.

The instant I walk through the doors of my own home, something feels ... off. I blame it on grief at first, and then I spot Campbell's silver suitcase in the middle of the foyer. I hardly have time to process the fact that she's here when she runs up to me out of nowhere and wraps me in her warm embrace.

"I came as soon as Oliver told me," she says, her head buried against my shoulder. "I'm so sorry."

Of course Oliver told her.

The man never wastes an excuse to be in contact with this woman in any way he can.

Holding my breath, I'm about to gently push her away when something comes over me. Instead I stand there. For whatever reason, I decide to let her hold me.

"I had no idea she was sick," Campbell says. "Why didn't you tell me?"

"She didn't want anyone to know."

Leaning back, her deep blue eyes scan mine and her delicate face softens. "You held it in this whole time? Is that why you've been ..."

Her voice trails to nothingness, the same nothingness that eats me from the inside.

"You don't have to answer that." She cups my face, a tender, unexpected move. And she looks at me with the kind of compassion I sure as hell don't deserve from her.

"You didn't have to come here," I say."

"Don't," she says. "Besides, Delia wouldn't want you to go through this alone."

She's not wrong—in fact, the more I get to know my future wife, the more I'm realizing she seldom is.

Slade—
In 365 days, we're going to be married. In my
younger years, I'd hoped by this point we'd be
exchanging love letters instead of hate mail.
Ha! Next month is our engagement party which
will kick off this entire shit show, and since
we'll be spending more time together from now
on, these letters will no longer be necessary.
(Were they ever though?)
All of this to say, this is my final letter to you.
The end of one era … the beginning of another.
Here's hoping this one's better.
Campbell (*age 23*)

Campbell—
Don't you ever get tired of hoping for things?
It's such a waste of time.
Slade (*age 24*)

Slade—

Okay, I meant for that to be my last letter to you, but since you asked a question, I wanted to respond. No. I never get tired of hoping. It's important that you know that about me as we go into this marriage. I will always hope for the best, even when things are at their worst. It's just who I am.

Campbell (*age 23*)

21

Campbell

"Oh, Campbell." My mom gasps as my bridal attendant fastens the final button and fluffs my veil. "You look so beautiful, I could just cry."

She's being dramatic per usual, but I, too, could cry.

Albeit for different reasons.

"What? What is it?" she asks when she notices the expression I'm wearing beneath the curtain of tulle covering my face.

My lower lip quivers. Crying on my wedding day wasn't on my BINGO card. I thought I'd be indifferent if anything. Masking. Putting on a good face so I could get through the day. But now that this day is actually here, it's not at all what I expected.

"What's going on?" Stassi takes my other side, placing her hand on the small of my back. "What's wrong?"

Tenley and Elise glance up from the other side of the room, their conversation turning abruptly silent.

"Everyone, could you give us a moment, please?" Mom asks. "Actually, we need to get going. Why don't you all head downstairs? There's a Mercedes van waiting to take you to the venue outside."

My bridesmaids collect their clutches and usher out in their matching lavender gowns with my attendant, hair stylist, photographer, and makeup artist following behind them.

Mom lifts my veil and gently places it behind my back. "You're supposed to be walking down the aisle in ten minutes. Julio just finished your makeup. Now is not the time to do this, Campbell. I'm telling you, whatever you're feeling, push it down. Deal with it later. Six hundred people traveled from all over the world to watch you two exchange vows. Don't embarrass yourself."

Her stare is frigid and her lips are terse against her teeth.

Instead of motherly advice, I'm getting a warning.

"He *hates* me," I tell her, holding back a brutal sob that wants to escape. My chest burns as I hold my breath until the sensation subsides. "He has *always* hated me ... and he always will. I can't do this. I can't marry him. I thought I could, but I'd rather—"

She grips my shoulders hard, but not hard enough to leave a mark on my skin.

"You're marrying him," she says, giving me a shake. "Pull yourself together and get over it. You don't have a choice."

"I don't need my inheritance."

"Don't be ridiculous." Mom throws her hands in the air. "You can't honestly expect to announce this at zero hour ..."

She continues ranting and pacing, but I tune her out.

Last month when Delia passed, I hopped on a plane as

soon as I heard. Within hours, I was at Slade's house—*our* house—waiting to comfort him the minute he walked through the door. While he let me hold him and keep him company through the week that followed, not once did he soften. I gave him some grace, of course. He'd just lost his mother. But it was the conversation we had after the rehearsal dinner last night that solidified everything for me.

"I'm never going to love you," he told me as he stole me aside on our way out. "I'm never going to be able to give you what you need. I'm never going to be the person you want me to be. I think you deserve to know that. I just don't want you going into this with your hopes up."

While hope shattered in my heart like a million tiny shards of glass, I wore my best poker face, remaining stoic and appearing unaffected.

"Tell me something I don't already know," I told him. "But I have to ask, is there someone else?"

"No," he told me without pause, though for all I knew, he could've been lying. Despite all of our letters and all the time we'd spent together, I still hardly knew the real Slade.

"Curious ...what's so awful about me that you won't even try?" I asked.

He answered my question with one of his own. "Who said it had anything to do with you?"

In ten minutes, I'm to marry a broken, callous stranger of a man.

I thought I could do it, but now ...

The idea of standing in front of hundreds of people, looking Slade in his hate-filled eyes, and promising to love and cherish and spend the rest of my life with him makes me want to scream, cry, and throw up—at the same time.

Mom begins to say something, only to be interrupted by

a knock at the door. Sighing, she cocks her head and gives me a once over.

"You're going to paint a smile on your face and be the happiest, most beautiful bride this world has ever seen," she says. "Whatever's going on, whatever your reservations are, we'll deal with them when you get back from your honeymoon."

I don't tell her there is no honeymoon—a decision Slade and I came to quickly and easily during the planning of this entire charade. My parents are under the impression we're spending ten days at some secluded resort in Bali, only we'll be in Palm Beach, each of us doing our own thing like two passing ships in the night.

"Deep breath, Campbell. You're going to be fine," Mom says before heading to the door. "Oh, Oliver. I wasn't expecting you."

My heart comes to a hard stop. Is he coming to tell me Slade is calling the wedding off?

Wishful thinking ...

"I forgot to give Campbell this earlier," I hear him say. A couple of hours ago, he stopped by with a gift from Slade. Months back, my mother reminded us it's tradition for the bride and groom to exchange gifts on their wedding day. I chose a vintage Louis Audemars pocket watch for him. He got me a gold and diamond pendant with our wedding date inscribed on the back. "It's a letter from Delia."

"Thank you. I'll be sure she gets it," Mom says.

"We're about to head out. The car is waiting," Oliver tells her.

"We'll be on our way shortly," she tells him. When she returns to my side, she hands me a white envelope with my name on it. "Don't read it now. We don't have time."

Nor would I want to—I'm already emotional. Reading

the words of a recently passed woman as I'm about to marry her beloved son would only complicate my already complicated feelings on the matter.

Placing the envelope in my suitcase, I carefully zip the compartment shut.

After the funeral last month, I was sitting outside talking to Oliver when he casually mentioned that Slade would always talk me up to his mom. He would gush about me because he knew how happy it made her that we were getting married. I realized then that it must have been why Delia claimed Slade "adored" me that day.

Oliver also shared that Delia had been sick for a while and that Slade had kept that from me at Delia's request. She didn't want to steal an ounce of our (perceived) thunder.

My heart softened—albeit only a tad—for Slade after learning all he had done to keep his mother happy and honor her wishes in her darkest hours. I thought for sure there was hope for us, that he had a sliver of kindness somewhere in him.

But after he said what he said last night, my hope is officially non-existent.

"I need to grab something from my room, but your father and bridesmaids are all downstairs waiting," my mom announces as she slides her phone into her pearl clutch and snaps it shut. "Why don't you head down there now? I'll meet you in a moment."

With that, she heads through the connecting door, into the adjacent suite.

I give myself one final glance in the full-length mirror, hardly recognizing the stranger staring back. My long blonde hair has been pressed into shiny, retro waves that waterfall down my shoulders. My face has been contoured and highlighted to the point that I look like I'm wearing an

Instagram filter. Feathery faux lashes accent my eyes and beneath my ivory dress, my curves are squeezed tight with shapewear.

The overpowering aroma of Chanel Number Five lingers in the air, capturing me in a prison-like cloud of rose, jasmine, lily of the valley, vanilla, and sandalwood. My mother insisted I wear it since she and my grandmother wore it on their respective wedding days and it was both tradition and good luck. She spritzed it all over me before I could protest.

Gathering the hem and train of my dress, I head to the hallway alone. My heart inches into my throat with each step towards the elevator bay, each beat a reminder that I could just ... run.

I could leave right now.

Not sure where I'd go, but I could figure it out.

"Oliver?" I spot him waiting by the elevators. "I thought you left already."

He spins on his heels, his face lighting when he sees me.

"Look at you," he says, his hands casually dipped into the pockets of his black suit as he takes me in. "Cleaned up nicely."

"I could say the same for you," I tease. "I thought you guys left already?"

It's not like Slade to be late for anything.

"Everything okay?" I ask.

The elevator doors open and we step inside. They say it's bad luck for a bride and groom to see each other before the wedding, but I've had my fill of tradition today. I'm willing to roll the dice on this one.

"Yeah, he just needed a moment to himself." He presses the button for the main level. "I think it really hit him today that Delia's not going to be here. He's fine though. He's ready."

"Ready to get this over with, I bet." I sniff a laugh. "That makes two of us."

It's a perfect eighty degrees when we get outside. Not a cloud in the sky. Two antique Rolls Royces—one black and one white—idle under the hotel portico. Slade and Victor are already in the back of the black one and my father is riding shotgun in the white one. The rest of the bridal party is piled into the Mercedes van.

"You've got this." Oliver nudges my shoulder before heading to the van.

"Thanks for the pep talk."

He shrugs, his bittersweet expression lingering a while. "I wish I had more for you."

"I hope your best man speech is better than this."

"Oh it is, trust me," he chuckles

"Campbell!" My mom trots outside in her heels. "You're dragging that beautiful train on the dirty concrete!"

I don't waste my breath reminding my mother that she basically kicked my bridal party out of the suite and then left me to get downstairs on my own. She helps me into the back of the white sedan, fussing under her breath about my dress all the while.

The black car takes off, en route to Saint Mary's Cathedral on Fisher Street.

"You look beautiful, Campbell," my father says. The wistful smile on his face is accented by the dampness in his eyes. I take it the warmth of my mother's slap has faded from my face, like it was never there to begin with. "Now, let's get you married, shall we?"

Mom shuts the door and prattles something off about

how the ceremony is already ten minutes behind and we haven't even arrived at the church yet.

"Relax, Blythe," he tells her before dialing up the radio. An oldies song plays from the speakers. "Let our girl enjoy her day."

If only I could.

22

Slade

"Friends and cherished family," Father Mark begins the ceremony. "We're gathered here today to celebrate a sacred, joyous union as we witness the merging of two souls in holy matrimony."

Two minutes ago, Campbell walked through the double doors on her father's arm, a vision of ethereal beauty and grace in a long white dress. She held her head high as her rose-colored lips spread into a soft, joyful smile that could fool the whole world.

There wasn't a dry eye in the place—save for perhaps mine—as her father gave her away, though technically he gave her to me twenty-four years ago.

"Marriage, my loved ones," Father Mark continues, "is a covenant rooted in the very essence of our existence. It's a profound commitment to grow together, to support one another, and to love each other without conditions. Today as we stand here in this sacred gathering space, we're reminded that love's not merely a fleeting emotion but a powerful choice to go through life hand in hand in unfaltering devotion."

Campbell gazes up at me through a fringe of dark lashes and her hands feel delicate and cashmere soft in mine, a reminder that this is the first time I've ever held them.

"Campbell and Slade, know that true love has brought you to this day, but it's your everlasting love that will carry you through the years to come," Father Mark says. "As you pledge yourselves to one another, know that it's within the journey that you'll find the true heart of love itself. You'll find it in the gift of giving and receiving. Sharing and supporting. Understanding and forgiveness."

I keep my attention trained on my bride, avoiding the temptation to sneak a glimpse of the empty space next to my father in the first pew.

"As you create your life together," the priest goes on, "keep in mind you're not losing your individuality. You're gaining a companion—one you'll need as you journey along life's long and winding paths. During the hard times, be compassionate listeners and relentless communicators. Speak only with an open heart but listen with understanding. Keep your words gentle and your actions kind always. Find comfort in each other's arms, for it's the safest haven you'll ever know. And as you stand here in front of this altar, remember that love is not confined by time and circumstance. It grows. Evolves. Thrives when nurtured. Every day, make an effort to keep the flame alive, to celebrate your partner in ways big and small, and most importantly, to be grateful to have one another."

Whoever gave Father Mark free rein to write his own speech should have given him a time limit. I exhale my frustration but keep my expression neutral. My patience is wearing thin already and we haven't even exchanged the rings. At this rate, we're going to be here until midnight.

"In times of tears and times of laughter, from this day forward, you'll never be alone," he continues. "Not only will you have each other, you'll have a sea of loved ones who will stand beside you, support you, and encourage you along the way. Lean on them and draw strength from knowing you have an army of love behind you."

Campbell's expression hasn't changed once this entire time. She hasn't squeezed my hand. Hasn't flinched. If anything, she's almost robotic. I've never seen her so ... controlled.

Last night, I pulled her aside and told her I could never love her the way she wanted to be loved. I might be a lot of things, but I wanted to give her one last 'out.' All night I lay awake in my hotel bed, wondering if I was going to get some middle-of-the-night text from her calling off the wedding. When the morning came and Oliver showed up with my tux in hand, I had my answer—she was planning to marry me anyway.

The reason, however, is anyone's guess.

I imagine I'll find out soon enough.

"May your love be a shining testament to all who bear witness today," Father Mark says. "As you exchange vows and rings, let these symbols serve as a reminder of the promises you're making to one another. I invite you to look into each other's eyes and remember this moment, for it marks the beginning of an extraordinary adventure that requires only love as your compass and faith in one another as your guiding light."

Oliver hands me the rings, and as I place Campbell's on her finger, I repeat Father Mark's vows. Campbell does the same.

"As a witness to your beautiful love and blessed commitment to one another, I'm honored to pronounce you Mr. and Mrs. Slade Victor Delacorte. May God bless your union with abundance. You may now seal your everlasting bond with a kiss."

I slip one hand around the small of her waist while the other cups her cheek, and then I lean in, claiming her rosy lips and dipping her back. To my surprise, she actually kisses me back, and we remain lip-locked for more than a handful of seconds. When I pull away, our eyes hold for a single endless moment. I lift my fist in the air, pumping it as if I'm the luckiest man on earth, which seems to rouse a pleasant reaction from the pews.

Not a single soul in this place has the faintest clue we're not the happy couple we pretend to be.

With my new wife by my side, we make our way down the aisle, hand in hand, nothing but dopey grins on our faces. The church organ plays a recessional song while everyone stands for us, cheering, celebrating, dabbing their happy tears with tissues.

"Ladies and gentlemen, the bride and groom would like to receive you all at the Hotel Chevalier Ballroom," Father Mark announces as we head towards one of the chauffeured Rolls Royces outside.

The driver gets the door for us, and I help Campbell with her dress.

The five seconds we're alone together, before the driver climbs back in, are the quietest five seconds of my life. If we had more time, I'd ask her why she chose to marry me after what I said last night.

She scoots all the way over, leaving an ocean-sized gap between us.

I keep my question to myself—for now.

Ten silent minutes later, we're the first to arrive at The Chevalier Hotel, where everything's in full swing for the night. Dozens of servers in black and white uniforms are stationed around the ballroom with trays of champagne and hors d'oeuvres and the band is set up on the stage in front of a freshly waxed dance floor. For the next four hours, we'll be hamming it up for the crowd before retiring to our honeymoon suite upstairs.

"Champagne for the happy couple?" A brunette woman I vaguely recognize as the wedding planner hands us each a flute. I have no idea where the champagne saucers we picked out that day are. I'm about to tell her Campbell doesn't drink champagne, but my bride graciously accepts a flute from her anyway and downs it in three swallows.

Guests begin to arrive in droves, the space growing louder by the minute. In the corner, a string quartet plays classical versions of modern love songs while everyone gets settled at their assigned tables.

Our bridal party arrives somewhere in the mix. Not unsurprisingly, Oliver is chatting up Campbell's friend Stassi, whom he was specifically told was off-limits. I smirk, rolling my eyes. Tigers don't change their stripes, not even at million-dollar weddings.

"You two are just the loveliest couple," an elderly woman says as she braces herself on my arm. I have no idea who she is, but the light of familiarity fills Campbell's eyes as they make small talk.

Behind the elderly woman is a middle-aged couple.

"Aunt Beth, Uncle Bryan," Campbell says, leaning in to give them hugs. "So glad you could make it."

"Wouldn't miss our favorite niece's big day for the world," the man says.

"You two sure do make a beautiful couple," the woman

adds, flashing a mile-wide beam. If I squint hard enough, she looks like a younger version of Blythe. If I had to guess, they're sisters. "Such a beautiful ceremony, too."

"Thank you," I say, winking. "I planned it myself."

"Don't let Blythe hear you say that," the woman chuckles before they move on.

It isn't until another couple comes up to us that I realize we've formed an unofficial receiving line. Ten more minutes of painful small talk go by before the wedding planner notices, intervenes, and ushers us to the head table. I've barely sat down before she places a microphone in my hand and tells me to welcome everyone.

My face hurts from smiling and I loathe being put on the spot, but I do what I have to do.

"Hi, everyone," I say, rising. A hush falls over the room as all eyes turn our way. "Campbell and I just wanted to thank you all so much for joining in our special day. As Father Mark said earlier, love is not just a fleeting choice, but a powerful choice." I swallow the irony of my words. "Campbell and I have known one another pretty much our entire lives. This may sound cliché, but I knew from the first time I met her that she was going to be my wife someday. Those of you who have the pleasure of knowing Campbell already know that she's special. She's optimistic. Easygoing. Quirky—in a good way, of course. She's kind and generous and thoughtful. She's never met a stranger. Those of you who are only meeting her for the first time tonight, let me tell you, the beauty you see on the outside doesn't hold a flame to the beauty she possesses on the inside. It's an honor to be standing here beside this incredible woman as her husband and life partner. Thank you all, again, for cele-brating with us tonight."

The massive crowd applauds, followed by the raucous

tinkle of silverware against stemware as they prompt us to kiss.

Campbell stands, her ocean blues searching mine as if to silently ask how much of that speech was genuine.

Leaning close, I cup her face and seal my lips hard against hers—a punishing sort of kiss.

She never should have married me.

Earlier today, Oliver attempted to give me a pep talk, saying I had to pretend to be happy for one night and one night only, that we had the rest of our lives to live miserably ever after. He was trying to lighten the mood, of course, but it only reinforced the reality of the situation.

As soon as we sit down, Oliver takes the mic, delivering a best man speech that might as well be a roast of me. One-liner after one-liner garners bursts of laughter and giant smiles. I chuckle at a few of his jokes as well, almost forgetting the reality of the situation.

Across the way, I spot my father at his table, seated next to an empty chair where my mother should be sitting. Once again, I distract myself by taking in my bride and slipping back into my mask.

After we buried Mom last month, my father pulled me aside and said, "Life is hard, Slade. As long as you have someone nice to spend it with, that's all that matters in the end. You can have all the money in the world, but if you don't have someone to share it with, someone who truly loves you for you, you're the poorest man who ever lived."

Oliver wraps up his speech before handing the mic to Stassi.

"Hi, everyone," she says. "I'm Stassi, the Maid of Honor, and Campbell's best friend since grade school. When she first told me she was marrying Slade ..."

Stassi delivers a speech more heartfelt than comedic,

garnering more happy tears than laughter as she rattles off all of the reasons she knew Campbell had met The One. Just as I was pretending to be happy for my mother's sake, Campbell was doing the same thing in her own way. I can't imagine it was easy for her.

Once her short, sweet diatribe is finished, a line of servers in black and white emerge from behind swinging doors, platters full of food. As we eat our first meal as husband and wife, our guests clang on their glasses no less than eight times, wanting us to demonstrate our love with yet another kiss.

"If I could get the bride and groom to the middle of the dance floor," the lead singer of the wedding band announces once plates are cleared. "Mr. and Mrs. Delacorte, it is our privileged honor to perform the song your late mother chose for your first dance."

My stomach falls to the floor, but on the outside, I maintain my composure.

I had no idea this was going to happen. I thought we were dancing to some meaningless contemporary Top 40 song Blythe had chosen months back. Searching the crowd, I find my father. He gives me a nod, confirming that my mother did, indeed, choose a special song for us.

Taking Campbell by the hand, I lead her to the middle of the dance floor, slip my hands around her waist, and pull her against me as the band begins to play *Make You Feel My Love*.

While the lyrics are poetic and poignant, I tune them out.

The last thing I want to feel—the last thing I deserve to feel—is Campbell's love.

23

Campbell

"Can you unbutton me?" I ask Slade when we get to our honeymoon suite. Today was easily the longest day of my entire life. My feet are on fire, my ribs ache from the shapewear, and my face hurts from all the smiling I did today.

"Turn around," Slade says, his voice low.

All night, he lavished me with his attention, his eyes holding both a heaviness and a mysterious glint that made it impossible to look away and even more impossible to know what was real and what wasn't. Granted, he told me last night he could never love me, but there were certain moments today where I felt ... adored.

His fingers work the first button, then the second, grazing my skin ever so slightly. With each unfastening, I can breathe a little easier, so I drag in the long, slow, deep breaths my lungs so badly craved throughout the day.

We must have danced for hours hand in hand, arm in arm, laughing and making fools of ourselves but in the best way—at least for all intents and purposes. In reality we were just actors playing parts, but experiencing that much amiability from Slade for the first time in twenty-four years has, in a way, tilted my world on its axis.

"It was a nice wedding, wasn't it," I say when he gets to the last section of buttons. Pressing my arms against my chest, I keep my dress from falling down. There's no need to be shy at this point, yet somehow I'm feeling more vulnerable than ever in this dauntingly quiet hotel room, just the two of us, no more fanfare or watchful gazes. "Everyone seemed like they had a good time."

He says nothing.

"I'm taking a shower," he announces when he's finished. I wait for him to disappear in the bathroom before letting the dress fall to a heap on the floor. I shimmy out of my shape-wear, tossing it aside, as the spray of the shower sounds from the en suite.

Our suitcases are resting side by side on the other side of the room. Someone must have placed them there while we were at the reception. Unzipping mine, I filet it open and locate my pajamas—a matching baby blue tank top and shorts made of the softest jersey T-shirt material. I almost thought about packing lingerie … just in case … but I didn't want to jinx anything.

After our conversation last night, I know I made the right call.

If he's incapable of ever loving me, why would I so much as consider giving my body to him? And as far as babies are concerned, we can do IUI or IVF. If Slade doesn't want my heart, he sure as hell isn't getting my body.

I'm about to shut my bag and get changed when I remember the note Oliver delivered earlier. Unzipping that pocket, I retrieve the crisp white envelope with my name ornately scribed in Delia's delicate cursive. Slipping my pajamas on, I shuffle to the king-sized bed, shove the red rose petals aside, and splay out in the middle before carefully tearing the seal on the letter.

Dearest Campbell—

If you're reading this, unfortunately it means my time on Earth has come to pass. There are so many things I'd have said to you today had I been there, but given that some things in life are beyond our control, this letter will have to suffice.

Firstly, it has been both an honor and a privilege watching you grow from the sweet little baby who always sported a smile when she saw me to the beautiful young woman who has embraced her unconventional birthright. Despite this marriage having been arranged on your behalf, it's important for you to know that neither myself and Victor nor your parents would have forced the two of you to go through with any of it if we didn't think you'd be the perfect pairing.

The four of us have no doubt that you and Slade will continue the remarkable legacies of the Delacorte and Wakemont families with pride, honor, and grace. I have no doubt that under your guidance, your children and your children's children will do wonderful things for this world. My only regret is that I won't be around to see it. Please know that wherever I am, part of me is still with you all and will be until we're reunited again someday.

That said, there's something else I wanted to say: please go easy on Slade.

I can imagine what you're thinking—I should be telling him to go easy on you.

Don't worry, I have. Slade received his own letter this morning. Whether or not he has yet to read it is anyone's guess. But as I was saying ...

As Slade's mother, I may be a little biased, but I'm confident in saying what I'm about to say because I know him best—or rather, I knew him best.

It may be hard for you to believe, but Slade has a heart of gold. It's the reason he worked so tirelessly to convince me you two were head over heels in love. (I played along because that's what good mothers do) and it's also the reason he kept my illness a private matter.

Since Slade was a child, I've been battling this rare and ruthless disorder. Far too many times, he witnessed my brushes with death and prepared himself for the worst. His formative years were a rollercoaster of emotions and with each birthday that passed, I watched my son grow colder and more distant from everyone except for me.

I've seen some of the letters the two of you exchanged over the years. While they were amusing at first, I always hoped they would shift as the two of you grew older and embraced your destiny. They say hindsight is 20-20. If that's the case, I surmise that perhaps if I'd never been sick and he'd never been repeatedly faced with the reality losing someone he held so dear to his heart, that it might be easier for him to form attachments.

So again, I say: please go easy on him.

I've heard people describe my son as an enigma before, but sometimes we have a tendency to complicate things that are simple. This may sound counterintuitive, but believe me when I tell you that the more Slade pushes you away, the more he needs you.

There.

That's the key to his heart.

I'd have given it to you sooner, but I was waiting for the right time—and then I ran out of time completely.

All the love and all the best wishes as you forge these roads called life together.

Your mother-in-love,
Delia

PS—I've included the lyrics to Make You Feel My Love on the other side of this letter—keep them in a safe place and read them whenever you need a reminder of how powerful love can be.

A thick tear slides down my cheek, splashing on the letter and diluting a spot of blue ink. Flipping the paper over, sure enough she's written out the full lyrics to the first song Slade and I danced to as husband and wife—a song she personally chose for us.

Folding the note, I tuck it safely back in my suitcase for now, and then I crawl under the covers, close my eyes, and fall asleep on my wedding night, a virgin with a head full of complicated considerations.

24

Slade

My *wife* is out cold when I emerge from the shower.

I had to wash this day off of me; the cocktail of perfume and cologne from the barrage of hugs, the smudges of lipstick faintly remaining on my cheeks from well-meaning kisses, the itchiness clinging to my skin from being prisoner to a wool and rayon tuxedo all day ...

And all the love.

So much fucking *love*.

It's all anyone could talk about.

You two look so in love ...

We just love weddings ...

There's so much love in the air tonight ...

The love you have for each other is so inspiring ...

You make the loveliest couple ...

Seeing the two of you reminds me that true love still exists and there's someone for everyone ...

I guess it means we looked the part, so there's that, but now that the fanfare is over, it's back to reality.

With damp hair and low slung joggers, I climb in beside Campbell, who is fast asleep with the most angelic expression on her face. For all I know, she popped a Xanax and peaced out.

Despite it being way past my bedtime, I should be doing the same thing, but I'm strangely wired.

Lying back, I stare at the ceiling, imagining how this night might have gone in an alternate reality.

Somewhere, in a parallel universe, we rushed to our honeymoon suite, I tore her out of her gown, and she ripped me out of my tux.

Somewhere, in a parallel universe, I carried her to the bed, sampled every sinful curve of her body, and greedily succumbed to the invitation her sultry blues provided.

Somewhere, in a parallel universe, she is my refuge from the storm and I am her safe place.

Somewhere, in a parallel universe, I am recklessly, dangerously in love with this woman and we can't wait to start our lives together.

25

Campbell

"Thank you, Aunt Beth," I say Sunday morning, holding up the crystal vase she and my uncle gifted us. We're at my parents' house for brunch, opening our wedding gifts in front of a couple dozen of our closest friends and family.

Stassi is seated beside us, making sure everything is logged to a T while Elise hands us the next gift to open. Tenley's on wrapping paper duty, ensuring every ribbon and piece of tissue paper is collected and placed into a trash bag. Exhaustion colors all of our faces, but when it's their turn, I'll be doing the same thing for them.

"Your uncle bought me flowers every Saturday the entire first year of our marriage in that very same vase," she gushes. "I thought maybe the two of you could start your own tradition."

"That's a great idea." Slade's dark eyes dip to me and he wears the same loving smile he painted on his face all day yesterday.

This morning, he woke at six, went for his run, swallowed down all of his supplements, and took a twenty-minute shower—all before saying a single word to me. Meanwhile, I keep thinking about Delia's letter, wondering if her advice had any root in reality or if it was simply a dying mother's last request.

"Here, open this one next." My mother hands me a square box wrapped in white paper and a tulle ribbon. For the ninety minutes that follow, we rinse and repeat. It isn't until brunch is announced that we're afforded a break.

"Campbell, remind me where the two of you are honeymooning again?" My mother's longtime best friend, Gail, asks from the other side of the dining table.

"Bali," I say.

"Yes, but where specifically?" She blinks, sipping her almond mocha cappuccino. "My husband and I have traveled there quite a few times. We love the Alila Villas and those gorgeous overwater bungalows with the breathtaking views of the island, but nothing compares to Villa Puri Nirwana. When I tell you we were treated like *royalty* ..."

I turn to Slade, silently willing him to answer. We both agreed to tell everyone we were honeymooning in Bali—his idea—but we never discussed any hypothetical details.

"We've booked private property, actually," he tells her.

She lifts a knowing brow, as if she's painting a picture in her head of two lovebirds who need all the privacy they can get.

"I'm sure a respite from all this crazy wedding planning is just what the two of you need," my mother interjects. Never mind that she planned this entire thing and all we had to do was show up and smile for the audience.

By the afternoon, all three hundred gifts and cards have

been opened and documented for thank you note purposes, and we've bid our final guests adieu.

"When do you fly home?" my father asks.

For some reason, it only hits me now that "home" will no longer refer to the roof we're standing under right now, the roof I've lived my whole life under.

Slade checks his watch. "Jet should be fueling up now. We're scheduled to take off in two hours."

"So soon, eh?" Dad chuckles, blinking away the threat of wistful tears. He's been like this all weekend, and I've yet to find the right words to say because of the uniqueness of our situation.

Half of me wants to throw my arms around him, promise him I'm going to be okay, that I'll be happy and I'm going to have the best life (even if I'm not sure about any of those things).

The other half of me wants to remind him that he coerced his only daughter into marrying a man who can never love her—and for that, he should be sad.

I swallow it all down and turn to my husband.

"We've got a lot to do back in Florida," I say, feigning excitement. "And we still need to pack for Bali."

"Don't you have someone to do that for you?" my mother asks. "What's your house manager's name again, Slade? Phoebe?"

"Her name is Fiona," I remind her. "And Fiona does enough for us as it is. I can pack for myself."

My mother's blank expression suggests she doesn't understand. And she wouldn't. She's been waited on hand and foot since she was in diapers. While my upbringing wasn't much different, I could never bring myself to fully enjoy something so many people in this world didn't have.

I once overheard my father boasting to a friend that the

Delacorte family had so much money that our children's children's children wouldn't be able to spend it in their lifetimes. I took that as a challenge. Why should one family get everything when so many others have nothing?

"When do you leave for Bali?" Mom asks.

"Wednesday," Slade says without pause. Slipping his hand around the small of my back, he pulls me against him. Knowing it's not real makes every show of affection and soulful gaze a cruel slap in the face. Still, I smile through it, same as him.

"Can't wait." I grin and wrinkle my nose and cup his chin. I can ham it up just as well as he can. "We should probably get going. We have to pick up our luggage from the Chevalier before we leave for the airport."

My parents send us out with lingering embraces and wistful words that come off more scripted than genuine. In a way, they've been waiting twenty-four years for this moment. Maybe it gives them a sense of accomplishment or ushers in a new era. Either way, there's an air of finality around us and the longer we stand here, the less this house feels like it ever was my home.

"Safe travels, sweetheart," Mom waves from the front steps as we head to Slade's rented Mercedes. Dad slips his arm around her and sends us off with a nod. "Send pictures!"

The silence in the car as we drive away reminds me of last night in the hotel, when he was helping me out of my dress and had nothing to say except that he was going to take a shower.

26

Slade

My father once told me marriages are like business deals. I was eleven at the time and he had a tendency to go off on tangents, offering life advice in the form of rambling lectures that tended to go in one ear and out the other.

But that day, his words stuck with me.

"You've got your contract, of course," he rambled. "And you've got your financials, your communications, your commitment to making your joint venture be the most successful it can be. Once you separate the emotion from all of that, you realize that marriages can be managed in a way that everyone benefits. Everything is negotiable. Remember that, son. Everything. And not all marriages have to be built on love. If you're lucky, of course, they are. But not everyone's lucky. Sometimes people marry for reasons that have nothing to do with love at all—and that's okay. Don't believe all the bullshit you hear, and especially don't believe all the crap you see on TV. Some people are trying to sell more greeting cards and movie tickets and roses. Love—or the idea of it—is a lucrative business in the right hands."

He went on to clarify that he loved my mother more than anything in the world and that he was one of the lucky ones, but he'd seen many men ruin their lives all for something they thought was love, and he didn't want me to do the same.

"Whether or not you love Campbell is irrelevant," he told me that day. "As long as you approach the marriage like a business deal, you two will have a long, happy life together."

"Are you going to say anything or are we going to spend the next twenty years in radio silence?" Campbell asks when we're halfway to the airport.

Our luggage is already in the trunk as we checked out of our suite this morning. Maybe she'd had enough Blythe and Cedric for one day? They're decent people—in their own ways—but sometimes a minute of their company feels more like an hour.

"What do you want to talk about?" I sail through a green light, then another. At this rate, we'll be sitting on the tarmac with nothing but time on our hands as we wait for our scheduled departure.

"Um ... anything?"

"Is that a question or a statement."

"Both," she says.

Finally, we hit a red light.

"I'm not sure what there is to talk about." I keep my attention straight ahead, though I sense the liquid-hot sear of her watchful stare. "Is something bothering you? Oh, I know. Was it the bedazzled Lucite platter your Aunt Cindy gifted us? I thought it was hideous, too, but I wasn't going to say anything."

I'm being facetious, of course, but I don't see the point in discussing anything heavy when we've just survived an over-the-top wedding and we're about to be stuck on a plane together for the next several hours.

"I realize I'm asking the world of you, but would it kill you to be with me for two seconds?" she asks. "It's exhausting for me. It has to be exhausting for you, too. Can't we just ... stop?"

"What's the point?"

Campbell tips her head back against the headrest, groaning. In all our years of knowing each other, I've never seen her so defeated.

"This is going to sound crazy," she says, her voice soft and almost apologetic, though I'm not sure to whom she's apologizing. Herself, maybe? "But part of me really wanted to love you. And part of me still thinks I could. Which makes *no* sense." Her hands lift before falling lifeless into her lap. "Because you're pretty awful. You're kind of the worst."

Fair observation.

"And maybe I'm imagining it, but I swear I catch these minuscule glimpses of the person you could be if you put your guard down for two seconds," she continues.

"Wishful thinking."

She huffs, resting her forehead against the glass of the passenger window. Not another word is spoken until we're seated on my jet, and even then, she only breaks her silence to tell me she has a headache and she's going to try and sleep it off in the bedroom.

Somewhere, in a parallel universe, her words are an invitation rather than a deterrent.

Somewhere, in a parallel universe, we're thirty thousand feet in the air, unable to keep our hands off one another.

Somewhere, in a parallel universe, she's biting her lip and digging her nails into my back and I'm giving her every last inch of my love.

Campbell disappears behind the bedroom door in the back.

The snick of the lock follows.

She doesn't know it, but this is for the best.

27

Campbell

"I didn't realize the two of you weren't on speaking terms," Oliver says Wednesday afternoon after I catch him up to speed. Slade is at his office yet again, where he's been spending most of his time since Monday, and I'm doing my best to not show how desperate I am for a decent conversation. Yesterday, I followed Fiona around the house, helping her and chatting her ear off about every topic under the sun. She humored me and politely went along with it, but by the end of the day, she was practically sprinting out of here. I can't do that to her again. "How much longer is this going to go on?"

"I don't know," I sigh, staring at the ceiling as another episode of Below Deck plays on the TV. "Nineteen ... twenty more years, maybe?"

Oliver snickers. "You guys seemed so happy at the wedding."

"We deserve Oscars for those performances."

"Maybe he just needs some more time."

"He's had over two decades," I reach for my Diet Coke and take a swill, though I need to cool it on the caffeine because sleep has been elusive lately. As soon as we got back Sunday night, I couldn't take another minute of Slade's stifling silence, so I've been taking up residence in one of the guest rooms, and the bed isn't nearly as comfortable as the one in the primary suite.

"You want me to talk to him? Maybe there's something I could say ..."

"No, no." I shoot him a stern look. "I don't need you intervening in any of this. I appreciate the offer, but I think it'd just make things worse. Plus, I don't want to put you in the middle of this."

"You kind of already are."

"Shoot," I say. He has a point. "I'm sorry. I don't mean to."

Now that we're officially married and I'm living here full-time, I should try and make some new friends—or fly out some old ones. The girls really want to visit, and I want them to, but lately I've been avoiding solidifying any plans. I can play the role of a devoted wife for chunks of time here and there, but the thought alone of having to maintain that façade for several days at a time is exhausting. And there's always the chance that my friends will see through it and ask a million questions that I don't want to have to answer.

What I wouldn't give to be able to tell them everything ...

"Aren't you guys supposed to have a baby or something soon?" Oliver asks. "How does that work when you won't even say hi to each other?"

"So I'm not sure if you know this, but advancements in medicine have made it possible for two people to have a baby without having to touch, talk, or look at one another." I shoot him a wink. "In vitro fertilization. You should look it up."

"I know what IVF is. I'm not a moron. I just mean you guys are making this way harder on yourselves than it has to be."

"You should try telling your nephew that," I say, "because I'm well aware."

He squints, confused. "Is Slade making you sleep in the guest room? Because if he is—"

"—no," I cut him off. "I'm sleeping there by choice."

"Is Slade making you eat breakfast alone every morning?"

"No," I say. "But—"

"—but what? It sounds to me like you're pulling away from him too. It takes two, you know."

Damn it. He's not wrong. But it's not that simple.

"Okay, so if I just throw myself at him, if I just lay down like a doormat and let him sleight me and ignore me at every turn, then things will get better? Is that what you're saying?" I ask.

"Of course not." He goes to say something then stops, as if he's stumped himself.

"He's had twenty-four years to come around," I say. "I can't make him like me if he doesn't want to like me."

"I'm telling you, let me talk to him. I know my personal life is a hot mess, but I give really good advice and Slade looks up to me like an older brother. And before you tell me not to get involved, it's too late. I'm involved. I'm invested. That and it's depressing watching two people become the worst versions of themselves—no offense."

"You walked in on me stuffing my face with Cheetos and watching reality TV and I just told you I'm going to have an IVF baby with a man who literally hates me," I say. "It's fair to say I'm not exactly living my best life."

Oliver pops up from the sofa, sliding his phone in his khaki shorts pocket and resting his hands on his hips like a man on a mission.

"I'm fixing this," he announces.

"Please don't. Truly. It's not your problem to fix."

"Then at least let me say something to him. Wouldn't kill him for his old uncle to remind him what a fucking moron he's being."

The last thing I want to do is cause any hard feelings between them.

Before I can protest, he's gone.

28

Slade

I tap the envelope against the top of my dresser.

It's Wednesday night, we've been home for three days now, and I'm finally unpacking my suitcase from last week. The morning of the wedding, Oliver handed me an envelope. The handwriting on the front was instantly recognizable.

"You don't have to read it today," he told me. "But Delia asked me to give this to you in the event that she wasn't able to make it to your wedding."

My chest was on fire as I held that letter from the woman whose loss I was still deeply grieving, but I swallowed the burn until I could no longer feel an ounce of it, and then I stuffed the note in the back of my suitcase.

While it's been out of sight, it hasn't been forgotten.

Taking a seat on the edge of my bed, I rest my elbows on my knees and run my fingertips along my mother's distinct cursive handwriting. Gathering a long, hard breath that balloons in my chest, I tear the paper and unfold the note inside.

> To my beloved son on his wedding day—
> What I wouldn't give to be with you today.
> It feels like only yesterday that I held you in my arms for the first time, heard your cries, and felt your heart beat against mine. I'd say I loved you from the moment I laid eyes on you, but the truth is, I loved you from the moment you were a glimmer of hope in my heart.
> I remember the day you took your first steps at Nana and Papa's, how you held onto my fingers until you were confident enough to let go, and once you did, you were off and running so fast we could hardly catch you. Now you're about to take a monumental step into a new chapter of your life and while I wish I could be there to hold your hand (hypothetically speaking of course, I know you're a grown man), know that I'm with you in spirit.
> I know that your heart carries a weight today.
> Change is never easy.
> Loss is never painless.
> I worry that you're withholding your true

feelings from Campbell because you're afraid to love her and lose her. (Yes, Slade, I knew the whole time how you really felt about her ... a mother always knows).

My one request for you, my dear son, is that you give her a chance.

That's all I'm asking.

It may not happen at the snap of your fingers, and that's okay.

Much like daffodils don't bloom overnight, neither does love.

But I promise you, Slade, if you give that beautiful, kindhearted woman a chance, there will come a day when you'll wake up and realize the person beside you has become your entire world, and that realization will be the most splendid feeling you could ever dream of.

It's indescribable, truly.

It's something that can only be felt.

This cannot happen, however, with a guarded heart, and the idea of you never experiencing this breaks my soul in two.

Loving and losing is one of life's most challenging absolutes, but there is never reward without risk. A Delacorte, of all people, should understand that.

Your entire life, you've done everything I've

ever asked of you, so now, I'm asking for one final favor: give Campbell a chance.

Remember, I will always be with you.

True love never dies.

And love is a journey that isn't always easy, but is always worth it.

All of my love—

Mom

I fold the letter, slide it back into the envelope, and tuck it into my nightstand drawer, taking a moment to process her words. I was so hell bent on making her believe that I was happy that we missed the opportunity to have this conversation in person.

I was only trying to do the right thing.

The other side of the bed is cold and undisturbed. All Campbell has ever wanted was to try to make this work, and I've pushed her away so much that she won't so much as breathe the same air as me.

Sinking back, I drag my hand through my hair, exhale, and do the unthinkable.

I can't undo twenty-four years of cruelty with a single gesture, but maybe it's a start.

29

Campbell

"Ouch, ouch, ouch." I stub my toe on something hard on my way out of the guest room Thursday morning. Lunging for the light switch, I flick it on before bracing myself against the wall and massaging the throbbing soreness out of my left foot.

As my blurry eyes focus on the floor, I spot the culprit—a thin, leatherbound book.

Picking it up, I find no title on the cover or spine.

It's only when I page through it that I realize it's a journal.

Not just any journal.

Slade's journal.

Judging by the dates on the entries, this spans from his childhood—beginning around age ten—to as recently as this year.

Tucking it under my arm, I cozy up on the chaise in the corner and start from the beginning.

Campbell—

I don't know why I'm writing this since you're never going to see it, but I guess I don't really have anyone else to talk to about this. Our cat, Midnight, ran away last week. No one knows this, but I accidentally left the back door open. My mom loves that cat more than anything. She cries a lot. My father has people looking for it. If something happened to Midnight, I'll never forgive myself. Doesn't help that Mom has been really sick lately. The doctors don't know what's wrong. All I know is that Midnight makes her feel better and keeps her company when I'm at school.

Slade (*age 10*)

Campbell—
I sent you a really mean birthday letter. I didn't mean it. It's been a crappy week, that's all. I don't really want to write more about it. I just hope you had a good birthday and got all the things you wanted. That's all.
Slade (*age 11*)

Campbell—

In your last letter, you told me ten things about yourself and asked me to do the same. I told you I hated you ten times. The truth is, I don't hate you. I don't know you enough to hate you. I hate that I'm being forced to marry someone. I don't want to get married. I think girls are annoying (no offense, you seem nice enough). Anyway, here are ten things about me, even if you'll never see this:

1. I love books. But I feel like all my friends would make fun of me if they knew, so I only read at night, in bed, with a flashlight.

2. I'm really good at soccer.

3. My favorite color is hunter green.

4. I can beat anyone in chess with just four moves.

5. My favorite holiday is Halloween because it's

the one day a year that it's socially acceptable to be anyone except who you are.

6. I recently started teaching myself how to code, but my father says it's a waste of time and that I should be focusing on learning business strategies instead.

7. I secretly love theme parks. I say secretly because Florida is basically the theme park capital of the country and it's not cool to say you like them here. Don't tell my friends.

8. Someday I want to have a whole garage full of sports cars. Lamborghinis, Bugattis, Ferraris ...

9. Tiger Woods came to my house once for a party my parents threw. He told me I should always play to win, which I think is common sense, but I pretended it meant a lot to me when he said that.

Slade (*age 12*)

Campbell—
Your last letter to me mentioned you'd been thinking about trying to get out of this marriage thing. I can't tell you how relieved I was to hear that. I don't want to marry you either. I'm sure you're nice enough and all, but have you ever seen a happily married couple? Even my parents claim they love each other but they still fight sometimes. I don't want that. Do you? I'm still thinking of ways we can throw a wrench in this. I'll let you know ...
Slade *(age 13)*

Campbell—
Three words that describe me: observant, restless, secretive
My role model is: I don't really have one. I think we should all try to be the best people we can be without copying anyone else. Not that there aren't admirable people out there.
My favorite color is: hunter green, which I've told you before.
Slade (*age 14*)

Campbell—

Sorry I haven't written in a while. Technically I'm apologizing to a book and that's weird. But whatever. Mom has been sick lately. We found her unresponsive the other day and rushed her to the hospital. Dad is flying her to Sweden later this week to meet with some famous doctor there. I hope we get some answers. I don't know what I'll do if we don't. I hate watching her suffer.

Slade (*age 15*)

Campbell—
I lied to you about why my junior prom date
had the worst time. It's my fault. My friends
and I stole some liquor from my parents and
got pretty crazy. I said some things to her I
shouldn't have said, things she didn't deserve to
hear because she's a nice girl. I won't get into it
because I'd rather not repeat them. Every time
I see her at school, I know I should apologize,
but I can't bring myself to. I don't know why.
Sometimes it feels like there's something
broken inside of me.
Slade (*age 16*)

Campbell—
You're in Paris this semester, and while I would never admit this to you in a million years, I kind of miss getting your letters. Even though it feels like a chore having to write you back because I feel like we're too old to be pen pals and too young to not just text each other like everyone else in the world, but the days when I get home from school and find one of your letters waiting for me on my desk ... it's hard to describe ... but I guess it feels good knowing someone took the time and energy to write and send me something, even if you're only doing it because you have to.

Slade (*age* 17)

Campbell—
In your last letter, you compared me to a playground bully and suggested that maybe I did like you but I was just pretending not to. While I think it'd be easier if you were right, I can confirm that I'm not pretending to not like you. I don't like you. But I don't not like you either. Maybe that sounds harsh, but you should know that I don't like most people. If you're in neutral territory with me, that's not necessarily a bad thing. And hey, maybe it'll change one of these days. You never know. Besides, I'm pretty sure we're on the same page. You're not exactly fawning all over me, either.
Slade (*age 18*)

Campbell—
I'm sitting in my room, in the fraternity house you recently made fun of in your last letter, and I'm writing in a journal that no one knows I have because I keep it hidden. If any of my frat brothers found it, they'd have a field day. I tried journaling on my laptop in a Word document, but it just wasn't the same. Sometimes I feel like there are two versions of me. The one I present to the world and then the real me. Do you ever feel that way? I can't be the only one.
Slade (*age 19*)

Campbell—
I can't stop thinking about you making out with
that lumberjack guy. I don't know why, but it
bothers me. Maybe it shouldn't. But sometimes
I'll be sitting in class and I'll just think of this
meathead in flannel putting his hands all over
you and then I think about how you'd rather be
with him than me. I have no right to be jealous
and yet I am. There's a part of me that—
despite my best intentions—is growing attached
to you.
Make it make sense.
Oh, and if we're being brutally honest, I hooked
up with a girl at a party last weekend solely
because she looked like you.
Slade (*age 20*)

Campbell—
I don't care what you say, you were totally trying
to make me jealous by bringing up that
Instagram guy hitting on you. And I know I said
he was ugly, but we both know he's not. Once
again, I'm losing my mind. I wish I could go
back to the days when I couldn't care less about
what you were doing.
On an unrelated note, I had to cancel my spring
break trip this year. Mom is sick again.
Everyone thinks I'm going to Punta Cana, but
I'm going home to be by her side. The doctors
say this could be it. But they've said that a
dozen times before and she always comes out of
it. Either way, I don't want to be lying hungover
on some beach when I get the worst call of my
life.

I hope you're going somewhere fun for spring break.

And I hope all those horny drunk college guys keep their damn hands off you. I wish I could remind you that you're not some piece of meat and you deserve better than to be some asshat's one-night stand.

Slade (*age 2 1*)

Campbell—

You asked what we're going to be doing ten years from now. I told you I try not to think about it if I can help it, but I was lying. I think about it a lot actually. More and more. A decade from now, we'll be in our early thirties. We'll probably have a kid or two. And we'll be either really happy or really fucking miserable. It's anyone's guess.

Uncle Oliver thought he knocked up his last girlfriend, but it ended up being a false alarm. But the way he was acting, you'd have thought his life was over.

You seem like you'd be a good mom. Patient and kind and funny and all of that.

I have no idea what kind of dad I'll be. My old man isn't exactly Danny Tanner from Full House. He's more like Palm Beach's version of

**Tony Soprano. He takes no shit from anyone
and has his own way of showing love.**
Slade (*age 22*)

Campbell—

I haven't written you in a while because … I'll be completely honest with you since you'll never see this … but I started seeing someone. It wasn't serious. And obviously it was never going to go anywhere because of our stupid marriage arrangement. I guess I just needed to rebel, to feel like I could stretch my wings if I wanted to.

Her name was Tiffany and we went on five dates. She also looked like you (I know, WTF is my problem?). At first it was fun, but the more time I spent with her, the more I realized she was dull and vapid. She didn't push my buttons the way you do. She did nothing to make herself a challenge or hold my interest. She threw herself at me. What self-respecting woman throws herself at a man? You would never do that.

Anyway, I kept finding myself wishing she were you, but then I remembered that you think I hate you and I've spent twenty years convincing myself that I hate you and that's pretty messed up when I stop and think about it.
If I were a better man, I could apologize to you —face to face, not via postage stamp.
I'm stubborn as hell. That's something you'll probably figure out sooner than later if you haven't already. It's not something I'm proud of. Maybe it's a Delacorte thing. I don't know.
Anyway, even if you never know this, I'm putting it in writing—I'm sorry for being such a dick. Maybe someday I'll apologize in person.
Don't hold your breath though.
Slade (*age 23*)

Campbell—
I just got home from our engagement party, I
can't stop thinking about you (in ways I've
never thought about you before), and it's
fucking terrifying.
I think I might actually <u>like</u> you, Campbell, and
I don't know what to do with those feelings so
they're probably all going to come out wrong
over the coming year.
The older I get, the more I'm realizing I self-
sabotage.
I'm my own worst enemy.
And you just might be the best thing that's ever
happened to me—and you'll never know
because I'm too damn stubborn to admit it.
Slade (*age 24*)

30

Campbell

I close the journal and sit in the guest room in a daze as the morning light filters through the curtains and everything I thought I knew is tipped upside down. A million thoughts rush through my head, ugly, hopeful, and every color in between. Part of me wants to scream at him until I lose my voice, the other half of me wants to hug him.

But mostly, I'm *furious*.

31

Slade

The world never fails to fade away during my morning jogs. Today, however, is an exception. With each steady stride, I think about my wife. As the latest Huberman Lab podcast plays in my AirPods, I hear none of it. My thoughts are only on Campbell. She should be waking any moment, stumbling across the journal I slid under the guest room door last night after she'd gone to bed.

My watch beeps, indicating my heart rate has remained more elevated than normal during today's run. I've never been an anxious person, but not knowing how she's going to react when I get home isn't doing me any favors.

I round the corner to my street, spotting my white, three-story abode in the distance with its row of matching palm trees swaying in the humid breeze and the iron gate standing tall at the end of the driveway. This place has always been my fortress of solitude, but it has never fully felt like home for reasons I could never put my finger on.

Now that Campbell's living here full-time—and despite the fact that we're not on speaking terms at the moment—there's a warmth about that place that it never had before.

Trotting up the driveway, I stop at the front door to catch my breath and wipe the sweat from my brow before heading in.

The faint scent of Campbell's usual breakfast order—oatmeal, coffee, and avocado toast—is missing from the air this morning, which means either she isn't up yet or she read my letters and lost her appetite at my audacity.

My footsteps echo against the marble as I make my way into the silent house. Climbing the curved stairs, I head to my room to shower—only in passing, I notice the guest room door is wide open.

Peeking in, I find Campbell seated on the velvet chaise in the corner, the leather book closed in her lap. She's half bent over, her elbow resting on her knee as she nibbles on her thumbnail.

I can't read her to save my life.

"Hi," I say.

Her arctic blues flick up and she straightens her posture.

"What is this?" she asks, her brows furrowed. "Another one of your sick little games?"

Before I can respond, she jumps up, the journal clutched hard against her chest.

"All these years, you gave me nothing but cold, calculated hate ... and now you show me this?" She chucks the book at me, and I catch it.

"I wanted you to see it," I say. "I thought you should know the truth."

"That you lied to me all these years? That you were too prideful to admit it?" Her eyes are flashing wildly and her tone is incredulous as she storms closer. "Is this supposed to be redeeming? Do you want me to run into your arms and tell you it's okay? That we can just start over? What? What were you hoping to accomplish here."

She folds her arms tight, her pretty face cocked sideways and her messy hair falling in her face.

"I'm sorry I couldn't tell you these things before," I say. My father always says the best apologies are succinct and to the point, so I resist the urge to explain beyond this. If she read the entries, that should give her more than enough insight into my motivations.

"You couldn't have given me this a year ago?" she asks. "Or at some other point in the past fifteen years?"

"I wish I could have."

"I don't think you understand how awful the past year has been for me." Her voice breaks, marking the first time I've ever seen her on the verge of tears in my presence. "The way you've slighted me, cast me off, treated me like an obligation, faked your kindness ... the damage has been done." Marching closer, she shoves her finger against my chest. "The night before our wedding, you told me you could never love me."

"Yes, I said that. But I didn't mean it. I wanted to give you an out. It seemed like the right thing to do after the way I'd treated you."

"How can I ever believe anything you say again?" A handful of tears slide down her cheeks, but she swipes them away. "You're heartless."

I deserve that.

"I'm complicated," I say. "This whole thing is ... complicated."

"Complicated? Our entire relationship, or the lack of it, is a twisted web you spun, Slade. It's only complicated because you made it that way. Now you want to hide behind prose and feigned vulnerability."

"There are parts of me that are broken, and I've not been kind to you because of that. I was hoping we could work together—"

She claps her arms against her sides. "So now it's *my* problem to fix?"

"I don't want you to *fix* me. I don't *need* you to either. I'm just telling you I'm aware of the problem and how it has affected you. I'm apologizing. I'm trying to make this right ... if it's not too late."

"Then why did you tell me you couldn't love me?" Her expression is laser tight, angered. The air between us is thick with tension, impossible to breathe. "Why would you want to give me an out when you were falling for me?"

"Because deep down, I know I don't deserve you. I don't deserve any of what I have."

She rolls her eyes. "I just ... one hell of an actor. And there's no denying you can be persuasive. I have no way of knowing what's real and what's not with you given everything ..."

"Every word in that journal is raw. Real. Every emotion. Every regret." There's no denying the evolution of my handwriting and vernacular, but now is not the time to point out minor details. I want to focus on the big picture here—*us*.

Our future.

Campbell sniffs and massages her neck, staring at the floor. "Okay, so now that you've had your little change of heart, what's the game plan now?"

Her voice is laced with a hint of sarcasm, but her question is sincere.

"This isn't a game and there's no plan," I tell her. "We have to figure this out together."

"I don't know, Slade." Tipping her chin, she exhales. "You should have given me that journal years ago. Maybe, just maybe we'd have stood a chance at being truly happy together. Now we'll never know."

Our faces are mere inches apart now, the distance between us fueled by hurt, anger, and the undeniable magnetism I've always foolishly ignored. As tears continue to stream down her face, I'm tempted to swipe them away but I think better of it.

We're not there *yet*.

And who knows if we'll ever be there.

"I want the drowning kind of love. The can't-sleep-can't-eat-until-I-see-you-again kind of love. I want a love that stirs my soul and consumes my dreams. I want a love that's bigger than the ever-expanding universe," she says. "I'm sorry, Slade, but you will never be *any* of that for me."

Her words, perhaps intended to cut me deep, only serve as a challenge—a challenge I'm ready and willing to accept if it means showing her how very fucking wrong she's going to be about me.

As we linger in stifled silence, her mouth pressed firm and her gorgeous glassy gaze filled with pain, I can't hold back another second. Pulling her to me, I cup her face and crash my lips onto hers. To my surprise, she doesn't push me away, not at first.

"You think one kiss will erase all of this?" she asks as she searches my face, her lips swollen from the greed of my kiss.

"No, but I think it's a pretty damn good start." I pull her into my arms again and claim her full lips once more. This time she melts against me, lifting on her toes as her fingers trail through the hair at the nape of my neck.

"I hate that I love the way you kiss me," her words are breathless as we come up for air. The storm of emotions exploding between us is tumultuous, messy, unpredictable, but there's no denying they're real. "I hate that I'm letting you do this."

"I'll stop if you want me to."

"Don't," she bites back, tasting my tongue when her lips return to mine. "You're much harder to hate when you're not talking."

I sniff a laugh, unsure if that's a compliment or a directive, and then I glide my hands down her sides, cupping her curved ass over her thin pajama bottoms. I lift her into my arms, letting her thighs straddle my hips as I taste the end of her neck, sampling every pulse of her heartbeat.

"Let me make this up to you," I say.

"How do I know this is real?" Her arms rest over my shoulders. Never mind that my hair is damp with sweat, my body is sticking to hers, and none of this remotely fits into my strict morning routine.

Screw all of that.

I want this woman and I want her right here, right now—if she'll have me.

"Talk is cheap." I kick the bedroom door shut with my foot before laying her down on the guest bed. My cock strains against my shorts, throbbing more by the second. "I thought maybe I could just show you how fucking crazy I am about you."

A mix of uncertainty colors her pretty face, but I kiss it away.

I'll kiss her a thousand times if it helps my cause.

"I don't know if this can erase our past," she says as I pull her cotton camisole over her head.

"Who said we had to erase it?" I run my fingers under the elastic band of her shorts, sliding my hand between her thighs until I reach her damp slit. She's wet—for me, a man who has caused her nothing but grief her entire life. "I want to build on it; something new, something better."

She releases a soft whimper as I circle her clit with my thumb and slide a finger inside her.

With my free hand, I guide her thighs apart. The tension rippling through her body tells me she doesn't fully trust me yet, but the sounds coming from her fuckable mouth suggest she's willing to give me a chance.

Tugging her shorts down, I toss them aside and stand back to take a look at my gorgeous wife and her sexy vulnerability on full display.

"What?" she asks, brows knitting.

"Are you really a virgin?" Over the years, we exchanged a lot of bullshit in those letters.

"Is that an issue for you?"

Dipping down, I kiss her belly, which caves with my touch. "Of course not. I wanted to know if I should go gentle on you."

I shove my shorts and boxers down, kicking them off.

Reaching, she wraps her arms underneath mine and pulls me against her. Her breasts are swollen with arousal and her nipples are pert, teasing my skin with every exhalation.

"Who said I wanted gentle?" Her hips buck beneath me as her thighs widen even more.

"How do you want it?"

"Have you thought of this moment before?" she asks.

"A million times."

"Fuck me the way you always wanted to then." There's a curious glint in her eye as she twists my hair around her fingers. "I want to feel wanted by the man who made it his life's mission to make me feel anything but that."

Her words somehow turn me on and break my heart at the same time.

"You're the sexiest thing I've ever laid my eyes on," I tell her. "You should know that."

The morning sunlight dances through a break in the curtains, illuminating her creamy skin and her supple curves, but the one light I need, the one that captures my complete attention, is in her eyes when she looks at me.

Our union may not have been born in love, but somewhere, somehow, love has been there all along, hiding in the broken cracks, waiting for us to come around.

I kiss my wife's full mouth once more, our tongues melding as I press my hardness against her sex, teasing her as she squirms beneath me. Cupping her breast in my hand, I take her budded nipple between my teeth, giving it a gentle graze that elicits a quiet moan.

Every move, every breath, is a revelation, a step in the right direction.

Her fingers skim my arms, sending a current through me as I brace myself above her and when she gazes up and bites her bottom lip, it's all I can do to keep from immediately plunging myself deep inside her.

Her eyes, always filled with defiance and curiosity before, now shimmer with vulnerability and anticipation as our words fade and our bodies do the talking. I could tell her all the things I adore about her until I'm blue in the face, but all of that would mean nothing if I didn't show her how I felt.

"I want to feel you inside me," she whispers. Reaching down, she palms my cock, softly stroking it before positioning at her entrance. The dampness of her arousal is warm against my tip, and I exhale an impatient growl.

Despite how badly she wants this, she's still a virgin.

I don't want this to be uncomfortable for her.

It should be special and memorable and perfect—the opposite of everything else she's experienced at my hands.

"What are you waiting for?" she asks, writhing under me. I silence her question with a kiss before gripping my throbbing cock and sliding it inside of her, inch by inch, slow and gentle. She's tight, as if her body was made for mine but hasn't been broken in yet.

"Relax," I remind her as she tenses against me. "Breathe."

Campbell exhales, her nails digging into my back as I thrust in and out, slow at first, then gradually turning up the pace as I'm driven by a sense of urgency. The collision of our bodies only serves to make me crave more of her.

"You feel so damn good," I tell her, excitement lurching through as her body responds to mine, becoming softer, wetter, more pliant with every thrust. "You're a natural."

She kisses me. "Shh."

I drive deeper inside her, implored by her wanton gaze. I could do this all day. All night. All damn week. Silently, I decide to call out from work. How could I possibly leave this woman after this? I want seconds, thirds. I want to devour every last inch of her until she knows just how much I intend to right my wrongs.

"I think I'm getting close ..." she sighs, "don't stop, don't stop ..."

A few seconds later, my beautiful bride is twisting, writhing, bucking, and moaning. Burying my head into her neck, I breathe in her addictive sweetness and brace myself for the biggest release I've ever known—a release a lifetime in the making.

We collapse in an exhausted heap when we're done,

making it impossible to tell where her body ends and mine begins.

Peering up at me through a fringe of dark lashes, she smiles, and for the first time in my life, I feel something I've never felt before.

Hope.

32

Campbell

"Can I ask you something?" I cup my hand over my eyes, peering at my husband as he soaks up the sun in the lounge chair beside me. After the unexpected turn of events this morning, he decided to take the day off to spend some quality time with me. He's determined to prove he meant what he said, but I'm still trying to wrap my head around the fact that he said any of that at all.

For twenty-four years, this man gave me every reason to believe he hated me.

I'm still not one hundred percent sold.

When I first read that journal, I wondered if it was some little mind game he was playing. I thought maybe he was trying to get back in my good graces so we could consummate the marriage because he may be complicated, but he's still a red-blooded American man. While we *did* technically consummate it, nothing about the experience felt mechanical or detached—in fact, it was the opposite.

He was warm and tender and attentive—a stranger with a familiar face.

I saw him in a light I never knew existed.

"What is it?" He glances away from the biography in his lap and lifts his sunglasses to the top of his head. The scent of banana and coconut suntan oil and sea spray fills the air. Overhead, seagulls squawk and circle in search of food, but given that this stretch of beach is private, we're the only ones here, and we were too busy doing other things to think about packing snacks ... they're out of luck.

"Would you have married me if you truly hated me?" I have to know. "Was it always about the money and you just happened to fall for me? Or ..."

His jaw tenses as he considers his answer.

"And you have to be honest," I point at him. We talked about this earlier. From this day forward, our policy is honesty always, no matter what.

"My father's media company," he begins, drawing in a long breath. "They've garnered a reputation over the years for being quite biased—politically that is. One of the things my father has always told me is that, if you have money, you have power. In our case, our power comes in the form of a media conglomerate that has enough collective power to influence political elections and national and worldwide events. My plan has always been to disassemble the company completely and put it back together, rebuilding it on an unbiased platform."

I'm taken aback.

Not only is Slade capable of unlocking his heart, he's actually admirably ethical.

The familiar stranger I married clears his throat and continues. "They say you have to be the change you want to see in the world. I intend to be that."

"And you were willing to sacrifice your own happiness, forgoing a chance at being truly in love and building a life with someone, all so you could make this happen?"

He nods. "I don't want the Delacorte name to be synonymous with corruption and manipulation. When my grandfather first built this company, the media industry wasn't anything like the machine it's become now. He'd roll over in his grave if he saw what his little news corporation has become."

"Your father doesn't care?"

"He's part of the problem," Slade says. "He views it as it's his money and his company, so he should be able to further his personal agenda and political affiliations. We've had a lot of, uh, heated conversations over the years. For Mom's sake, we finally agreed to disagree. We don't discuss politics anymore."

"Does he know your intentions once you take over?"

"He does."

"And he's okay with it?" I ask.

Slade sniffs. "Deep down he knows I'm doing the right thing. He just doesn't have the energy or the motivation to do it himself."

His muscles tense and his breath grows slightly shallow, like this is a subject matter he doesn't enjoy discussing.

"What?" He wrinkles his nose when he realizes I've been staring at him a little too long.

"Who even *are* you, Slade Delacorte?" I ask, my words drawn out and colored with disbelief.

Reaching over, he drags my lounge chair closer to his before tossing his book in the sand and pulling me into his lap.

"I'm your husband," he says, a mischievous glint in his coffee-brown irises, "that's who."

Last night I went to bed alone, bitter, hopeless, disenchanted.

This morning I woke up, fought with my husband, lost my virginity, and now I'm straddling him on the beach, tracing my fingers along his rippled eight-pack abs while he looks like he's thinking of making a meal out of me right here, right now.

"This is all happening so fast," I tell him.

"I'm just as shocked as you are."

"Good. I'm glad it's not just me. I just don't want us to get ahead of ourselves, you know? Emotions were running high … and then we … and now we're … I just worry—"

Leaning forward, he silences me with a kiss.

"Campbell Wakemont wasn't a worrier," he says. "Campbell Delacorte shouldn't be one either."

My mouth tugs up at one side. After the priest pronounced us husband and wife at the wedding, I hadn't thought much about my new name. In fact, I haven't even begun the process of having it officially changed. But the way it sounds on his lips sends a thrill down my middle that I wasn't anticipating.

"You hungry?" he asks.

"Famished." After Slade took my virginity this morning, he took me a second time—in the shower. And after that, we went for a third round outside on the veranda, in broad daylight. The lower half of our bodies were wrapped in a blanket as he bent me over the railing and took me from behind. I never knew it was possible to have that many orgasms in such a short amount of time, but I'm being proven wrong about all sorts of things today.

We head back to the house, where Slade gives Fiona the night off and orders us a lavish feast from his favorite Greek restaurant downtown.

"You want to watch a movie?" I ask him later. "I know it's almost your bedtime and all, but I'm not ready for this day to be over just yet."

"Sure. Why don't you head to the family room and find something you like. I'll be back in a little bit."

"Back? Are you going somewhere?"

"Give me thirty minutes."

Thirty-eight minutes pass before the man returns. The rustling of plastic bags and the shuffling of footsteps grows louder as he heads my way. On the screen, I've cued up some historical drama that looks like the kind of thing he'd enjoy based on the biography he was reading today.

"What's all that?" I ask when he strolls in with an armful of goods.

"I stopped at the AMC and picked up some popcorn. I had them pop a fresh batch, so that's why it took so long." He places the tub on the coffee table. "And then I ran into the gas station to get some candy. Wasn't sure what you liked, so I got a little bit of everything."

He empties the bag next to the bucket of popcorn, forming a mountain of gummy bears, Snickers bars, Caramello bites, Twizzlers, and Raisinettes.

"I take back every bad thing I've ever said about you." I swipe the Twizzlers. "You clearly know the way to my heart."

Wearing a proud smirk, he settles in next to me and slips his arm around my shoulders.

Peering up at him, I drink him in for the millionth time today. Every time, it's like looking at a stranger—but in a good way. And I have butterflies ... actual butterflies ... with him for the first time ever.

"Who'd have thought?" I ask, though it's mostly a rhetorical question.

"Who'd have thought," he echoes back.

33

Slade

"Knock, knock, you busy?"

I glance up from my desk the following afternoon and find Oliver in my doorway.

"What are you doing here?" I ask. "You never come to the office."

He dips his hands into the pockets of his designer jeans, shrugging. "I was in the area. Thought I'd see if you had lunch plans."

"Ever heard of texting?" I deadpanned.

"Yes, actually. I texted you several times yesterday and you left me on read. I thought I'd make sure you were still alive and kicking. Last time I was over there, it sounded like things were a little tense with you and Campbell."

I roll my eyes. "All good now."

"Really?" The shock registers on his face in real time. "I mean, that's awesome. I was worried. She seemed so upset the other day and said you two weren't talking and she'd been sleeping in the guest room ..."

"No need to rehash everything."

"Sorry, yeah." He massages the back of his neck. "So it's all good now?"

"That's ... what I just said." My inbox chimes and I click on a message from the attorney handling the Franklin and Dodd buyout we're still negotiating. His message simply asks me to call him. I exhale my annoyance and reach for my phone. "Sorry. I was out of the office yesterday, catching up on everything. I can't do lunch today. Another time?"

Oliver slumps against the door frame, looking like someone ran over his puppy. With everything that happened over the past year, our brotherly bond has taken a bit of a back seat, and now that I'm married, my priorities are shifting faster than any of us ever expected.

"What are you doing this weekend? Maybe we can grab a beer down at the marina," I suggest, hoping to put a little light back in his eyes.

"Yeah, we should," he says, lifting his head. "I don't want to steal you away from Campbell though if you already have plans. I'm glad things are getting better. She's a nice girl. I figured it'd only be a matter of time before you finally realized that."

I spare him the diatribe about how I already knew but was too stubborn to admit it.

"You guys going to go on a honeymoon after all then?" he asks.

"I guess I hadn't thought about it yet." Two days ago, she wouldn't even make eye contact with me, let alone acknowledge my presence. Twenty-four hours ago, we were going at it like rabbits. I've hardly had a moment to process the winds of change, let alone contemplate taking her on a proper honeymoon.

Grabbing a pen, I write "call travel agent" on a sticky note and circle it twice. While I am it, I make another note to schedule a surprise visit from her friends. She could use a little pick-me-up after everything I've put her through.

"Anything else on your mind?" I ask my uncle since he's yet to budge.

Jutting his chin out, he shakes his head. "Nah. I'll get a hold of you later this week."

"Why don't you come over for dinner tonight? Campbell's planning to cook some big meal. There'll be more than enough."

Oliver sniffs a laugh. "I don't want to be a third wheel."

"Seven o'clock." I point to my watch. "Don't be late."

The second he's gone, I text my wife and tell her to set a third place setting later for Oliver, then I dial the attorney.

"Good news!" he answers in the middle of the first ring. "Franklin and Dodd have accepted our offer. As of January 1 next year, their holdings will become property of Delacorte Media Group. Congrats, Slade. I know you've been working hard on this deal."

Leaning back in my leather chair, I kick my feet up on my desk and take a second to appreciate my overwhelming good fortune this week. I don't know what I ever did to deserve any of it, but I'm grateful. Humbled, even, if one can believe such a thing.

It's 6 PM when I pull into the driveway. Before, I'd sit in the car, wasting time on my phone before heading inside where I was clearly not welcome in my own home. But now? I'm practically sprinting inside. Only the second I step foot into the foyer, I'm met with a thick haze and the sharp tang of burnt food lingering in the air.

"Campbell?" I call out.

"In the kitchen," she calls back.

I find her standing at the sink, frantically scrubbing some dish.

"Hey," I slip my hands around her waist from behind and kiss her cheek. "Everything okay?"

She turns to me, snapping off her rubber gloves, and looking like she's two seconds from crying.

"What's wrong? What is it?" I ask, sweeping a strand of her messy hair out of her eyes and tucking it behind her ear. The apron hugging her body is covered in miscellaneous food stains and resting on the counter is a dish so charred it's indistinguishable.

"So ... I burned dinner," she says.

"It happens."

"I'm sorry."

"Don't apologize," I say.

"I don't know what happened. I was watching these tutorials all afternoon on YouTube and I did everything exactly how they said, and I don't know? Maybe I used the wrong setting on the oven? I thought I could save the vegetables, but somehow those turned out both undercooked and overcooked."

I kiss her. "I'll order in."

"Can you sign me up for cooking lessons while you're at it?"

"I'm sure Fiona could show you a few things if you asked."

Staring at the charred dish on the counter, she bunches her lips at the side. "I don't know if that dish was expensive or not, but I'm pretty sure it's ruined. Turns out burned chicken is impossible to get off after it hardens. God, I'm so sorry."

"Stop apologizing. It's the thought that counts anyway." Leading her by the hand, I take her upstairs.

"Where are we going?" she asks, traipsing behind me.

"I'm starving," I tell her as we make our way to the bedroom. "And since you burned dinner, I have no choice but to make a meal out of you."

Sweeping her into my arms, I gently toss her on the bed, tear off her leggings, and bury my head between her thighs where I proceed to devour her until she's gasping, quivering, and begging me to stop.

Chicken is overrated anyway.

34

Campbell

The soft glow from the television illuminates the family room as the dramatic antics of the Below Deck crew unfolds on the screen. Leaning back into the plush sofa, I snap off another piece of strawberry Twizzler while Oliver makes some comment about the technicalities of some engine.

"Is there anything else you like besides boats?" I ask him. "I don't think I've ever heard you talk about anything else."

Slade chuckles. "Women. He likes women. The more unhinged, the better."

"Courtney was an angel. There'll never be another Courtney," Oliver chuffs. "And Lena. Oh my god, Lena. I'll never understood why she went back to that cheating bastard ex of hers."

"Maybe deep down she knew you were too good for her," I tell him.

"Yeah, that's what it was," Slade teases. "Had nothing to

do with the fact that he got hammered off his ass and proposed a threesome with her best friend."

"I'm sure there's a nice girl out there waiting to meet a nice guy like you," I say. Oliver is definitely more of a free spirit, but there's always been something lonely about him, almost as if he's hiding his emptiness behind his larger-than-life persona.

"Don't give him false hope. All the good ones are taken," Slade razzes him some more. This is what they do, and I've quickly learned it's their love language. They give each other crap because they care. "And I got the last one."

Slade squeezes my knee and gives me a wink.

It's only been a week since we turned this new corner, but each day has only gotten better. At some point, I fear there'll be nowhere to go but down. But I'm trying to enjoy the unfolding of this strange new normal instead of wasting precious time worrying about a hypothetical scenario.

Oliver's phone chimes and he checks it. "Sweet."

"What?" Slade asks.

"My Schaeffer Flybridge is ready for the weekend," he says.

"Your what-what?" I ask.

"It's a fifty-eight-foot yacht I just added to my fleet. Some guy in Jupiter bought it last year and never took it out. The thing's never even been out of the marina," he says.

"Isn't fifty-eight feet kind of small for a yacht?" I ask, though I'm only giving him crap because of all the numbers he rattles off every time we watch this show together.

"The thing about my industry is, I have to have something for everyone. Not everyone can afford to rent a two hundred footer," he explains. "I've got to cater to all kinds of clientele."

"I bet for what you paid for that Flybridge, you could have bought yourself a Bugatti," Slade says.

"But then I wouldn't be able to borrow yours," Oliver quips back before lunging for the remote and hitting the pause button. "You know ..."

Slade and I exchange looks and rolled eyes. We know exactly where he's going with this.

"I know what you guys are going to say, but just hear me out," Oliver continues, "Slade, you let me borrow your cars all the time and you never ask for anything from me. And Campbell, I know you're not a boat person, but what if you, me, and Slade took the Flybridge out on her maiden voyage? It could be, sort of, like a wedding gift from me to you guys. It's a smaller yacht, so we won't need a full crew. In fact, I could man it myself. And I'll stay out of sight. You won't even know I'm there."

"I don't know." I wince. "I'd rather not."

"You guys haven't even gone on a honeymoon," Oliver says. "Or anywhere for that matter. You've been holed up here ever since you got back from the wedding last week. Why don't you come out on the boat this weekend, two days of rest and relaxation. No distractions from the rest of the world. You can lay out and drink and soak up the sun and pretend you're in the South of France or something—my treat."

"You don't have to do that for us," Slade tells him.

"I know. But I want to. You've always done so much for me," he says. "I'm just happy for you guys, is all."

I shift, uncomfortable as I steal a glance at my husband, searching for a sign that he's on my side, only there's something in his eyes that makes me think he's actually considering this. I'm sure if I put my foot down, he'd back me up, but with everything going so well lately, I don't want to rock the proverbial boat over a ... boat.

"What do you think?" Slade asks me, his tone tinged with genuine consideration. "Could be something fun to do this weekend. It's not like we have plans. And he's right—we haven't taken a honeymoon."

I laugh. "No offense, Oliver, but a romantic getaway with you sleeping in the next room isn't exactly my idea of a honeymoon."

"You won't even know I'm there." Oliver places a hand over his heart, sitting straight. "Swear on my life. It'll be like it's just the two of you, the open sea, and all the first-class luxury you can imagine. Top shelf drinks, cashmere linens ..."

I bite my lip, contemplating as he rattles off a list of amenities. I'm still not sold. The idea of being on the open water doesn't appeal to me no matter how many perks he throws in, though I have been feeling cooped up lately and a change of scenery might be nice.

"Look," Oliver says, cocking his head towards me and resting his arm on the back of the couch. "I just want to give you two a chance to create some beautiful memories. And also I want to prove to you that you're wrong about boats. They're safe and fun and you're missing out. And if at any point, you want to come back to shore, just say the word and we'll go, no questions asked."

"How far away will we be?" I ask.

"Three hours, max," he says.

Glancing at Slade, I lift my brows.

"I think it could be fun," he says. "If all we have to do is show up, I mean ..."

I sigh, not wanting to be the cog in the wheel. "You're sure it's safe?"

Slade frowns, "Do you honestly think I'd put us in any kind of danger?"

"Feel free to check out my safety ratings and inspection records," Oliver says. "If I were some slime bag renting out dilapidated scows, do you think I'd still be in business? Hell, I wouldn't even be insurable."

I hate this idea. I do. But if Slade comes, maybe it won't be so bad.

"Fine," I say. "But only if there's an endless supply of seasickness tablets on board and you show me how to use all the safety equipment."

"I'll give you the full rundown before we depart," Oliver promises. "We won't leave until you feel confident about everything."

Maybe I'm overreacting, but growing up off the coast of Maine, you hear so many boating horror stories—that compounded with my grandfather's freak accident gives me pause.

Oliver rubs his hands together, grinning from ear to ear. I'm pretty sure we just made this man's entire year.

"All right," he says, "so why don't you two meet me at the Gas Lantern Marina Friday, slip number fourteen, say around noon? I'll have you back by Sunday." Rising, he turns to me, "It gets a little cold on the water at night, so pack some sweaters."

I salute him. "Yes, First Officer Oliver."

"It's actually Captain Oliver," he corrects me.

Slade rolls his eyes.

"Okay, I'm out. I've got some things to line up for our trip," Oliver says. "You two lovebirds get plenty of rest and I'll see you in a couple of days."

"I hope I don't regret this," I tell Slade when he's gone.

My husband tugs me into his lap, runs his fingers

through my hair, and leans in to kiss me. "I thought he'd never leave."

"Wait, did you only agree to this whole yacht thing because you wanted Oliver to leave?" I ask.

"No ..."

I squint. "Mm hm."

Slade chuckles. "No, seriously. I didn't. I think it'll be a nice little weekend getaway. And maybe it won't be the worst thing for you to get over your fear of boats, especially living here."

Dozens of old stories from back home flick through my mind like microfiche at a library.

"If you don't want to go, we don't have to go," he says, and with his words the excitement that was radiating off of him a few moments ago grows dim.

"We'll go," I say. I don't want to, but I'll do it for him.

If Slade can get over his fear of opening up, I can get over my fear of open water.

35

Slade

"So what happens if we break down?" Campbell asks as Oliver gives us the safety tour Friday afternoon. We've only been on his yacht twenty minutes so far, and she's yet to let go of anything. When she's not holding onto a railing, she's holding onto me for dear life. I almost feel bad insisting we do this, but I think it'll be good for her.

"I've got a Zodiac Nautic on board," Oliver says. "It's an inflatable dinghy that fits three people. That or I could call the Coast Guard or one of my guys at the boathouse. I promise you, Campbell, there's no getting stranded out here."

She eyes the open deck of the stern. "It's weird how it's just ... open."

"Well, you don't use it when the ship is moving," I tell her. "It's meant for lounging and sunbathing when you're stationary."

My explanation does nothing to get the horrified look

off her face, but she's yet to declare she's getting off, so that's a good sign.

"Let me show you your accommodations," Oliver motions for us to follow him to the lower level of the yacht, where a cozy yet well-appointed bedroom is flanked by an en suite bathroom. On the other side of the ship is a smaller bedroom and bathroom as well as a full kitchen. "Anything you need, anything at all ... I've already thought of it."

He leads us to the kitchen, where he yanks open the fridge and shows us the pre-made meals, snacks, Evian waters, and adult beverages he's stocked.

"Okay, so we went over the safety protocols, I showed you where the life vests are and the satellite phone and how to use the radio in case of an emergency," Oliver counts off his fingers. "Am I forgetting anything?"

"I think that's it," I say.

"You ready to earn your sea legs, Campbell?" Oliver nudges my wife, who's so tense she practically falls over like a statue.

"Yeah, let's go," she feigns enthusiasm, maintaining a death grip on my forearm.

My uncle slips his captain's hat on and trots upstairs to the helm wearing the dopiest grin I've ever seen. I know it means the world to him that we're here, and while half of me thinks this will be good for Campbell, the other half of me knows he needed this. Without my mother around, he's lost the only real sense of purpose he had—the only sense of family he had, too, and now that I'm married and starting a new chapter in my own life, he's taken even more of a backseat in the Delacorte lineup.

"Why don't you head down to the cabin and get changed into your swimsuit? I'll fix us a couple drinks and meet you on the console. " I tell her.

Her eyes nervously search mine before she rises on her toes, gives me a peck, and heads below deck. Ten minutes later, she walks out in a neon peach bikini, a white sarong tied around her waist. I bite my lip, wishing we were truly alone right now.

"Here you are." I hand her a handcrafted cocktail, clink my tumbler against hers, and make a toast. "Here's to a weekend we'll never forget."

Drinking in my beautiful wife as we disembark, I take a moment to appreciate how far we've come ... while also realizing we're only getting started. In a way, this trip is a metaphor, symbolizing the adventure that lies ahead as we overcome our fears, grow together, and attempt to have fun while we're at it.

I sync my phone to the Bluetooth speakers on the deck, pulling up a playlist I downloaded before we left. The farther we get out to sea, the weaker the cell signals are—if we can even get one at all.

Her favorite song from the latest The 1975 album plays, instantly putting a smile on her face. She curls up against me, sipping her drink, humming along to the music as the marina grows smaller in the distance.

"See, it's not so bad," I tell her.

"I guess ..."

I squeeze her against me for a little reassurance. Glancing up, I spot my uncle behind the wheel of the yacht, aviators over his nose and his attention focused on the waters ahead as he pays us no mind.

The gentle rhythm of the waters and the warmth of the midday sun beating down coupled with my best girl in my arms fills me with an overwhelming sense of peace. Closing my eyes for just a second, I only intend to rest them. But by the time they open again, my music has stopped playing and the sun is sitting lower in the sky. Checking my watch, I realize we've both been passed out for a few hours.

Campbell stirs when I shift. "Did we pass out?"

"Yeah," I say. "Must've needed to catch up on sleep."

She checks her phone.

"It's four thirty," I tell her.

"I'm not worried about the time; I was just seeing if we had any service." Her mouth pulls down at the sides. "No bars."

"They don't have cell towers in the ocean."

"Thank you, Captain Obvious," she elbows me. "Or should I say First Officer Obvious?"

"See, you're already learning all the lingo."

She rises, tugging her sarong into place. "I'm kind of hungry. What do you think he has for snacks?"

"Everything." I follow her to the kitchen, where we help ourselves to the assortment of finger sandwiches, sliced fresh fruit, and gourmet cheeses.

"You're going to have to roll me out of here on Sunday," she says as she stabs a square of gouda with a toothpick and pops it in her mouth. "Or maybe toss me off the side of the boat and I'll just float home."

"Oh, hey, you guys are finally up." Oliver leans against the doorway. "I was getting worried for a second. Make sure you're staying hydrated okay, being out here with all that sun during the day can really do a number on you if you don't stay on top of it."

"Shouldn't you be steering the ship?" Campbell asks, eyes wild.

Oliver chuckles. "We're anchored for the evening."

"You can anchor in water this deep?" she asks, confused.

I lean in. "Don't get him started unless you want a full lesson on the technicalities of underwater parachutes."

"Not everyone has the attention span required for such riveting topics," Oliver shoots me a look. "But if you ever want to know how that works, I'd be happy to draw it out for you."

"I'll keep that in mind," Campbell says, reaching for a slice of watermelon. "Thank you."

"Did you guys want me to heat up your dinners?" Oliver asks.

Campbell places her hand on her stomach. "I don't know if I could eat a whole meal right now. Maybe later?"

I nod. "We'll hold off. Thank you though."

"Sounds good," Oliver says. "I'll be upstairs if you need me, otherwise ... I'll make myself scarce."

"I have a surprise for you," I tell Campbell as we finish our snacks. "But it's in the bedroom."

"Mr. Delacorte, you've had me twice today," she pretends to be appalled, but the smile on her face says she's thinking what I'm thinking. "But I suppose one more time won't hurt ..."

Slipping my hand over hers, I take her to the bedroom where a bottle of Cristal is nestled in a bucket of ice (thanks to Oliver), along with the two champagne saucers we picked out when we did our registry shopping.

"I know you said you're not a champagne person," I tell her. "But I promise you've never enjoyed champagne the *proper* way before."

"Oh, with the bigger surface area and all that," she says. "I remember you explained it to me before. I still don't think it'll make that big of a difference, but I'll try it. For you."

"That's not what I meant," I say. She cocks a brow. "Here. I'll show you."

She watches in silence as I uncork the bottle and pour the shimmering gold liquid into our matching saucers and place them aside. Then with one tug, I untie her sarong, letting it fall to the floor before unfastening her bikini top. Taking a sip of champagne, I leave a small amount of liquid in my mouth before tasting one of her exposed nipples.

She releases a breathy sigh as the cold and bubbles mix with the warmth of my tongue on her flesh.

Swallowing, I take another sip and move for her mouth next, letting the champagne pass from my tongue to hers.

She shivers against me and I pull her into my arms.

"You're right," she says, "I've never had champagne like this before."

And I'm only getting started ...

Slipping my fingers under the waist of her bikini bottoms, I tug them off. She stumbles back onto the bed, giggling in anticipation.

With a champagne saucer in hand, I trickle some onto her stomach, which caves in response to the merciless temperature. Pressing my lips against her warm skin, I drink the bubbles from her belly button before pouring another splash lower and repeating it until I'm between her thighs.

Tipping the saucer, I let a splash drip down her slit before slowly running my tongue along it, collecting every drop. Over and over, I drink champagne from between her legs, swirling the cold bubbles with my tongue against her most sensitive area. She sucks in a breath, her body trembling as she grips fistfuls of bedding, and it isn't long before she's writhing against my mouth, sticky with Cristal and arousal.

Sweet intoxication.

36

Campbell

Slade's half of the bed is empty when I wake Saturday morning. My head is pounding and my mind is dazed and my stomach turns. The ship is rocking more than it was before. Or maybe I'm just hungover.

After Slade's champagne adventure last night, we got a little carried away. It wasn't until we were deliriously spent that we wandered out for a snack shortly after midnight, fed our faces, then sauntered back to our room to crash.

Shrugging into a cashmere robe, I tie the belt and head out.

"Slade?" I call, bracing myself against the nearest wall as the yacht leans.

I check the bathroom, debating whether or not I should grab a quick shower since I'm sticky from last night, but something doesn't feel right. Climbing the stairs out of the cabin, I'm met with the bright morning sun and the sound of waves lapping against the side of the ship.

"Slade?" I yell again. "Where are you?"

I can hear someone talking, but I can't tell if it's Slade or Oliver. Heading up to the helm next, I'm expecting to find Oliver behind the wheel, only he's nowhere in sight. It's just Slade, pacing, dragging his hands through his hair.

"I'm going to fucking kill him," Slade says.

"What? Slade, what's going on? Where's Oliver?"

"That son of a bitch is dead to me. I'm going to destroy him, he's—"

"—hey," I grip his arm, giving it a shake. "You going to tell me what's going on?"

"Jesus, Campbell." His eyes come into focus and he stops pacing. "Don't panic ... but I can't find Oliver."

"What do you mean, you can't *find* Oliver?"

"He's ... gone."

"What are you talking about?" I hear his words crystal clear, but they're not computing. It's like my brain refuses to comprehend what he's saying.

"I ... I ... came up here this morning to ask him something and he wasn't there, so I checked his cabin room and the bed was made. It didn't even look like he'd slept there last night. So then I checked around the rest of the ship." He bites his lower lip for a moment, nearly drawing blood. "It's like he was never here ... I don't understand ..."

"Slade, you're scaring me."

Placing his hands on my arms, he steers me to a nearby seat. "I'm sorry. I'm just trying to figure out what to do."

"Can't we radio the Coast Guard or whatever?" I distinctly remember Oliver carefully giving me the safety rundown yesterday and there being a myriad of emergency options.

"He cut the wires." Slade crouches down, his hand in his hair again. "The bastard cut the wires to the radio. He took the solar flares. He threw all of the food and water overboard—at least I assume so because the kitchen is empty. He must've drained the gas tank somehow, or maybe he didn't fill it all the way before we left, but either way, we're on E. The satellite cell is gone, too. Even the life jackets."

"What?" The panic in my voice sends a tightness to my throat. "What about that boat? The emergency one he talked about? The inflatable?"

"It's gone too. I'm guessing that's how he got out of here." He rises, pacing again. "That fucking bastard left us here to die."

Slade takes the seat next to me.

"I'm so sorry, Campbell," he says, staring blankly ahead, a shell-shocked look about him. "I can't believe he would do this."

"We're going to die here, aren't we?"

Two weeks ago today, we said the words 'til death do us part.

The irony of that isn't lost on me.

37

Slade

"You have to drink something," I tell her. It's been twenty-four hours since Oliver left us stranded somewhere in the Atlantic. I hand her the champagne bucket filled with melted ice. It's all we have for water. Apparently Oliver thought of everything—going so far as to shut off the water filtration system and drain the onboard tank.

The bastard had to have been planning this for a while.

"It's all we have," she says, her tongue smacking against the roof of her mouth. Her eyes are looking hollower by the hour. The average person can survive up to three days without water, but being out here, under the hot sun, might accelerate that. I promised Campbell she'd be safe, that I wouldn't let anything happen to her. If anyone dies on this fucking boat, it's not going to be her.

Hunger pangs sound from her stomach, but she says nothing. I must have torn this ship upside down earlier looking for something edible, only to come up empty-handed. I'd have settled for a fishing rod or a net, too, but again, Oliver thought of everything.

"You need to sit down," she tells me. "Stop moving so much, stop pacing, conserve your energy."

She closes her eyes, massaging her temples. For a moment, I'm hit with a flashback of my mother in one of her debilitating states, where nothing provided her relief or comfort from her pain.

"I'm going to kill him," I say for the millionth time since yesterday.

Campbell says nothing. We both know in order to kill that man, I'd have to get off this boat alive, and it's not looking like that's going to happen anytime soon.

"Maybe we should lie down," she says, her voice slow and lacking a shred of energy. She's fading already, and we're only twenty-four hours into this. "We don't have food or water, but we have each other."

It's the only thing we have, literally.

It's too hot to lie down in bed, so I spread out a blanket on the floor of the helm, under the shade. It must be a hundred degrees outside, which means we're hardly getting relief from the sun. Yesterday we figured out pretty quickly that Oliver also sabotaged the generator, rendering the air conditioner useless.

"I'm sorry," I tell my wife of two weeks.

"Shh," she rests her head against my shoulder, closing her eyes. "Save your energy."

Unless some random boat happens to pass by, there's no point. It would take divine intervention, and it's been my experience in life that miracles don't happen.

"I love you, Campbell," I say. I've never said those words before to anyone. "I've loved you for years, even if I didn't realize it."

"I love you too," she says. "You've grown on me these last couple of weeks."

She wears a weak smile for me.

While I should be focusing on her, on what could very well be our final days together, all I can think about is all the things I want to do when I see Oliver ... *if* I see Oliver. This entire thing is about money. That's the simplest explanation. What a fool I was to ever worry that he would try to steal Campbell out from under me. It was never her he wanted. It was the Delacorte money. If I die, Oliver will be the last remaining heir to the Delacorte fortune, as the prenup specifically prohibits Campbell from collecting anything other than what was previously agreed upon.

With my mother gone and with me out of the picture, Oliver will get *everything* once my father passes.

"I'm going to miss this," Campbell sighs. "If we don't make it out of here, I hope we can still be together ...wherever we go next."

Holding her tight, I kiss the top of her head. "Me too."

The rocking motion of the yacht is oddly soothing.

I realize, now, that we're probably drifting at sea.

Oliver likely ensured we were no longer anchored before he left—making it that much harder for any search and rescue efforts to locate us.

By the time nightfall comes, there's an eerie peacefulness washing over me. If I die tonight, at least I'll die with the woman I love by my side. It's better I focus on that and not the fact that Oliver must have laced our food and drinks with something to knock us out. There's no way each of us could have slept through all the shit he was doing to sabotage our chances of survival. It must have taken him hours.

"Campbell," I whisper, in case she's asleep.

"Yeah?" She sucks in a frigid breath through her chattering teeth. It's colder out here than Oliver initially led us to believe, though I'm willing to bet that was intentional too. I hold her closer, tighter, but I'm not giving off much warmth myself.

"I just want you to know," I say, swallowing the dry lump in my throat. "We would've had a great life together."

"I know."

"I was going to take you to Bali as a surprise," I tell her. "My travel agent was putting together a honeymoon for us. I was going to ask you to marry me there."

"We're already married."

"Right, but you deserve a *real* proposal," I say. "And a *real* wedding that actually means something. Maybe on a mountain in the clouds, just the two of us."

"I'd have loved that." Her voice is wistful as she splays her hand across my heart.

"I wanted it to be a surprise."

"It's the thought that counts, you know." She snickers as she feeds me the same line I fed her the night she burned dinner. "You know what I'm thinking about right now?"

"What?"

"That if I wasn't so tired and sticky and sweaty and thirsty and hungry, I'd be jumping your bones."

I manage to laugh, no small feat all things considered.

"Does that thought count?" she asks.

Pressing my lips against her forehead, I say, "In this case, yes. Yes, it does."

38

Campbell

I must be dreaming, because there's a guy in head-to-toe navy blue standing at our feet.

"Ma'am, ma'am, are you okay?" The uniformed man crouches down, gently shaking my leg. This has to be real. I felt the warmth of his hand. Sitting forward, I rub my eyes, which are dryer than sandpaper, and squint until he comes into focus. "I'm Officer Ramirez with the United States Coast Guard."

A woman in the same uniform climbs the stairs to the helm, a bag with some medical symbol strapped over her shoulder.

"Slade," I nudge him, but he's still out. "Slade, wake up. We've been found."

My stomach knots when he doesn't open his eyes, and for a second, I fear the worst. Yesterday Slade and I deduced that Oliver must have drugged us. At first, we assumed it was just so he could grab all the gear off the boat and leave without us waking up, but if ...

I can't finish the thought.

I can't stomach it either.

I'm going to be sick.

"Please, you have to do something," I scream at the guardsmen, despite them already working on him. In my irrational state, it doesn't feel like they're doing enough. "Slade, *please!*"

"Ma'am, you're going to have to remain calm," the man tells me.

I'm gripping his arm, willing him to wake, holding onto him with every ounce of tattered, desperate strength that remains.

"He has a pulse," the female officer says to her partner. "Sir, sir. Can you hear me?"

"We haven't had anything to eat or drink in days," I tell them, though I'm not sure how many days. Two? Maybe three? My brain is foggy and my tongue is rough against the roof of my mouth, making it challenging to speak.

Officer Ramirez retrieves a bottle of water from the medical kit, uncaps it, and hands it to me, but I'm too focused on Slade.

"Slade, *wake up* ... you have to wake up ..." I shake his shoulder as hard as I can. After a few seconds that feel like decades, his eyelids flutter open. Throwing my arms around him, I bury my head against his chest, grateful he's still alive.

Everything happens in a vacuum after this. The next thing I know, they're transferring us to a long white ship with the words US COAST GUARD and a thick red stripe on the side. We sit together in a daze while a commanding officer asks us questions and another officer relays information into a radio. It's as calm as it is chaotic, as surreal as it is tangible.

My husband sips his electrolyte water, staring vacantly ahead, a wool blanket wrapped around his body. They told us not to drink too fast or we could get sick, though I don't think I could chug anything if I tried. I barely have the energy to lift the bottle to my lips.

"How did you find us?" Slade asks one of the coast-guardsmen, blinking slow.

"We received a tip from Boat Watch, a national volunteer organization," he says. "Someone spotted your vessel via sea plane and it matched a BOLO report that had just come in yesterday out of Palm Beach."

"Bolo?" I ask.

"Be on the lookout," he explains.

"What day is it?" Slade takes a sip of water, his lips chapped and almost colorless.

"It's Monday, sir," the man answers. "9:52 AM."

That means we weren't reported as missing until yesterday.

One more day could have been the difference between life and death.

"We should be back to the shore in a few hours, so hang tight," the female officer tells us. "An ambulance is going to meet us there and take you to the Lower Keys Medical Center for evaluation. They might want to keep you overnight for observation."

Lower Keys? I had no idea we'd drifted that far south.

Resting my head against Slade, I close my eyes, promising myself I'll never take the gift of life for granted so long as I live.

Victor is waiting with my parents, Stassi, Tinley, and Elise at the hospital when we arrive. My mother throws her arms around me, genuine tears springing from her eyes as she squeezes me so tight I can't breathe—ironic since the last time we touched was when she shook me on my wedding day while she had that crazy look in her eyes. I'd planned to bring it up eventually, but that conversation's going to have to get sidelined as we deal with this.

"I thought you two were in Bali on your honeymoon," she says, cupping my face. "Why weren't you in Bali?"

Stassi and Elise exchange confused looks. Tenley watches us, waiting for an answer.

"Blythe," my father says, shooting her a look as if to tell her now is not the time.

They place the eight of us in a private room together as various nurses, doctors, and staffers shuffle in and out taking vitals, starting IVs, and assuring us we're going to be fine.

"Where the hell is Oliver?" Slade's jaw is clenched, much like the death grip he's had on my hand since we were transferred to the Coast Guard ship. His eyes are darting, alert as they can be, as if his vigilance could possibly save me from any other unexpected threats. I suspect it's going to take a while for him to calm down.

"Hiding like a coward." Victor forces a hard breath through his nostrils. "Biding his last taste of freedom until we find him.

As chance would have it, Fiona spotted Oliver driving around town Saturday afternoon, which seemed odd to her since we were all supposed to be on the yacht until Sunday. She stopped at the house to see if we were home, only to discover we were still gone. When she tried calling our cell phones, they both immediately went to voicemail since we were out of range. From there, she contacted Victor and told him what she knew. Within hours, he'd contacted the police, my parents, the Coast Guard, and hired a private search and rescue team.

"If you're up to it, the police would like to ask you some questions," one of the nurses tells us when she pops in.

"Send them in," Slade says. "The sooner we can press charges, the better."

One uniformed policeman and a plain-clothed detective step inside, introducing themselves before firing off question after question.

From the sounds of it, they have to get a judge to sign off on the arrest warrant, and since all evidence points to this being premeditated, he'll be charged with two counts of attempted murder in the first degree. In the state of Florida, those charges can often carry as much weight as if the murders were successful.

"Let's just skip the legal bullshit," Slade says when the officers leave. "Put me in a room with him. I'll make sure he gets what he deserves."

"The consequences he'll have to face will be far worse than anything you could ever do to him," Victor says. "His life is over. He'll spend the rest of it behind bars. No more yachts. No more beautiful women. No freedom. And no trust fund—though I did some checking into it. Turns out there is no trust fund. He's blown through it all."

Slade's jaw clenches, and while he says nothing, I'm certain we're all thinking the same thing.

"He'll have to liquidate his assets to pay for his legal fees. Then again, I have it on good authority that he's borrowed against every last yacht in his fleet. There really isn't anything left to liquidate," Victor says. "I told our father that twenty-five was much too young for him to have full control of his inheritance, but he refused to listen."

"You doing okay?" Slade turns to me. He's asked me this

same question at least a dozen times in the last few hours. I'm not sure if he keeps forgetting or if he's simply worried about me, but I give his hand a squeeze and offer a weak smile.

"I'm fine," I assure him. "Just grateful to be here with you."

39

Slade

I wake up before the sun and roll to my side, watching my wife sleep. We've been home for almost a week, and despite the fact that Oliver was located and taken into custody four days ago, I find myself hypervigilant and overprotective of Campbell.

For as long as I live, I'll never forgive my uncle for what he did, but Campbell likes to remind me that being angry won't change what happened.

Regardless, I can't stop ruminating, thinking about what would have happened if Fiona hadn't seen Oliver cruising around town that day and hadn't had the gut instinct to check for us at home.

I let my wife sleep, trekking downstairs to make myself a coffee. In the time that we've been back, I've forgone my militant morning routine because I haven't been able to stomach the thought of leaving Campbell alone. Never mind that the threat is neutralized—I can't wrap my head around the fact that I never saw it coming.

Before, I could've listed a million shady things Oliver was capable of, but murder would never have been among them. He had issues just like everyone else, but he was always so happy, nice, fun, the kind of guy who lived in the moment and never had a care in the world.

I don't know if I'll ever look at anyone the same after this.

Seated in the breakfast nook, I peer out the windows at the ocean waves crashing in the distance and the various assortment of boats lining the horizon. Rising, I close the shades with a dramatic pull before skulking back to the table. I can't even enjoy the view from my own house without being reminded of that weekend.

For two years, I've called this house my home and I was beginning to look forward to sharing it with Campbell—only now, much like the cars in my garage that are covered with Oliver's grimy fingerprints, it's tainted.

I have no choice but to sell everything.

We need a clean start.

I finish my coffee, rinse the mug, and place it in the jam-packed dishwasher. I gave Fiona a month off, paid, as a small token of our gratitude, but I intend to do much more for her once I get my bearings. The house might be a little less sparkling than usual and we're ordering takeout like it's our job, but it's the least I can do for Fiona after everything.

Grabbing a dishwasher tablet from under the sink, I spot the crystal vase Campbell's aunt and uncle gave us for our wedding. I remember her aunt saying something about her husband giving her flowers every week for the first year of their marriage, and how it was important to have traditions.

Heading outside to the terrace next, I clip a handful of vibrant purple bougainvillea before returning inside to make Campbell's breakfast. Ten minutes later, I'm carrying a tray of oatmeal, avocado toast, and fresh flowers upstairs.

"Oh, good, you're up," I say when I find her in the bathroom washing up. I place the tray on the bed. "I made you breakfast."

"You didn't have to do that," she says when she returns, greeting me with a spearmint-flavored kiss. "But thank you. Where'd the flowers come from?"

"The terrace."

"You did that arrangement yourself?"

"If by arrangement, you mean I cut them and put them in a vase with water, then yes."

She laughs. "I'm impressed."

"You recognize the vase?"

Chewing, she inspects the flowers closely. "Aunt Beth's vase?"

"Yep. I thought maybe we could start our own tradition."

"I like that," she says, "but let's make it our own. I love flowers, but I don't think something should have to die just because it's pretty. Kind of cruel not to just ... let it live, you know?"

RIP our wedding flowers—though there was no talking Blythe out of that.

"Fair enough. Any ideas?"

Placing the breakfast tray aside, she leans over and reaches for me, pulling me back into bed.

"I have a few," she says with an impish smirk as her hands dip beneath my waistband. Kissing me, she strokes my cock. "Morning sex. Morning sex should be our tradition."

"I could get on board with that." I abandon her mouth and work my way down her neck before pulling her shirt over her head. Lately she's been sleeping in nothing but a T-shirt. Stopping, I take a second to admire her in all her exposed glory.

"What?"

"I wish you could see how fucking sexy you are," I say. "If you had any idea, I think you'd just ... your mind would be blown."

Campbell laughs, swatting at me. "*Stahhhp.*"

"Stop what? Telling my wife how smoking hot she is?" I scoff. "Never."

She rolls her eyes, humble as ever, though the smile she's fighting tells me she secretly enjoys when I fawn over her. The first time we made love, she made it clear that all she wanted was to feel like I desired her.

I spent over twenty years making her feel the opposite of that.

I plan to spend the rest of my days making sure she never feels that way again.

Turning onto my back, I shove my sweats down and pull her onto my lap. I'll take this woman any way I can, but there's something about watching her ride me that makes every other position pale in comparison. It's the intense concentration on her face as she grinds. It's the way her hair cascades down her shoulders when she throws her head back, messy and wild. It's the way she bites her lip when she's almost there ...

I don't know that I'll ever get enough of this woman.

"I like this tradition already." Campbell's breathless when we're finished. She's lying on my chest, my drained cock still pulsing inside her. Her heart beats against mine, practically in sync. Her nipples graze my flesh as she situates herself, reviving my hardness. I could easily go for another round, but we've got some packing to do. "So what's the plan? You going into the office today? You haven't been in once since we've been back."

She sits up and carefully climbs off of me, my seed spilling down her inner thigh.

"I'm taking an extended leave of absence," I say.

She balks, though I can't blame her for being confused. "Really? Why?"

"Because I'm taking my wife on our honeymoon."

Grinning, she claps her hand over her mouth, bouncing with excitement.

"We leave tonight," I tell her. "I'm taking you to Bali and I'm going to marry you all over again, on top of that mountain in the clouds, just like I promised."

Campbell cups my face in her hands, dipping in to kiss me.

"I love you so much," she says.

"But I love you more."

40

One Week Later

Campbell

The soft caress of the Balinese breeze plays with my hair as I stand on the edge of the world, atop a mountain where clouds float like a gentle embrace all around us. Bali, with its lush landscapes, vibrant culture, and serene beaches, captured my heart the moment we landed.

This past week has been a whirlwind of adventures. Slade and I explored the bustling streets of Ubud with its intricate temples and fragrant markets, tasted street food so flavorful it practically burst in my mouth with every bite, and when we couldn't eat any more, we danced under the stars to the tune of gamelan music playing from a nearby festival.

But so far my favorite thing about being here with Slade

are our quiet mornings watching the sunrise off our terrace, where the sun casts a golden glow on all of the dew-kissed greenery.

If Heaven is real, I think we've found it.

"You ready?" Slade asks as he takes my hands in his.

I nod, my stomach filled with more butterflies than I've ever felt in my life.

We're getting married—again.

Only today it's just the two of us on a mountain in the clouds. No fanfare. No witnesses. Just us. We figured we needed a redo after everything. The first time we exchanged vows, our words were empty and our hearts were elsewhere. Today though, I feel every part of him in my soul, and I can't wait to pledge my commitment.

Slade is dashingly handsome in a simple white shirt and pressed khakis, the sunlight adding a golden hue to his bronzed skin. He smiles at me, his loving gaze holding the raw depth of emotion that was missing on our wedding day.

"Should I go first?" he asks when he notices the tears pricking my eyes. They're happy tears, of course, but there's no hiding them. And in true Slade fashion, he notices everything.

"Please," I say with a laugh.

"This isn't easy for me," he says. "You know I hate talking about my feelings."

"I know." I squeeze his hands.

"But, uh." For a moment, he appears to be choked up, but that moment passes. "For the longest time, I was a man who built walls around his heart, certain that what lay inside was neither worthy of giving nor capable of receiving it. I associated love with loss and uncertainty, believing if I could avoid love, I could avoid the pain that inevitably happens when you lose someone you care deeply about.

Campbell, I made a lot of mistakes, and there are a million things I would do differently if I had the chance. But as we build our future and no longer focus on the past, I want to stand before you and give you my word. From now until the end of time, I promise to be the man you saw in me when I couldn't see him myself. I vow to cherish you, even when times are tough—especially when times are tough. I'll listen, truly listen to your dreams, fear, hopes, and laughter, ensuring that you never feel alone and that you're supported in all that you do. I vow to remind myself daily of the gift I've been given, this second chance at a love I never thought I needed, wanted, or deserved. And I'll work every day to be deserving of that love, of your trust, and of this beautiful life we're creating together against all odds. You're the other half of my soul, my favorite part of every day, and my best friend. I promise, Campbell, from this day forward, I'll love you with every beat of my heart."

Tears prick my eyes as I soak in his words. He swipes them away with his thumb, offering me a tender smile. I'm not sure how I can top that, but I'll try. Reaching into the front of my dress, I pull a small folded note from my bra.

He snickers, amused, and I roll my eyes. It's not the most glamorous move, but I'm terrible at memorizing speeches and I wanted to make sure I didn't leave anything out.

"I wrote this last night, when you were sleeping," I tell him as the clouds continue to embrace us and the ocean waves serenade us with their symphony below. "Slade, for as long as I can remember, I knew you were going to be my husband. While everyone else got to experience the wonderment of not knowing what their life had in store for them, I always knew. Only what I didn't know was that I would one day fall in love with you. Throughout our tumultuous beginnings, one thing always stood out to me—this glimmer of something deep and profound within you. You were a fortress that I could never break through. But over these last several weeks, I've learned you were never a puzzle to be solved and that I could never break down your walls no matter how much I wanted to. You had to tear them down yourself, brick by brick, when you were ready. Today as I stand before you in a place that fittingly feels like a lost paradise, I offer you my genuine love and commitment. I promise to be patient, to understand that healing and growth take time. I vow to see the potential in us, even when we can't always see it ourselves. I pledge to never try to fix or change you but to encourage you as you discover the best version of yourself. I love you for who you are today and for the man who continues to unfurl before me with each new day. But above all, I promise to cherish this delicate flower that is love, to let it thrive and bloom in its own time, and to honor its beauty for the rest of our lives."

Slade lifts his hand to my jaw, lowering his lips to mine as we seal our promises to one another on a mountain in the sky.

"I love you," he says.

"I love you too." I throw my arms around him, inhaling his intoxicating cologne as it mingles with the earthy scent surrounding us as he kisses me long, soft, and deep. Who'd have ever imagined I'd one day feel safe, treasured, and adored in the arms of the man who once loathed my very existence?

"There's one more thing," he says when he pulls away a moment later. Reaching into his back pocket, he retrieves a folded stack of papers.

"What's this?"

"Our prenup," he says before ripping it down the

middle. "Our marriage is not a business deal. What's mine is yours, now and forever."

Tossing the torn sheets in the air, they fall all around us, until the wind carries them down the mountain and into the infinite sea below.

I'm speechless.

Slipping his phone from his pocket next, he cues a song. Make You Feel My Love.

With his hands on my waist, he pulls me against him, stares so deeply into my eyes that I swear I feel his love in my soul, and then he presses a tender kiss against my lips.

"Mrs. Delacorte," he says. "May I have this dance ... every day for the rest of our lives?"

"You may, Mr. Delacorte. You may."

41

Slade

I take a seat and lift the receiver to my ear, blood boiling beneath my skin on what's already a record-scorching day.

Fitting, I suppose.

On the other side of a glass partition is the very definition of a waste of space.

Oliver lifts the receiver on his side. He looks frailer than the last time I saw him, his physique practically swimming in his garish orange jumpsuit. It's a far cry from all the designer labels he's accustomed to, and it's safe to assume the prison fare isn't up to his standards either, hence why he's dropped a few pounds since being here. His head is shaved. Gone are his thick, russet locks, the ones he used to run his hands through when he'd spot a beautiful woman.

"You look pathetic," are the first words out of my mouth.

Oliver's eyes drift down. It's a wonder he can even look at me at all.

"I'm glad you came," he finally speaks. "There's a lot I wanted to say to you."

I chuff. "Oh, yeah?"

Leaning back, I sport an expressionless face as I prepare to hear him plead his case to my deaf ears. There's not a single word that exists in the English language that will change the way I feel about him.

Not now.

Not ever.

"I wanted to tell you how sorry I am." His careful gaze floats to mine again, but he winces as if he's afraid to keep it there for too long.

Good.

He should be fucking terrified.

He's lucky we're on two opposite sides of a wall and there are half a dozen guards on standby or this wouldn't end well for him.

I haven't arranged for it yet, but I know people who know people on the inside. If he thinks life behind bars is bad now, he has no idea that his life is about to get insurmountably worse in every way imaginable.

Our eyes hold in a stand-off of sorts. I assume he's trying to read me so he can gauge where to go next with this conversation, but I keep poker-straight.

This asshole has manipulated me—and our family—for too long.

Not to mention, he manipulated Campbell into befriending him, confiding in him, trusting him to take her out on the water.

"I made a mistake," Oliver says, his lower lip quivering. "It's just ... you've always had everything. Our whole life. You've always been the golden boy. And the fact that you were basically getting to inherit the entire Delacorte fortune all for marrying the girl of my dreams? I was jealous, Slade. More than jealous actually. I was spiteful. I resented you and I wanted you to lose everything. I'm sorry. I messed up. So big. I wasn't thinking straight. I was desperate. I was—"

"Shut up. You've said enough. You tried to kill my wife. You tried to kill me," I say. "After everything I've done for you ... after everything my father and mother did for you? You were more than my uncle, you were my brother, my best friend, and the fact that you did what you did ..."

My fist clenches and from the corner of my eye, I spot one of the uniformed guards watching me. I can't cause a scene or I'll be asked to leave.

Lowering my voice, I say my final piece. "You left us to die, but you're the one who's dead now. You're dead to me, you're dead to my father, you're dead to Campbell, you're dead to the world." Pointing to the door behind me, I add, "I just want you to know, while you rot in here for the rest of your life, that not a single person out there is going to miss you or give a flying fuck about you ever again. I hope it was worth it."

Slamming the handset into its cradle, I walk out, head held high, turning my back on the one person I never dreamed would betray me, and when I get home, I find refuge in the arms of the one woman I never dreamed would love me.

Life is strange and unpredictable.

But it always has a way of giving us exactly what we deserve in the end.

Epilogue

5 years later

Slade

Mom—

It's been a little more than five years since we said goodbye, so I figured it was time to send you an update. It's Thanksgiving today, and I've snuck upstairs to write you this letter.

Dad brought your old recipe book over and Fiona is making your famous sage brown butter dressing. It won't taste the same without your special touch, but we thought it would be a nice way to honor your memory. Why we haven't done this sooner is beyond me, but we've decided it's going to be a tradition going forward. We do that now—traditions. We're like some corny All-American family you'd see on a 90s sitcom, but we're loving every minute of it.

Can you believe that? You're probably cracking up wherever you are, watching me chase my kids around, host my in-laws, and talk about family traditions. You'd also get a kick out of watching Dad become a grandfather. He retired a few years ago, passing the company reins to me, and when he isn't on the golf course, he's at our house tossing the twins in the pool and giving them "pony rides," tickling them until they're doubled over with laughter, and playing infinite rounds of CandyLand and Chutes and Ladders. It'd been so long, I almost forgot this version of him existed. It's good to have him back.

Campbell is the most incredible mother, too. She dotes on our babies hand and foot. She reads them every book under the sun. Sings to them. Gets down on the floor and plays with them. Takes them to music classes, readings at the library, and everything else she can do to expose them to all the little meaningful things this world has to offer. She even refused to let me hire a nanny. We still have Fiona, and she's a great help around the house, but as far as the kids go, it's just the two of us—well, mostly Campbell. The kids prefer her over me anyway, though everyone tells me that's normal. I guess I get it. You were always the one I'd run to first instead of dad. Mothers just have that something special that most men don't. But I digress.

Adelia and Adrian turned four last month. Their birthday is the day before Halloween, so we had a costume birthday party. It went about how you'd expect when you combine twenty small children and a plethora of sugar all in one place, but they had the time of their little lives and Campbell documented every minute of it so we can look back someday and relive every second of it.

I see so much of you in Adelia. She's got your mile-wide smile, dimples and all. And like you, she has an abundance of energy, always trying to cram as many activities into one day as she can and inevitably passing out in some random place in some strange position. Last night we found her asleep under her bed, flashlight, coloring book, and crayons scattered around her.

Adrian is our old soul. He's serious and inquisitive and loves all things nature. He's always bringing in random small bugs and animals he finds outside, much to Fiona's dismay. Like his old man, he seems to have an affinity for the written word. We're building him an entire wall of bookshelves for his room next year. If you were here, I have no doubt you'd spend hours reading to him.

As the kids get older, I've been telling them more about you. We kiss your picture goodnight at bedtime, and sometimes I try to make up those silly songs you always used to come up with on a dime, the ones that would get stuck in my head for days. I'm not half as good as you in that department, but I try and that's what counts, right?

Also, Mom, I wanted to tell you that you were right. About everything. Not that you needed to hear that. You were never one of those people. But I took your advice, and I gave Campbell a chance and I'm happier than I've ever been. She's happy too. I make sure of that every single day. You said it wouldn't happen overnight, but it almost did. I think deep down, we always had feelings for each other—we were just too young (and stubborn) to understand and appreciate them.

Everything I have and everything I am would never have been possible without your patient and loving guidance, and I plan to instill that same wisdom into my kids as they grow older. All three of them. Well, number three isn't here yet, but she will be soon—we're due at the end of December. She wasn't planned, but I can't bring myself to call her an "accident" or an "oops" because we couldn't be more excited to add another little Delacorte to our crazy household.

That's another thing—I never realized how much I'd love being a dad. The first time I held them in my arms, my chest felt so full I thought it was going to explode ... Now I know how you felt wanting to ensure my happiness and success in life. I get it. But while it's tempting to want to give them the world, I know the one thing they need the most from me is to feel loved.

I so badly wish you were here to see them grow, to share in our joy, and to be that wonderful grandmother I always imagined you'd be. But I take solace in the fact that a part of you lives on in them, in the light of their eyes, their laughter, and their zest for this crazy thing called life.

Anyway, I hear Campbell calling for me, so I better wrap this up. I think it's almost time to eat. Just wanted to check in with you and let you know that I finally understand

everything you said in that letter you
wrote me.

I love you, Mom.

I miss you.

And I promise to keep making you proud.

Forever in my heart,
Slade
PS—Thanks for the baby clothes.

Extended Epilogue

1 Month Later

Slade

Dear Campbell—
You're currently in a hospital bed, about to
give birth to our third child. I wanted to tell
you all of this myself, but the doctors just
gave you you're epidural so you can get a little
bit of rest, and I don't want to wake you, so
I decided to write you a letter instead.
We should do that again—exchange letters.
Love letters, obviously.
Another tradition to add to the roster ...
Anyway, just wanted you to know that
you've got this, and I'll be right beside you,

holding your hand (or if it's anything like last time, getting the bones of my hand crushed into a million tiny pieces). Not complaining though. You know I'll always take one for our team.

By the end of tonight, we should be a family of five. It's crazy to think about. I know it's going to be an adjustment for us all, but I can't wait to see Adelia and Adrian as big siblings and I know some of our greatest memories are yet to come.

You're the definition of strength, grace, and beauty.

Thank you for bringing my children into this world, and when you're ready, let's do it again.

I love you forever—

Slade

PS—You'd look really fucking hot in a mini-van. Just saying.

Coming Soon!

Stassi's story releases September 7th, 2023!

SAMPLE
You or Someone Like You

CHAPTER ONE

SLOANE

"Can I just say . . . you make one hell of a me." My twin, Margaux, eyes my reflection from across the room before flinging her lavender velvet comforter off her legs. "Ugh."

Dashing to the hall bathroom, my sister's bare feet skitter and slide against the slick hardwood floors of our Midtown apartment. The clank of the toilet seat hitting the ceramic tank behind it sounds next, followed by god-awful retching that sends a flash of sympathy nausea to my middle. In the midst of everything, my stomach rumbles as if to remind me I haven't eaten since breakfast—not the wisest move when I'm about to go on a blind date with a total stranger on Margaux's behalf.

Dating—in and of itself—is hard enough.

Serving as someone's dating avatar? It's a whole new level of insanity that's going to require a substantial amount of liquid courage.

"I'm never eating leftover sushi again," Margaux says when she returns. Climbing beneath her blankets again, she rests her arm across her forehead like a sickly Victorian woman on a fainting couch. She's always been a glutton for sympathy, though. Anytime she has so much as a sniffle, you'd think she were dying of the Black Plague. Pointing across the room in my direction, she adds, "And I mean it this time."

"Sure you do." I wink and fix my attention on the pearl buttons on the cardigan I'm borrowing from her closet before running my palm along my fresh honey-blonde highlights.

"You should curl your hair," Margaux says. Food poisoning aside, she can't help but micromanage me. Despite being a mere two minutes older than me, she takes her big-sister role seriously, often wearing it like a badge of honor. At least that's what I tell myself. It very well could be that Margaux is just a control freak who lives to call the shots.

"What? No." I wrinkle my nose and fasten the last button on my sweater. Despite it being June and an agreeable eighty degrees out, she insisted that this is what she had planned to wear.

"I literally curl mine every single day," she says. "You can't play the part without dressing the part, and that includes how I do my hair."

"But if he's never met you, how would he know you curl your hair every day?"

I was twelve the first time I attempted to wield a curling iron. It was an utter and complete failure of an ordeal, and I walked away smelling like singed hair and sporting a burnt spot the size of a postage stamp in the middle of my forehead. I've been curling iron celibate ever since, and I've vowed to embrace my stick-straight hair until my dying day.

My sister can pry my flat iron from my cold, dead fingers.

"It's not about that," she says. "It's about authenticity. You're standing there in my heels, my skirt, and my cardigan. You're wearing my bracelet and my perfume and my lipstick. Your modern bob just looks low-key jarring with everything else going on."

She's not wrong about that last part. The lace and pearls on the sweater juxtaposed with the dainty gold tennis bracelet, hip-hugging wool pencil skirt, and classic red lip would be better served with loose, cascading waves, something romantic and feminine.

But there's no time.

And even if there were, I'd still give her a hard and resounding no.

"I thought you weren't trying to impress this guy? I thought you were just going on a date to appease your boss? I don't see how any of this matters." I bite my tongue to keep from pointing out that control-freak Margaux has entered the building, and she needs to take a back seat because she's knee deep in a bad case of food poisoning and I'm five minutes from climbing into an Uber, walking into a restaurant, and meeting some stranger as her.

She's not exactly in a position to be running the show.

"I just got my hair done this morning," I add, "which means I won't be curling a single strand."

The last time I pretended to be Margaux, I was twenty-one, and we were college seniors back in Ohio. She'd hit the frat parties a little too hard during finals week and all but promised me her firstborn child if I'd take her art history exam as her. Seeing how art history was (and still is) my favorite subject in the entire world, it was an easy yes. Hell, I'd have done it for fun because that's the kind of nose-in-a-book, head-in-the-clouds girl I was back then. I lived and breathed art in all its forms. Contemporary. Renaissance. Neoclassical. Cinematic. Literary. Undiscovered. Controversial. If it had a creative pulse, I couldn't get enough.

Meanwhile, Margaux lived and breathed boys, boss-girl besties, and being seen.

We may share facial features and a shoe size, but that's where our similarities end. Our personalities are night and day. If we didn't look undeniably identical, I might question our genetic relation.

"Fine, whatever," she says with a relenting sigh.

"Relax." I make my way to the side of her bed, adjust her blankets, and give her a reassuring smile before handing her the TV remote and her cell phone. "I've got this. Just rest, watch a funny movie, scroll TikTok, and try to refrain from puking your guts out again, okay?"

Sinking against her pillows, she nods. "I'll try."

"I'm going to grab you a ginger ale and some buttered saltines, and then I'm out." My watch vibrates on my wrist, letting me know my Uber driver is almost here. My stomach somersaults. Even though this isn't my blind date, it's nerve racking all the same.

A first date is a first date is a first date.

I head to the kitchen and return with her drink and crackers and collect my phone, keys, and purse off her dresser where I'd left them earlier. She'd cornered me the second I got home from work—a mere fifty-two minutes ago—and begged me to go on her date tonight. Apparently she's gunning for a promotion, and her boss keeps dropping hints about setting her up with her single nephew. Coming from personal experience, I know what it feels like to not have the job you want, the job you've worked your entire life to have. I'd hate that for her.

"Sloane?" Margaux calls out before I leave for the night.

"Yeah?" I turn back, leaning against the doorjamb.

"Don't try too hard, okay?"

"What do you mean?"

"I don't want him to like you . . . I mean me," she says. "I don't exactly have the best track record with relationships."

It's true. All Margaux's romantic endeavors tend to go down in flames. The splits are rarely mutual and always accompanied by some dramatic fanfare. I love my sister, but I'd pity any man who attempts a relationship with her. There aren't a lot of men who can handle her larger-than-life persona and her boss-girl energy. She's not some diminutive wallflower with stay-at-home-wife ambitions. She has a personality, and she likes to call the shots. Most men tend to be more intimidated by her than anything. She's yet to find her equal, even in a city of millions.

"If I dated this guy . . . and if for some reason it didn't end well . . . Theodora could have me blacklisted from the industry." Sitting up, she adds, "Be nice. Be pleasant. But maybe don't flirt with him. Maybe . . . maybe just be boring."

Of all the things my sister has asked of me in our twenty-seven years on this planet, this one takes the cake.

"Can you do that?" Her round baby blues are filled with hope. "Can you be boring?"

"According to you, I already am, so it shouldn't be that hard," I say with a little more sarcasm lacing my voice than I intended. It's not easy being the introvert of our duo, to be made to feel like some kind of social pariah for not having twenty best friends on speed dial, for preferring a quiet

Friday night in to an expensive blacked-out blur of a night out.

"Stop." Margaux rolls her eyes, her expression softening. "You're not boring. You're just . . ." I hold my breath, waiting for her to replace the word boring with some adjacent term that'll only serve as a backhanded compliment. Something like quiet, reserved, or introverted. "You know what I'm trying to say. Anyway, thank you for doing this. Truly. Thank you."

My watch vibrates, letting me know my ride is here.

"What's this guy's name?" I adjust my purse strap over my shoulder before tugging at the itchy lace sticking out from my collar. "I don't think you've told me yet."

"Roman Bellisario," she says. "Theodora showed me a picture of him once. Dark hair, dark eyes, razor-sharp jawline, tall . . ."

Margaux's voice grows distant as she continues to describe him, and the world around me fades away by the second.

I don't need to hear another word.

I know exactly who he is.

"My ride's downstairs." I swallow a hard lump that has suddenly formed in my throat. "Guess I'll . . . see you in a few."

Before I shut the door, my sister calls out a quick good luck—which is ironic because that's exactly what I'm going to need to get through tonight.

CHAPTER TWO

ROMAN

I trace a fingertip against the side of a perspiring crystal tumbler, focusing on the indentation on my left ring finger where my platinum wedding band has resided for the past ten years—three years too long, if you ask my aunt Theodora.

If it weren't for the mindless chatter of bar patrons around me, I could almost hear her voice gently scolding me for still wearing it, not mincing a single word as she reminds me I'll never find another woman with that thing on my finger, all but referring to it as deadweight.

But that's kind of the point.

I don't want another woman.

I want the one I had before she was heartlessly ripped from this world without warning by some spineless coward who hit her with their car and fled the scene before they could answer for what they did. The fact that the bastard is still out there, living life like nothing ever happened while our lives were permanently altered, is something I've yet to get over.

I don't know that I ever will.

Not even sure that I can.

"Another one, sir?" The young, overly friendly bartender points to my empty drink. He can't be much older than twenty-two or twenty-three, if I had to guess. Judging by the stars in his eyes, life hasn't screwed with him yet.

But it will.

Sooner or later, it always does.

I check the time on my phone—my blind date should be here any minute.

"Might as well." I slide the glass his way, and he uncaps a bottle of top-shelf Macallan, pouring two fingers' worth and then some, like he senses I'm on the cusp of something

. . . unnatural. I've never been one to let nerves show, but I imagine I'm giving off the kind of vibe that tells everyone within a ten-foot radius that this is the last place I want to be tonight. "That's good. Thank you."

I take a sip and scan the restaurant portion of the bar in search of the poor woman my aunt sent to "save me from myself."

Her words, of course.

For the past few months, she hasn't stopped telling me about one of her employees at Lucerne Product Development, some blue-eyed, blonde-haired, bubbly "fun-time girl" who would "pull me out of my shell" and "usher me back into the world of the living."

I didn't waste my breath telling her blondes have never been my type.

And I love my shell—it's impenetrable.

It's Teflon and Kevlar and Fort Knox.

It's where my daughters are.

It's my entire world . . . what remains of it, anyway.

While I've no doubt been existing with one foot in the grave and the other one in the land of the living, there's no time stamp on grief. It takes however long it takes. I'm not going to hurry it up so my meddling-but-well-intentioned aunt has one less thing to worry about.

That's the thing about death—it's inconvenient as hell, and there's not a damn thing anyone can do about it.

Nevertheless, Theodora is the most persistent person on the face of the earth. She refuses to take no for an answer—which is how I ended up here . . . at the bar of some hotel restaurant in Gramercy Park, waiting for some poor stranger who's likely only doing this as a favor to her insistent boss.

Sliding my phone from my pocket, I pull up the

Lucerne Product Development site, tap on the employee directory, and type in the name my aunt gave me: Margo.

Zero results.

Exhaling, I change the spelling, this time searching up Margaux.

The first result, Margaux Abbott, looks old enough to be my grandmother—white hair, chained glasses, librarian frown and all.

The second listing, Margaux Sheridan, matches Aunt Theodora's description of blonde and blue eyed. A blinding white smile that takes up the entire lower half of her face alludes to the bubbly part. I zoom in, examining her as if I'm looking for clues to some mystery—or a sign that tonight's not going to be an awkward, uncomfortable, complete waste of time.

Pale-pink earrings in the shape of large-petaled flowers hang from Margaux's ears in her company directory photo, and her lashes are much too long, dark, and thick to be natural. A triple-layer pearl necklace is fastened around her neck, and a diamond cameo brooch adorns her lapel. I can't be sure if she's going for a coastal grandma look or if this is some kind of a joke.

Darkening my screen, I return my phone to my pocket and my attention to my scotch.

"Mr. Bellisario?" A petite hostess dressed fittingly in head-to-toe black places a palm on my shoulder. "Your table is ready."

Drink in hand, I follow her to a corner booth with a single flickering candle, a pristine white tablecloth, and a small vase of three red roses in full bloom.

It's so romantically cliché it's almost laughable.

Once seated, I take a deep breath, get my shit together, and steal a glance around the room. All around me, silverware clinks against china and stemware. Voices drone on, conversations layered one on top of the other. The smell of expensive perfume and aftershave dances through the air, mixed with the savory scents of a five-star dining experience.

Everywhere I look are couples, their faces painted in soft candlelight as they gaze across the table at one another with stars for eyes. This restaurant gives a whole new meaning to the phrase "Love is in the air."

Theodora chose this place on purpose, I have no doubt.

I haven't been on a first date since Emma, and the day I married her, I promised she'd be my last date.

My forever date.

Death has a way of changing things, though, of making agreements null and void whether you like it or not.

I check the time, resisting the urge to roll my eyes at the fact that the allegedly effervescent Ms. Margaux Sheridan is eight minutes late. I'll give her seven more, and then I'm leaving. If there's anything I've learned in the past three years, it's that life is too short for the things that don't matter —like blind dates people agree to under duress.

For a moment, I visualize my life as sand falling through the center of an hourglass, each granule representing a second I'll never get back. When you lose something—or in my case someone—it forever alters your perspective on things.

All a person has, truly, is their time.

Everything else is inconsequential.

"I'm so sorry I'm late." A breathy voice pulls me from my muddling thoughts. Glancing up, I'm met with frosty Alaskan-blue eyes, a fringe of dark lashes, and hair the color of glazed honey and summer sunshine. "Traffic was terrible getting over here, and the Uber driver refused to take a different route and—never mind. I'm here. That's all that matters, right?" Her full lips pull into a nervous smile before she extends her hand like she's about to interview for a job. "Margaux. Margaux Sheridan. It's nice to meet you."

She's no Emma, but at least she has basic manners.

That and she's not the worst thing in the world to look at. Far from it. I'd have to be blind not to notice the subtle, radiant beauty emanating off her, quietly commanding my attention. Not that I have any intention of doing anything with said attention, but maybe tonight won't be the worst thing I've experienced in a while.

Could absolutely be worse.

"Roman." Rising, I meet her buttery-soft hand with mine and give it a firm shake better suited for a business meeting than a date, and then I wait like a proper gentleman as she takes the seat across from me.

Studying her in the quivering candlelight that filters the space between us, a strange twinge of familiarity hits me— like I've seen her somewhere before. I've never set foot in my aunt's building downtown, so it wouldn't be that.

"I'm sorry . . . Have we met before?" I ask.

She squints as if she's studying me. "Um, no? I don't believe so?"

"You look familiar." My gaze narrows as I try to place her, but my concentration is interrupted by our server.

"I get that a lot." She orders a cucumber gin and tonic before turning her attention to the food menu.

Sniffing, I say, "I took you as more of a rosé kind of girl."

"I would never." A flicker of a grin crosses her full lips before fading completely, like it was never there to begin with. Nerves, perhaps. I won't hold it against her. "There are rosé girls, then there are cucumber-gin-and-tonic girls. I can see how you might mix us up, but trust me, we're night and day."

Witty without being flirty.

I can respect that.

"Fascinating," I say with a gracious smile to compensate for my sarcasm. "So, Margaux, tell me about yourself."

I hate this.

I hate every damn second of this.

It's not who I am. It's not who I want to be. It's not where I want to be.

My muscles are riddled with tension, perhaps in an attempt to keep me from crawling out of my skin.

"Oh," she says, eyes sparking as if she's surprised by my question. That or she's nervous. I tend to have that effect on people—but tonight I'm doing my best to not come off like a giant prick allergic to happiness. It's the least I can do since she got dressed up and came all this way. "Um, what all has Theodora told you about me?"

"Very little, actually." I don't want to offend her with the fact that my aunt sold her as a good-time girl. To Theodora's generation, that sort of label has other connotations. I also don't want to offend her by confessing that I asked zero questions because I have zero interest in pursuing anything beyond this insufferable evening. "What has she told you about me?"

"Not a whole lot." She looks around the restaurant, though whether she's searching for our server and her drink or taking in the scenery is beyond me. It's all the same, I suppose. Tucking a strand of glossy hair behind one ear, she returns her serene gaze to mine.

"Okay, so on that note," I say as if I'm conducting a work interview, "let's start with you."

This is excruciating.

And it's clear I'm going to be doing the conversational heavy lifting tonight.

"What do you want to know?" She blinks at me with those baby doll eyes of hers, and I'm not sure if there's a single thought behind them.

My jaw tightens, and a dull ache floods the sides of my face as a tension headache forms in real time.

Margaux toys with her pearl necklace, tugging on it as if it's almost choking her. In the process, the top button of her cardigan has come undone, revealing a hint of creamy skin, but the rest of her is conservatively covered despite the early-summer heat wave we're having. When she's finished fussing with her necklace, she pulls at the itchy-looking lace collar of her sweater.

Nothing about her looks comfortable.

Nothing about her looks like she wants to be here either.

Perhaps we have something in common already.

CHAPTER THREE

SLOANE

This is painful.

Physically painful—all the way to the marrow of my bones.

I'm baking in this sweater and filtering every word that comes out of my mouth in an attempt to ensure that I'm dreadfully boring per Margaux's orders. My back hurts from sitting straight and proper and my face hurts from smiling and my head hurts from nodding.

It's taking everything I have not to wince and cringe my way through this clunky, flavorless conversation.

I take a generous swill of my gin and tonic, which isn't kicking in fast enough.

If Margaux were here—like she was meant to be—she'd breeze through all this small talk with a smile on her face and a witticism on the tip of her tongue. That woman has the art of conversation down to a science. She can talk to anyone, anywhere, about anything, and make it look like child's play. She can walk into a room full of strangers and walk out with five new best friends and an invitation to be in some stranger's wedding.

Me, on the other hand? I'd rather stick a rusty needle in my eye than talk about the weather, mayoral candidates, whatever new restaurant opened up in the East Village last week, or my favorite Hamptons hot spots. Superficial topics have never appealed to me.

At least I'm killing it in the uninteresting department, though I can't tell whether Roman's eyes are glazed over because of his half-empty glass of liquor or because I'm quite literally boring the man to tears.

"Food's taking a while, isn't it?" he asks only a few minutes after we order.

I get the sense he wants the evening to hurry along just as much as I do.

"Places like this aren't exactly known for their speed," I say in the most monotone voice I can muster in accordance with Margaux's rules. "Plus, I think it's only been five minutes."

Who knew three hundred seconds could feel like three hundred years?

He takes a substantial sip from his glass. I swear each drink that passes his lips is bigger than the one before it. The next time our server stops by, he'll be due for a refill, and the night is exhaustingly young.

I steal a look around the restaurant—it's all I can do to distract myself from the fact that I'm sitting across from Roman Bellisario . . . a notoriously elusive and demanding New York art collector whose reputation I'm far too familiar with, given my line of work. As the director of the Westfeldt International Art Gallery in SoHo, I've conversed and negotiated with his personal curator more times than I care to count, though this is the first time I've ever been face to face with the jerk himself.

Only so far, he's yet to be a jerk.

Bland, maybe.

But not an asshole.

Certainly not the arrogant dumpster fire of a man I was anticipating.

I imagine he's on his best behavior, given that this is a first date. Fortunately for him, he won't need to maintain the illusion that he's actually some kind of decent person because this first date will be our last date too.

Our paths first crossed three years ago, and in one of the worst ways.

"So did you grow up in the city or . . . ?" His voice tapers into nothing, like he doesn't have the energy to finish his sentence. The lack of excitement in his tone tells me this small talk is just as painful for him as it is for me. There's no twinkle in his eye that hints he's enjoying a single second of our evening so far.

"Ohio," I say. "A small town about forty miles north of Columbus. You?"

I keep the details to a minimum to avoid the risk of diving into any kind of conversation with meaning. This needs to be bare bones, dry, stilted, and forgettable.

"Born and raised here," he says. I can't be sure, but I

swear he's stifling a yawn. He dips his head down and checks his phone.

I do the same.

"Sorry—it's my sitter," he says a moment later. "If you'll excuse me, I'll be right back."

With that, he leaves me alone at the table, disappearing into some hallway behind the hostess stand. Pressing my lips together, I wrap my head around the fact that Roman Bellisario is a dad.

There isn't a fatherly thing about this man.

He's a ruthless negotiator, a nepotism trust-fund type— the last kind of person I can picture tucking in a child at night or reading bedtime stories or doing the whole tooth fairy, Easter bunny, Santa Claus thing.

Though I imagine he has paid help who do that for him.

Most people like him leave the child-rearing to the salaried, résuméd professionals.

They outsource.

I nurse my drink as I wait for his return, and I take the opportunity to check a few work emails.

Our food arrives in his absence, and for a moment I contemplate whether he made the phone call up so he could bail. You never know with people, and to be completely honest, it would be a bold but fair move.

No one should have to suffer through this a minute longer than necessary.

From the corner of my eye, I watch the couple to my right. His hand brushes hers from across the table. She reaches to catch a drip of red wine from the corner of his mouth. In the midst of it all, he can't seem to take his eyes off her for a single second. They're connected, entranced, infatuated with one another.

It's been years since I've had that, and 99 percent of the

time I don't think twice about it. Dating . . . sex . . . relation-ships . . . it's all taken a back seat these days while I focus on my career. The art-collector world is intricate, strategic, and all about who you know. Any spare time I have is spent on fostering my professional connections. I'm on an elevator to the top, and I have no plans to disembark anytime soon.

"Apologies," Roman says when he (shockingly) returns. "It's the first time in years that I've left the girls alone for more . . . they wanted to tell me good night before they went to bed."

Nearly choking on my drink, I clear my throat. "Girls? You have daughters?"

Being a father is one thing.

But being a girl dad? Completely different ball game.

"Two," he says. His dark eyes illuminate for the first time tonight. "Adeline's five and Marabel's four."

I've never been one to fawn over children and babies—to be honest, sometimes they scare me. They seem so deli-cate, so unpredictable, so fueled with unbridled emotion. But the idea of this tall, dark, and grumpy megawatt million-aire melting over his two little girls is . . . kind of sweet.

Immediately I picture two little darlings with velvet ribbons in their hair, patent leather Mary Janes, and dimpled grins. Like two little Eloises living at the Plaza.

And their names . . . I could melt.

Straightening my shoulders and clearing my throat, I remind myself I'm on a very simple mission. No need to complicate it or get off track. Besides, he could be the best dad in the entire world to them, but it doesn't change the way he treats other people—especially in my industry.

There's no excuse for being a grade-A asshole.

Ever.

Biting my tongue, I swallow my curiosity away to keep

from asking about his ex. Even if this were a real date, the question would be completely out of pocket.

"So what brought you all the way here from Ohio?" he asks.

"A—" I stop myself before I blurt out the word art. "All the things the city has to offer."

I give myself an invisible pat on the back for that save.

"Right, but why Manhattan? Why not Chicago? Los Angeles? London? What brought you here?" he asks.

Bless his heart—he's making an effort now.

Though there's still a lack of enthusiasm in his dark-brown eyes or a hint of genuine interest in his monotone Bruce Wayne voice.

Roman slices into his filet mignon, forks it, and lifts it to his full lips. Two dimples flank his mouth as he chews, and his jaw muscles divot. There's no denying the man is attractive. Some might even argue he's hotter than sin. Broad shoulders, a permanent poker face, and Big Dick Energy tend to do that to a man.

Fortunately I'm not the shallow sort—and even more fortunately, I'm not here for myself.

"Came here in high school for a school trip." I leave out the part about the trip being an Alice Calhoun High Art Club trip. "Fell in love and instantly knew it's where I wanted to live after college."

"Where'd you go to school?" he asks. "And what'd you study?"

Again, there's very little interest being conveyed beyond his actual words, but since he asked, I'll answer. Each question, each bite only brings us closer to the inevitable end of the evening.

"The Ohio State University," I say, which is the truth.

But I give him Margaux's major. "I studied marketing with a minor in communications."

"That's how you ended up in product development, I take it?" He forks another bite of his steak, and I deduce he'd much rather be putting a fork in this date.

It's funny—as much as Theodora was pushing for Margaux to go out with her nephew, I'd have assumed he at least wanted to take her out. Now I get the sense that he's merely doing her a favor.

"Exactly." The fewer words I utter tonight, the better. No need to wax poetic about the brand deals Margaux brokers—specifically the ones with social media influencers wanting to start a skin-care line or branch into athleisure or whatever "merch" is trending at the moment. I don't pretend to know half of what she does on a daily basis. All I know is she's really good at it. One of the best. "You?"

"Beg your pardon?" he asks, though I'm quite certain he heard me clear as a bell.

"You?" I repeat.

"What about me?" His eyes glint, as if he's keen to the fact that I'm using as few words as possible, as if he finds amusement in making me ask a proper, fully formed question.

"Where did you go to school and what did you study?" I ask. While I'm well aware of this man's reputation in the art-collecting underworld of the city, I don't know much about him otherwise.

There's no Wikipedia page on Roman Bellisario.

No website.

No red carpet charity gala photos.

Nothing.

At least there wasn't anything when I googled him years

ago after he had me fired from my dream job over an honest mix-up.

I'd seen him at my old gallery a handful of times, walking around like he owned the place. Negotiating prices on nonnegotiable pieces. Demanding private showings before or after hours. No one ever told him no. He was one of their biggest clients.

"NYU," he says, washing down his answer with a sip of amber-colored liquor. "I studied art history. Had every intention of advancing my degree and pursuing a career in higher education. Teaching, to be specific." He pauses, his attention flicking down for a beat. "Still think I'd have made one hell of an art history professor, but I guess things don't always work out the way we plan them."

"What stopped you?" I can't help myself.

I also can't help myself from imagining him commanding an auditorium full of young minds, his broad shoulders and generous biceps straining inside a tweed jacket, his messy hair and tortoise-framed glasses giving him that dark-academia edge that's all the rage right now. The front row would be filled with girls, all taking notes, all raising their hands for a chance to be in his hot seat, if only long enough to ask a single question.

As much as I hate it, the man is speaking my language. My skin is on fire, sparked with the electric urge to wax poetic on favorite painters, periods, and Picasso pieces. No doubt he's a man who knows his stuff, and I'm sure he could teach me a thing or two.

But Margaux wouldn't know a Picasso if it hit her in the face.

Margaux would talk about a Taylor Swift or Bruno Mars concert she attended at Madison Square Garden last month or some trendy, hard-to-find candle she hunted down in a boutique on Bleecker.

Still, I'm pleasantly surprised by the fact that he's not just some old-moneyed jerk trying to pad his portfolio with priceless works of art he can use for tax-evasion purposes down the road (it's a thing).

"My father." A hint of a wince colors his handsome face, and a divot forms along his jaw. "It wasn't the Bellisario way, or something along those lines. Feels like a lifetime ago. I try not to think about it too much."

"What's stopping you now?" I ask. If I had to guess, he looks to be somewhere in his midthirties . . . surely he's not still living under his father's thumb? If he's got enough cash to drop millions on Stefan DuMonde paintings and Ophelia Finnegan sculptures, he's got enough cash to pursue his PhD.

"Between running my father's company and raising my daughters, my spare time is limited these days."

"Do you have help?" I ask before clarifying. "Raising them?"

I shouldn't be engaging in this conversation, taking it to deeper levels and veering off the small-talk beaten path, but surely a question or two won't hurt.

"I have hired help, if that's what you're asking," he says.

His lips press flat like he wants to say more but changes his mind.

"I'm sorry. That must be difficult," I say.

"It's not the way we planned it, but it is what it is."

I would love to know what exactly "it" is.

Did they divorce?

Did she suddenly decide motherhood and marriage weren't for her and fly the coop?

Did she somehow tragically pass away?

What was her name?

What was she like?

And most importantly, what kind of woman can turn Roman Bellisario from a bona fide heartless bastard into a doting girl dad?

A hundred other questions flood my mind, but I wash them down, one after another, with my cucumber gin and tonic.

"Anyway." He tosses back the remainder of his drink before placing his fork and knife at the bottom of his plate.

He's done with dinner.

Probably done with this conversation too.

I don't say another word. I simply work on finishing my duck à l'orange and cauliflower mash.

"I'm sorry." I point at my still-full plate between bites. I've always been a slow eater, but tonight it seems especially that way.

"Take your time," he says, though I can't tell if he means it, if he's being sarcastic or gracious or all of that or none of that. All his mixed signals make him impossible to read.

Roman checks his phone . . . again.

Taking one more bite, I place my napkin over my plate to signal that I, too, am done. I'm still hungry. Famished, actually, given that I accidentally skipped lunch today. But no need to drag this date on longer than necessary. I'll hoover a bowl of Reese's Puffs over the sink like a heathen the second I get home if it means cutting out of this early.

Roman drags in a long, slow breath, pinches the bridge of his nose, and turns his attention back to me. I brace myself, preparing for some uncomfortable speech or phony excuse that'll put us both out of our miseries.

"I'm sorry," he says. "I haven't done this in a long time . . . the dating thing . . ." He begins to say something again, only to stop and pause. "Look, you seem nice and all, and I know my aunt meant well when she set this up, but I'm just not—"

His speech is cut short by the server, who presents a leather folder with tonight's bill. Lifting his finger, he motions for the man to wait, and then he retrieves three crisp hundred-dollar bills.

"Keep the change," he tells the guy, who walks off with raised eyebrows and a subdued smile on his face. Turning back to me, he continues, "My wife died, Margaux. Three years ago. To say it's been difficult would be the understatement of the century. I'm not really looking to move on. Not anytime soon, anyway. I'm focusing on my business and my daughters, and I don't really know how someone new would fit into any of that."

"You don't have to explain yourself." I stop him before he can continue since it isn't necessary.

Exhaling, he leans back, as if he's relieved, as if all the pressure has been released from the room.

"I'm pretty career focused myself," I say. "I'm flattered Theodora thought of me in this way, but I think we can both agree we're not a match."

Roman tosses back the final few drops of his drink before giving a nod, and he even flashes some semblance of a smile. While he doesn't seem like a happy man, there's no denying he's happy about this.

"I'm sorry about your wife," I say. And I mean it. He might be a colossal asshole who had me fired, but he's still a human being sporting a gaping hole where his heart should be. "Your daughters are lucky to have a dad who puts them first."

I would know.

Our father always put us first, even after my mother left

him. We were his everything, his reason for existing. He made that crystal clear. He was hurting, but he still kept room in his heart for us. He never did get over my mother, but it wasn't for a lack of trying. She was it for him. Everyone else paled in comparison.

Roman returns his wallet to his pocket, an official signal that this date is over.

Reaching for my purse, I rise from the table. "Thank you for dinner."

"My pleasure," he says, though he doesn't mean it, I'm sure. It's just one of those things you say without thinking.

We leave the dining room together, head past the hostess, and weave through pockets of waiting patrons before hitting the sidewalk.

Stopping next to a newspaper rack, we give each other one final awkward smile and nod. No goodbye, good luck, or words of formality necessary. A moment later, he checks his phone for the millionth time tonight. If we were on a real date, it'd be a red flag, and I'd take it personally.

"Hm," he says, though he doesn't elaborate.

His mouth turns down at the sides.

I don't ask.

It's not my business, and it doesn't matter.

"All right then . . . ," I say to myself before turning to leave. Starting my walk home, I feel almost weightless as the stress of the evening evaporates into the city air. I Ubered here out of necessity earlier, given that time was of the essence, but nothing beats a Friday-night walk in an emptied-out Manhattan. The smells. The sights. The sounds. The people-watching. It's like being a fly on the wall of the most interesting place in existence. It's one of my favorite little pastimes, if one can call it that. Margaux always teases that I absorb my surroundings as if by osmosis. "See you around, I guess."

He lifts his phone to his ear, his dark brows knit. I don't think he heard me, nor is he aware that I'm walking away.

As he said earlier, it is what it is.

It's an expression I've always found banal yet somehow applicable to every situation in existence. Growing up, my father always taught us that we can't always change a situation, but we can always change our attitude toward that situation. Sometimes the best attitude a person can have is simply acceptance.

Chuckling to myself as I leave, I accept that this was the strangest date I've ever had in my life.

I'm four blocks into my journey when I bump into Roman at a crosswalk. Had I noticed him any sooner, I'd have kept my eyes down, only now it's too late. We're staring at each other, separated by four people and a restless standard poodle with a Louis Vuitton collar.

"Hi . . . ," I say, though it comes out as more of a question than a greeting.

"My driver had a family emergency," he says with a slight air of annoyance.

"You didn't want to Uber or . . . ?" I ask. There's always the subway. Or a yellow cab. Buses, of course. He has options. Trekking home in those expensive-looking leather loafers seems like it should be the last of them.

A brunette woman between us looks at him, then me, then rolls her eyes, as if our conversation inconveniences her. She pops a white earbud into her ear and steps aside, leaving a gap where she once stood.

"You headed uptown?" he asks, ignoring my question.

"Midtown," I say. The crosswalk light changes, indicating it's safe to walk. "You?"

"Upper East Side," he says.

Somehow in the process of making our way across the street, we wind up behind the four people and the poodle, the two of us walking side by side.

A block later and we're still walking . . . together.

It's strange, even stranger than the date we just ended, but I'm not going to be rude and suddenly veer off onto some side street only to risk bumping into him again.

My goal tonight was to be boring, not weird.

Huge difference.

Soon, though, that one block becomes two, which then becomes three, then four, and before I know it, we're approaching my street, and we still haven't breathed a single additional word to one another.

The second my building comes into view, I nonchalantly dig my keys out of my purse, jangling them as if to wordlessly let him know I've reached my destination. I'd thank him for walking me home, but I don't know if that's what he did? We simply happened to be going in the same direction on the same route at the same time.

"This is your place?" He breaks the silence.

I point toward the front door of my building. "This is me."

He stops in his tracks. His Italian shoes look out of place on this humble stretch of Midtown street.

"This building," he says, scratching at his temple. He points at the brown structure with matching front steps and the black iron railings and a sign that says The Mayberry—Established 1912. "This one right here?"

My gaze narrows as I attempt to wrap my head around what he's getting at. Does he want me to invite him up for a nightcap? Or god forbid, a one-night stand? I don't care how disarmingly attractive this man is, I could never let him into my home or my pants.

He stands frozen beside me, contemplative, lost in thought, staring at the steps like he's seen a ghost. Snapping out of it, his gaze lowers. He runs his hands through his dark hair before blowing a hard breath between his full lips.

"I'm, um, going to head up now . . ." I jingle my keys once again. He looks straight at them as he rakes his hand along his jaw. "Have a good rest of your night."

His eyes drift toward my hand before settling on a cracked section of sidewalk.

"Jesus Christ," he mutters under his breath.

He's visibly upset about something.

Meanwhile, I've never been more confused about anything in my entire life.

"Everything okay?" I can't, in good conscience, leave him like this.

Is he diabetic? Is he having an episode?

His lips press together as our eyes meet. The streetlight above paints harsh shadows on his chiseled face, so I'm unable to accurately gauge his expression.

"Where did you get that key chain?" he asks.

I lift my keys, isolating the canary-yellow enameled H with the red leather lover's knot—a limited edition Halcyon key chain I happened to get during my tenure at the very gallery he got me fired from.

Years ago, we were attempting to broker a deal with an up-and-coming artist who went by the pseudonym Halcyon. Much like Banksy, Halcyon preferred to be faceless and nameless. An enigma known only for what they created and not what (or who) they were. Only Halcyon hasn't reached near the notoriety that Banksy has over the years. The average person wouldn't have the faintest clue who Halcyon is.

And to this day, no one knows.

They only worked through a third-party representative who kept their identity anonymous, and they haven't produced anything in years.

A cold flush of panic sears through me, and heat creeps along the back of my neck. It was a mix-up over a Halcyon piece three years ago that cost me my job. I'd sold a piece entitled You or Someone like You to a local collector for a sizable sum—the biggest sale my gallery had made that entire year—only to learn Roman had reserved it with another staff member. It was an honest communication mix-up. We didn't find out until it was too late.

It was a whole thing that I'd sooner wipe from my memory if I could.

"This one?" I ask.

"Yes." His reply is impatient, pressing. "Where did you get that?"

The yellow key chains with the lover's knots were made in a limited batch for promotional purposes, and I managed to nab one of only ten in existence. Being that it's a collector's item, it's slightly frivolous of me to use it as an everyday item, but its sunny yellow color makes me happy every time I see it, and it'd be a shame to let it sit in some box in some drawer collecting dust. Besides, it's a symbol of resilience to me. Mix-up or not, the sale of that piece was (and still is) my biggest to date.

To me, this key chain represents strength and perseverance.

I didn't let that firing get the best of me. If anything, it only made me tougher and more determined than ever to make it in my industry. I know how it feels to love your career more than anything in the entire world. As different as Margaux and I are, we're both dedicated, loyal, hard-working professionals. If being on this date tonight helps my sister get that much closer to her promotion, it's a small price to pay.

"Someone gave it to me a few years back," I say, feigning a foggy memory in hopes he won't pry any further. Then again, Halcyon is a popular topic among those in the art-world know. That said, Halcyon hasn't produced any work in years. Word on the street is that it was some PR stunt or get-rich-quick scheme, and that Halcyon (whoever they are) went back to their day job. I don't want to believe that, seeing how the paintings Halcyon made were visually stunning and original master-pieces. Guess we'll have no way of knowing until the face-less, nameless person behind the paintbrush steps forward.

If they ever do . . .

"You like Halcyon?" I ask. It's a stupid question, I'm sure. Every art collector loves Halcyon. Even if they don't like their work, they like how much their work is worth. Art that has only appreciated in value sevenfold since Halcyon quit painting.

I stop myself before asking if he owns any Halcyon pieces.

He never revealed during dinner that he collects art—only that he wanted to teach art history once upon a time—and it's a tidbit I only know because of my profession.

Margaux wouldn't know any of this.

"How do you know who Halcyon is?" he asks. But before I can answer, he adds, "I told you I was an art history major at NYU, that I wanted to be a professor, and you didn't mention you were a fan of one of the most obscure artists in the city? Someone only those in the know would . . ."

He stops talking.

I wrinkle my nose. I'm not sure what he's getting at.

"I'm sorry—I'm terrible at small talk," I say, hoping that's an acceptable answer. "I guess I should've worked that into the conversation, huh?"

His piercing stare burns into me. I shudder, worried he's somehow piecing everything together. I should have said my sister is an art dealer and gave me the key chain as a gift. Maybe that would've sufficed? Maybe he wouldn't have thought anything of it and let it go instead of pinning me into place with the weight of his scrutinizing glower.

I'm seconds from accepting the fact that the jig is up when his expression softens, and he waves his hand.

"I'm sorry," Roman says. "Forget I said anything. Just . . . forget all of this."

Before I get the chance to reply, he's making his way up the block.

And to think, I was worried about being the weird one tonight.

Halcyon key chain in hand, I traipse up the steps and head to my apartment, grateful that this night is over and that I'll never have to deal with Roman Bellisario ever again.

END OF SAMPLE

Read Now!

About the Author

Winter Renshaw is a Wall Street Journal and #1 Amazon bestselling author of contemporary romance novels that have sold nearly 5 million copies all over the world. An Iowa native and a graduate of Iowa State University, Winter still calls Iowa home, where she resides with her husband, three children, and their extremely spoiled dogs.

Winter also writes psychological suspense under her Minka Kent pseudonym. Her debut, THE MEMORY WATCHER, hit #9 in the Kindle store and is currently being screen-adapted in South Korea. Her follow-up, THE THINNEST AIR, hit #1 in the Kindle store and spent five weeks as a Washington Post bestseller. Over the years, her suspense work has been nominated for International Thriller Writer awards, mentioned by The New York Post and People Magazine, as well as optioned for film and television.

She is represented by Jill Marsal at Marsal Lyon Literary Agency.

Connect at www.facebook.com/authorwinterrenshaw,

winterrenshaw.com, or follow her @winterrenshaw on Instagram!

Visit www.winterrenshaw.com for free content or to apply for the ARC Reviewer Team.

Never miss a new release! Sign up for Winter's MAILING LIST!